D1592489

TO WED A HIGHLANDER

The de Moray Druids Collection

KERRIGAN BYRNE

OLIVER HEBER BOOKS
& GNARLY WOOL PUBLISHING

HIGHLAND WARLORD

First Witch:

"When shall we three meet again,
In thunder, lightning, or in rain?"

Second Witch:

"When the Hurlyburly's done,
When the Battle's lost and won."

Third Witch:

"That will be ere the set of the sun."

~ William Shakespeare, Macbeth

CHAPTER 1

25TH OF SEPTEMBER, 1066

T*his bridge is where I die*, Bael thought, as five thousand Saxon warriors drove what Vikings they didn't slaughter back across Stamford Bridge. The scents of blood and battle filtered through the thick copse of trees lining the River Dewent. Their full leaves blocked the view of the massacre being wrought on the West bank, and so Bael's Berserker remained leashed for the moment.

"I warned you," he muttered to Jarl Tostig, who pulled his horse to an abrupt stop next to him at the mouth of the bridge. "Those men were not safe on the west bank, and now our forces have been cut in half by Goodwin's army."

"How was I to know the fucking Saxon King's army could march nineteen leagues like it was nothing? They weren't supposed to be here. They act like they fell upon us by accident." Tostig drew his sword, trying to hold his antsy stallion in check, and spat on the ground. "Now trap them on the bridge and kill them *all*."

Bael's hand tightened on his double-bladed axe, his beast yearning to do exactly that. "I can kill a hundred on my own. Maybe more. But not five thousand." He turned to the unwise Jarl beside him, feeling more antipathy than anything. "If you do not make peace with this King Harold, then many of your raiders are going to Valhalla today."

"I do not pay you gold for talk of peace, Bael, I pay for your axe." Behind the fire in Jarl Tostig's blue eyes, Bael read a different emotion. Fear. "York fell to your rage. Northumbria cowered before it. And Scarborough burned to the ground. Now go. Prove your worth to the Gods, before they forsake the half of you that's worth anything."

Years ago, that barb would have angered him.

Bael yawned, scratched an itch on his back with the edge of his axe, and shrugged. He didn't miss the widening of the Jarl's eyes as he did this, knowing that the axe he wielded like a child's toy would take most warriors two hands and a great heave to swing.

Wishing he'd at least had time for ale and breakfast before marching to his death, Bael ambled toward the bridge, rolling his shoulders and feeling the chilled wind feather over his bare chest. There was something different about this wind. Something mysterious that shimmered over his senses and pricked at the beast within him.

Power lurked in those trees. *Nie*, not power. *Magick*.

Perhaps a Valkyrie waited in preparation for so many Viking deaths.

"It has been an honor raiding alongside a blessed warrior of Freya such as you," Tostig called after him.

"I wish I could say the same," he yelled over his shoulder, twirling his axe a few times.

Foolish Jarls. Fighting for even more foolish kings who cared more for treasure than they did the survival of their own people. Perhaps it was good he died today. He didn't like what this world was becoming. Families, clans, and villages joined into bigger towns and cities, swearing fealty to rich and greedy men who called themselves kings. Power no longer belonged to the strongest, the bravest, and the most just, but to the cunning and the silver-tongued. This should not be the way of things.

Bael had to shoulder through retreating Vikings once the bridge narrowed, and he ordered them to form a shield wall behind him. When the English broke through, his men might still stand a chance.

Inside he both mourned and rejoiced for those brothers already fallen. He would see them soon in the halls of Valhalla. Would drink with Freya and have a place in her long-house.

Finally.

Blood stained the tunic of a wounded Viking warrior limping across the planks of the bridge supported by narrow stone walls. The Berserker beast rippled beneath his skin, rising to the surface. Vibrant greens and the colors of autumn faded from his sight until everything was grey and sharp as if he were a hawk.

The retreating Vikings ran, not to escape the advancing Saxons.

But him.

Bael embraced the rage building inside him with the strength of a storm surge. It rolled along his veins, pouring through his blood like liquid fire. It was as savage as hatred. As pleasurable as lust. The swell of his muscles tightened his skin until only the swing of his axe could appease the brutal urge to bathe in the blood of his enemies.

The Saxons wore helmets and shields. Their armor gleamed, reflecting the sun like waves on the sea as they perused the fleeing Vikings. They'd been too long away from the north. Too long away from the stories and legends of the Berserkers. So when they saw the lone giant on the bridge they didn't tremble. They didn't flee. They advanced, running at Bael as though competing for who would be the first to claim his life.

The first slice of his axe took two heads at once and yet another on the backswing. Bael let out a roar that warned the Saxons he could not possibly be human. His weapon was part of him, part of his beast. His eyes, now black voids of abysmal rage, saw only prey. His nose only smelled blood and death, and reveled in the potent perfume. When the bodies began to pile, he climbed over the corpses to get at his enemies. He killed so many, their blood and limbs littered the river with gore.

Their weapons caused no pain, though his only armor was a fearsome helm made of bone and iron. The Saxons broke upon him like waves on the black cliffs, spraying blood and falling away, only to press forward again. His world dissolved into nothing but blood-lust.

This bridge was going to be where Baelsar Bloodborn was fated to die.

He couldn't fucking wait.

MORGANA DE MORAY struggled to take a breath. Tugging at the thick bonds that imprisoned her wrists behind her back and her ankles together, she tried to find a position that would alleviate the pressure on her ribs. Draped like she was over the saddle of a tall Saxon warhorse, the feat proved impossible.

Lifting her head from the horse's flank, she peered out over the autumn field strewn with dead Northmen. The Saxons marched away from her toward a narrow break in the tree line that ran along the river. For once, she felt blessed that her captors hadn't fed her much, because she would have added any food in her stomach to the battle gore littering the fields. The smell, alone, was enough to sicken her, but the sight of so much slaughter. So much blood. It was overwhelming.

If she didn't make her escape now, she might never again have the chance. Morgana knew where this ended when the Saxon King Goodwinson was done with her. On a pyre, burning for witchcraft. Her options were to flee or die, and she planned to live. Had too much to live for. Her Druid brother needed her alive. Her people needed her powers.

The *world* needed her help to save it. Even these bloody Saxon oafs and the blood-thirsty Viking pillagers they'd chanced upon. If any of them survived this battle, it would be for naught if she and her cousin, Kenna, didn't make it home to the Highlands in time for Samhain.

Morgana renewed her struggles, focusing on freeing her feet from her boots, which were bound together. Her thick stockings allowed for some movement. If she could just peel her slender feet out of them, she might have a chance.

As she shimmied and worked, she cursed the entire masculine breed. *Men.* Why was it always kill-first-think-second with them? They'd abandoned their horses on the east bank because, from what she'd gleaned from their calls, Stamford Bridge was too narrow to support more than a horse or two, and the Viking's long-spears would rid them of too much good horseflesh.

So they'd sacrifice men—soldiers—but not their horses. It was truly a wonder that men ruled the world. They held some particularly unbalanced priorities.

Morgana grunted, feeling one of her boots give, taking her stockings with it. Rejoicing, she kicked it off, much to the irritation of her very alive, very powerful equine conveyance.

"Steady," she crooned. "Steady on." Wincing as the stallion pranced, jarring her middle, Morgana murmured a sleep spell she'd memorized as a child, praying that it worked on animals as well as it had her nurse.

Thankfully, it did, and the beast stilled, allowing her to kick off her other boot and stocking, taking her bindings with them. Wriggling her body and reaching with her toes, she went limp, sliding down the side of the horse and landed in the cold mud with bare feet.

Heart racing, Morgana used the horse's body as a shield and surveyed the rapidly emptying battlefield, considering her options. Something caused much excitement at the bridge, which remained hidden from her view by the thicket of trees. Too many Saxons lingered in the freshly harvested fields for her to make her way west, and the preponderance of the army made a bolt north impossible. The Saxons pressed toward the old Roman road, eager to claim victory from those across the river.

Home lie north and west. The river threaded directly to her east, and she had to make it to the cover of trees without being seen. She needed to reach the water, and fast. There had to be a jagged branch upon which she could free her wrists from their thick leather bonds, and use the cover to develop a plan of escape. Even if she had to flee to the south and make a large circle back west and north, that would be a better choice than remaining here.

Sending up a prayer to the Goddess for strength, safety, and concealment, Morgana took two bracing breaths and broke from the dozing horse, dashing toward the trees. It amazed her how incredibly difficult running with her hands bound behind her could be. Balance without the use of her arms proved surprisingly problematic. Dry stalks of whatever had grown in this field poked at her bare feet through the mud, and scratched at her shoulder when she stumbled and fell.

Scrambling back to her feet, she didn't dare to look behind her, in case death in the form of a Saxon arrow whistled toward her. Better that than a pyre and her flesh melting from her bones, she thought, and forged ahead, doing her best to ignore her bleeding heels. Once she found water, she could heal them.

Plunging into the tree line, she willed the tears blurring her vision to cease. She'd never forget the violence and horror of this day. Never rid her memory of the cruelty of men toward their enemies. And for what? She couldn't fathom. She only knew that men—good men, family men—became monsters when ordered to be. And they killed without remorse. They were given permission by their kings and their Gods to spill blood upon the earth. The most precious and potent combination of water and life.

The forest ground was damp and mossy, strewn with freshly-fallen leaves. She slowed to look for jagged rocks, but couldn't see any in her immediate vicinity. The trees still blushed with youth and their branches were thick with foliage and smooth with health. Her tender feet relished the soft earth beneath her, but she needed to find something—anything—to cut her bonds with.

The thin line of trees suddenly gave way to a very slim river-bank. Morgana's first impulse to fling herself into the water and let the current carry her to safety disappeared with horrific alacrity.

Blood stained the river and filtered into pools of mud. Disembodied limbs bobbed in little gruesome fleets, swept downstream by the lazy autumn pull of the current. Morgana stifled the scream tearing up her throat. Though water was her element, Morgana couldn't bear to be engulfed by all that death and gore.

She swallowed bile as a man's head floated by, his sightless eyes frozen in a stare of terror that fixed upon her until disappearing around a gentle bend.

A fierce roar clawed at her bones with an icy chill and drew her frantic eyes to a stone bridge upriver. Though it was far enough away that she had to squint, what Morgana saw stopped her breath.

Vikings. Hundreds upon hundreds of them crouched behind a shield wall on the east bank. But the blood-lust palpably emanating from the army wasn't what froze her feet to the mud. It was the carnage wrought by the lone giant slaughtering count-less Saxons on the Stamford Bridge.

Blood wept from the wooden slats. The water climbed the riverbanks, displaced by the weight of the dozen men dispatched with just a few strokes of his colossal axe.

The survival instinct to bolt warred with a different impulse. An unnatural one. This giant, the one who'd emitted that terri-fying roar was like her. Different. Powerful.

Magical.

Mesmerized when she should be repelled, Morgana leaned her shoulder against a tree, and crouched low, willing her breath to slow.

The stone wall of the bridge mostly hid his legs, but the giant's torso was bare except for the strap across his chest that would secure that impossible axe to his back. That and the blood of the fallen drenching his skin. His features were hidden by distance and a fearsome helm of iron decorated by skull bones.

Arrows seemed to glance off his flesh. The swords of his enemies found no purchase even if the blows rang true. The bridge could only support men about four shoulders wide, and four men could never hope to fell a warrior such as this.

He killed like other men danced, with light feet for bones encumbered by so much muscle, and swift, unpredictable movements for such a large weapon. He was a bard of blood. A legion of one. A painter whose brush only knew the color red.

The Viking not only held the bridge, he took it. Grinding forward through bone and flesh with a hoard at his back and a throng in front of him.

Morgana ached to run, but something locked her feet in place, her toes sinking into the soft earth of the riverbank. She was witnessing something epic. A feat of man that would be recorded in the ages until the end of times.

And yet... Morgana stretched her Druid senses. The ones that told her he was a man, and more than a man. He roared like a beast. He moved with the speed of a Fae. Swung his axe with the strength of a God. He had to have killed fifty, nay, a hundred men, and he didn't show the first signs of tiring.

Movement beneath the bridge caught Morgana's notice. A barrel bobbed in the river's slow current. She squinted harder, trying to make out the long protuberance from the barrel's edge from where she stood. She recognized it too late. The Saxon concealed within sprang from where the blood and entrails of his brothers-in-arms dripped on him from the bridge, braced one hand on the stones, and drove a long-spear between the slats, impaling the Viking warrior in the thigh.

A howl rent the afternoon, and still the giant fought on, cleaving clean through a shield and embedding his axe into the skull of a man. Kicking the body off his weapon, he roared again as a second spear lodged in his back, this one just beneath his ribs.

And yet more men fell before him. But his movements began to slow. Blood flowed from his back and thigh with startling speed.

Hot tears branded Morgana's cheeks, and she couldn't reach up to wipe at them. Didn't understand why she already mourned for this lone, violent beast. A strangled gasp escaped her as the spear found purchase a third time, again in his back. Shoulders heaving, the warrior's head dropped and his magnificent body swayed before plunging over the stone wall and into the river, his blood mingling with that of the countless men he'd massacred.

CHAPTER 2

S axons took the bridge and flooded the east bank. Instead of spreading and breaking upon the Viking shield wall like a wave, they pierced through like an arrow. The screams of rage and pain rose above the gentle song of the trees. The gurgles of throats filling with blood drowned out the gurgle of the river.

Morgana couldn't bear to look. Instead, she followed the slow progress of the giant as the current carried him downstream from the bridge toward her. In moments, he would pass her and his body would be gone forever.

Not today, she decided. *I need you.*

Ignoring the roiling in her stomach, she inched both her feet into the freezing river and reached out with her magick. *Bring him to me*, she told the current. *Bring me the warrior.*

The river obeyed. The Viking's body slid along the bank, magickally avoiding rocks and the water's other gruesome occupants, until the current deposited his impressive weight in the mud at her feet. Most of his thick frame remained submerged, the water not strong or fast enough to propel him with any force.

His features, all but an obstinate jaw and lips too full to be concealed by his few days growth of beard, were hidden from her by his fearsome bone and iron helm. The water leached blood away from hair the color of volcanic stone.

Gods but he was massive.

She needed to touch him in order to know where to send her magick. How could she possibly do it with her wrists bound behind her? Healing magick was intimate, internal. Generally she had to lay her hands on a wound, on a body, to diagnose and provide a cure.

She cursed her bonds once again, futilely testing their strength, and winced as the leather bit into her skin.

Damn. That left her only one choice. Trying not to think of what polluted the river, Morgana dropped to her knees beside his alarmingly still frame, grateful that the water had lifted much of the blood from his skin.

Willing her heart to slow, she pressed her ear to a chest the texture of firm Highland stone and almost as deep as it was wide. No breath lifted his ribs. No pulse moved the blood through his veins.

But life still flowed within him.

So did magick.

Alarmed, Morgana fought to remain calm as she closed her eyes and used her ear and cheek to connect with what blood was left in his body. *Where are your wounds?* She knew he'd been stabbed three times, but she needed to assess what damage had been done on the inside, and she doubted her ability to roll him over even if she had the use of her hands. He was simply too heavy.

His blood connected to hers as no other patient had before. A clear and instant knowledge of the damage seared her mind. The wound in his thigh was mostly meat and vein. But blood leaked from both of his lungs, and would prove fatal any moment.

This mythical savage needed breath. He needed the punctures in his lungs healed. Since she couldn't reach his back, she'd have to do it a different way.

Taking strength from the water flowing around her knees, Morgana chanted a spell of healing against his chest. Willing his wounds to mend like she never had hoped before.

Nothing changed. In fact, she could feel his life draining out of him with every moment that passed. A frantic panic welled within her.

"Stay with me, warrior," she implored, moving to kneel at his shoulder. "Do not cross to the Otherworld just yet. I need you." Taking the loamy air deep into her chest, she brought her lips close to his and breathed her healing spell against his mouth.

"*EARTH IS OUR BODY.*

  Fire, our soul.
  Air, our breath.
  Water, our blood.
  Flesh knit to flesh.
  Vein to vein.
  The Goddess blesses you.
  Be whole again."

AN IMPULSE BORNE of pure feminine urge pushed her to make a hasty, desperate move, and she fused her mouth to his, breathing her magick into his lungs.

It should have taken but a moment, the space of a short and powerful breath.

But once her warm lips were pillowed by his cool mouth, Morgana was seized by a typhoon of such shocking sensation; she lost all sense of place. The green of the forest, the chill of the water, the sounds of rampant bloodshed all faded as something as subtle as a whisper and as deafening as the truth rushed around and through her. It reminded her of holy days, when planets aligned in their orbits, or when full moons coincided with a solstice or equinox. It was a foreign and potent magick. Masculine. Dominant. Binding.

Before her overwrought brain could process movement, she was shackled to a chest by bands of pure iron, and being devoured by a mouth that was cold no longer.

Pulled onto an enormous body bowing with the first breath of life, Morgana knew she should panic. That she should struggle. But she didn't. It would have been fruitless. There was no escaping a hold this powerful.

The Viking ripped off his helm and sat up, dragging her into his lap and cradling her body into the cavern of his. Once again, Morgana found herself a captive. For something about this kiss was stronger than any length of rope or magick spell could ever be.

There was a hint of the divine in his savage lips. A glimpse of the eternal.

And just like that, she was bound.

The Viking ripped at the front of Morgana's bodice; effectively breaking the spell and dumping her soundly back into reality.

"No!" she gasped, ripping her mouth away from his.

To her utter shock, he stilled, though his big hand nestled in the valley of her breasts, spreading unsettling warmth through her. She became equally frozen as she looked up into his face.

By the Goddess, she was cradled in the lap of a monster.

Morgana often felt when she looked out into the absolute black of a moonless night, a bereft sort of expectant danger. Like the darkness peered back at her, studied her weaknesses, and reached into the places of her soul where magick resided that should never see the light.

If one concentrated that darkness, that trepidation that lifted the hairs on the back of one's neck and caused even the bravest of men to avoid the shadows, it still wouldn't have aptly described the pure black emptiness of the Viking's eyes. He seemed to study her in that way she imagined the nighttime did.

Those fathomless pools of onyx roaming her face as though *she* were the peculiarity.

She remained locked with the beast in a moment of stunned visual discovery. Aside from his eyes, or lack thereof, the rest of his face was undoubtedly male. Or would be, if the Gods of war, those fiends of destruction, ever *created* a warrior's features.

Nothing about those broad and brutal planes were ever meant to please the eye. His chin and jaw, set in sharp angles, thrust forward with unyielding menace. A forehead positioned in an eternal scowl shadowed those already impossibly dark, deep-set eyes. Scroll tattoos toyed with his hairline and disappeared into his abundant dark hair.

But his lips.

Morgana's gaze latched on to them with a desperate fascination. Those lips were the Goddess's compensation for his frightening demeanor. She'd never before seen lips like that on a man. The rest of him would *have* to be so alarmingly masculine in order to claim such a luscious mouth.

"What are you?" she breathed the question. For surely a creature such as he was not of this world.

He didn't answer. Instead, his hand lifted from her chest to her cheek. With a tenderness that shocked Morgana, the Viking explored her own features with the thoroughness of a blind man. A soft ticking rumble, like that of a contented cat, began to emanate from somewhere within his massive chest. It echoed through her in the most unsettling way, the vibrations rocketing a strange awareness directly to between her legs.

Morgana submitted to this, wondering if his sight was, indeed impaired by the soulless voids of his eyes.

A slow recognition began to permeate her memory, one her brother, Malcolm, and her cousin, Kenna, had discussed in awe-struck whispers after pouring through tomes in Dun Moray's library.

Morgana had never been much for the hours of scouring spells and memorizing the legends of her Druid people as her brother and cousin were. She learned from the forests, from the rivers, from the elders of Moray. She would rather read the faces of her people than a dusty old book.

But this story she remembered, because she found a brutal sort of romance within it. One of a Northman blessed by the war Goddess Freya with preternatural strength and stamina. When he saw blood, he unleashed a beast of battle with black eyes and sharpened teeth. An unstoppable beast who slaughtered indiscriminately, unable to decipher between man, woman, or child. What had Malcolm called them again?

Berserkers.

By the Gods. She was bound in the clutches of one of the most lethal creatures to ever walk the earth. And, according to Kenna, who paid particular attention to this part, the only possible way he would refrain from murdering her was if—

She gulped, her eyes peeling wide and her mouth dropping open.

If he'd claimed her as his mate.

CHAPTER 3

It was because she'd kissed him, Morgana realized with a dizzy sort of exhilarated horror. In bringing him back from the brink of death, she'd bound him to her for life.

The battle began to spill back toward the bridge, Vikings and Saxons alike using the trees across the river for cover and ambush. With an animalistic noise, the Viking stood taking her with him, and began a frantic search of the ground around them.

"Put me down, and I'll bring you your axe," Morgana offered. "You'll be needing it."

The Berserker reluctantly complied, and she yet again decided to forgo touching the river with anything but her feet as she commanded the heavy axe toward them.

"Do you think you could untie me?" she ventured.

Instead, the demon-eyed warrior shocked her by snatching his weapon from the blood-soaked river, securing it to his back, and gathering her into the safety of his chest before striding through the trees with unnatural swiftness.

"Not that way!" Morgana protested, renewing her fruitless struggles against her bonds. "It's too dangerous. We should go downriver."

She would have called the sound that escaped his throat a

scoff if the idea that a beast like him making such a sound wasn't so ludicrous.

The Berserker clutched her tighter as they broke from the tree line and crossed the near-empty west bank battlefield. Sickened, Morgana was grateful to turn her eyes away from the massacre and bury her face against the strength of his chest. Without a doubt, this place would become a graveyard of sun-bleached bones and drifting souls for centuries.

She heard the shocked exclamations of the few Saxons who stayed behind to thrust their swords through injured Vikings or to pull their wounded from the battlefield. Peeking from the safety of his chest, Morgana was astounded to see that even on foot, they moved with the speed of a galloping horse. Arrows sliced through the air, but none of them found purchase.

Before long, she and the Berserker had traveled west over countless fields of purple meadow thistle, and over short stone hedges of farmland. He never seemed to tire, his breath remaining even against her cheek. Morgana could barely contain the gratitude she felt toward him for helping her to escape the horrors of the English-Saxon horde.

The terrain gave way to rolling emerald hills and lush valleys of grazing beasts. The hills seemed to present a challenge for her transport, and a few grunts and hitches of breath escaped him when he climbed.

Cresting a hill, they spotted a stream winding through a vale lined with trees that were short but still thick with vibrant autumn foliage. As though he read her mind, the Berserker made for the copse of trees, his gait becoming increasingly uneven. Ducking into the cover afforded by low-hanging branches, he took her to the water's edge and set her feet on the soft mossy ground.

Morgana felt a bit unsteady, and was glad when he didn't move away. He crowded his massive body against hers, dipping his neck toward the crown of her head, and taking deep pulls of breath against her hair.

Though she wasn't as afraid as she knew she probably should be, Morgana didn't feel ready to meet those fathomless obsidian eyes again just yet. Now that they'd escaped the battle, just what did this beast of muscle and magick plan to do with her?

Or—*to* her.

The possibilities sent a trembling thrill of fear laced with a dark excitement washing down her spine and pooling between her legs. The puzzling reaction of her body to his nearness both troubled and stimulated her.

The breath in his chest shortened and hitched, as though he tested the air like a hound scenting something delicious. The sound he made was laced with sin and need, and Morgana found herself once again pulled against the wall of his body, the black voids of his eyes conveying the most unmistakable of intentions. Against her belly, the thick column of his sex pulsed behind the layer of his trews, full and hard.

He meant to have her. To *take* her.

"Wait!" She would've held up her hands against him, were they free of the bonds, and her shoulders tensed with the need to have them back.

He stopped. Though he grunted his frustration at her, and bared teeth just a touch too sharp to be human.

Morgana felt the blood drain from her face, but she met his savage displeasure with all the courage she could muster. If he treated her roughly, she could try the sleeping spell on him, and hope it worked upon another creature of magick.

"I-I don't know if you understand me," she ventured, realizing he might not even know her language, let alone any verbal form of communication. "But I would ask one more thing of you." She stepped back and turned, offering him her bound hands. "Untie me?" she tried again.

He didn't hesitate before reaching for her wrists and pulling her leather bonds apart as though he ripped a piece of spun linen.

Morgana turned and gaped at him, rubbing one wrist, and

then the other as the uncomfortable tingle of feeling rushed from her shoulders all the way down to her fingertips. "I thank you, warrior," she sighed, testing her aching shoulders.

He made an animalistic sound of distress, his hands shackling her forearms and lifting her wrists for inspection. The skin was raw and angry, but not broken. He growled at the marks, and then lifted them to his lips. Those soft, full crescents of skin brushed against the thin flesh covering the veins of her wrists, and her pulse flared beneath the slight pressure of his mouth.

His dark beard, only long enough to be soft rather than rough, provided an entrancing contrast in sensation as his hot tongue escaped to venture over her newly sensitized flesh in a long lick.

She felt that lick elsewhere, and her lips parted on a gasp of equal parts dismay and delight.

His eyes latched onto hers, and his grip tightened. She got the impression his gaze sharpened and dulled, like he fought to maintain his focus. His breath became more labored, and he blinked as though fighting something.

Doubt lanced through her, causing her to wonder if he only toyed with his prey before devouring it. Needing to be free and regain her bearings, Morgana tugged on her wrist, but he refused to relinquish it.

"Let me go, Berserker," she ordered in a voice much stronger than she felt.

Again, he complied, a whisper of hurt furling his brow before he suddenly crashed to his knees with a hard grunt of unmistakable pain. A pool of blood had gathered around him, and Morgana noticed the bronze of his skin had taken on a pale tinge.

Only then did she remember his leg.

"Oh *no*," she cried. Her healing breath would not have reached the spear wound in his thigh. Only his lungs. He'd run with her as his burden all this way with such a deep and painful wound.

His torso swayed, his lids fluttering as though they battled consciousness. Morgana caught him as he fell forward, and did her best to lower his heavy trunk to the ground.

"I'll heal you," she promised, pillowing his head upon the moss before moving to tug at his trews. The wet animal skin clung to his boulder-sized thighs as though it had claws, but she didn't stop wrestling with them, using her powers to pull the water from the material.

In order to save his life, she needed to get him naked.

CHAPTER 4

B ael returned to consciousness with the aimless drift of a
feather upon a breeze. To fall was inevitable, but the
journey was unhurried. Small perceptions permeated his senses
one at a time. His nose twitched at the smell of earth and moss
and clean water. Though, something else drifted upon his breath.
The aroma of ripe fruit and exotic spices. Cinnamon, maybe. He
filled his lungs to the brim, catching the unmistakable scent of a
woman.

A maiden of Valhalla, perhaps? Or a Valkyrie come to lead
him to his eternal glory in the halls of Freya?

His hearing returned second, pricking to the tranquil sound
of a stream and the wind rustling through trees and across blades
of summer grass. A soft song harmonized with the soothing
sounds, the voice achingly sweet and dripping with innocence.
Bael didn't recognize any of the words, but then he had not yet
learned the language of angels.

Awareness of his body came next. He was on his back,
pillowed by soft ground and moss. His skin bared and roughened
by a gentle, yet chilly breeze. Though his thoughts were sluggish
and muddled, he felt clean and vital and—powerful. Coursing

with more magick than his usual fledgling abilities, he felt as though he could run until he ran out of earth.

Opening his eyes, he found a blanket of stars winking through a canopy of trees. Night in Valhalla? Did the Gods sleep? Or did they use the darkness as his body obviously wanted to now? For fucking.

His dark vision was unchanged in this place, honed to shades and shadows, but just as sharp as in the daytime. A moon hung heavy in the sky and painted the night an eerie blue.

How could this be?

He turned toward the sound of the brook and the chanting sing-song voice, and knew he must be dead, because his heart stalled and his breath froze for long enough to kill any man.

The bathing woman knelt in the shallow brook, her back to him, cupping water and splashing it over her shoulders. Her skin looked soft and luminous in the moonlight, and Bael's eyes couldn't help but follow the glistening rivulets as they ran down the column of her spine. She was the culmination of every warrior's desire. Nothing but soft curves and pale skin. The opposite of his own utilitarian body, her every lush dip and round flare was meant to please, entice and satisfy.

Bael stood. His mouth flooded and his sex pulsed impossibly harder, fuller, and more insistent than ever before in his life.

At last. This bathing siren was *his* for the taking. His reward for a century of loneliness, war and bloodshed. He'd done everything asked of him by the Berserker elders, even those younger than himself. He'd endured the censure and disgust of those who cursed his tainted blood, and stood as a dark stain among a horde of fair-skinned, light-eyed warriors.

There was a myth among the Berserker temple, one that promised the most fearsome, and most valiant warriors would be led into Valhalla by one of Freya's handmaidens. Before being welcomed into the hall of the All Father, Odin, the handmaiden would first bathe him while he rested his battle-weary bones, and then fulfill his every sexual desire, no matter how dark or inconceivable.

Now that he'd died in battle, fighting for the survival of his Nordic kin who would never truly accept him as one of their own, Freya had granted him the gift of her handmaiden.

Bael could hardly believe it. For a long time he'd yearned for death, for a release from his empty prison. If he'd have known heaven would be so sweet, he would have invaded England by himself to ensure his demise decades ago.

His desires were neither dark nor devious, they were simple and they were few. He had no use for exotic rituals or the increasingly shameful pleasures sought by the men in his army. He merely yearned for the feel of a woman's flesh so long denied him. For a touch of softness in this hard and brutal existence. To feel her lie beneath him and cradle him inside her warmth until he lost himself. He craved both acceptance and release. And here was the woman who would grant him a taste of that, if only for a night.

Mine.

Bael's beast growled a claim so strong, a dawning stroke of need and elation lanced through him, followed by a crippling wave of lust and possession.

No, Bael thought. Things were different here in Valhalla. He wouldn't have to worry about mating.

The woman's song died on a gasp, and she blindly turned toward him, the tips of her full, luxuriant breasts covered by wet and heavy hair.

He'd never been driven to his knees by any living soul, no matter how hard they tried, but the eruption of frenzy those full breasts released nearly buckled his legs from beneath him.

Staggering forward, Bael splashed into the stream, yanked her up from where she knelt, and stole the protest from her mouth by sealing it with his own. She tensed against him at first, but then melted with a sound of surrender. Her body was cool and damp from the stream against his heated flesh. She felt good. Invigorating. Her lips seemed soft and familiar, as though he'd kissed them before, sampled their sweetness, and reveled in their pliant warmth.

It had been decades since he'd felt the touch of another. Fifty years since a woman had pressed herself against him as she did now. Bael had almost forgotten what a woman felt like, but he knew without a doubt that no other woman he'd ever touched came close to the sensual perfection of the one in his arms.

The scent of her, ripe fruits and spices, frayed the edges of his sanity.

With a moan, equal parts pleasure and torture, Bael ran his hands down the dramatic slope of her back as it dipped into a narrow waist and flared into an ass that overflowed his kneading palms. Gods, she couldn't *be* any more perfect than this. He cared little to feel bones beneath a woman's flesh. He wanted substance and softness. To fill his big hands and feast his eyes on every inch. He much preferred the luscious shape of her body to the hard, muscled shield maidens of the north, or the skin-and-bone whores his men paid for.

The way her flesh slid along his as she drew her hands up his arms and across the span of his shoulders to twine about his neck, unstitched the last fibers of his self-control. Digging his fingers into her ass, he hefted her against him and split her legs to wrap around his trunk.

Bael even liked the way she gasped in shock and clung to him with her arms and knees as though his actions surprised her.

Yes. Her long legs would be wrapped around parts of him until morning dawned in Valhalla. His waist. His head. Bael planned to feast on her flesh and her sex. To feed her his own. To take pleasure in the sweetness of her voice as she came for him and spill his release inside her again and again.

Gods, it had been *so* long. A lifetime.

Carrying her to the soft mossy bank without separating their fused mouths, he lowered them both to the ground and covered her body with his.

Tonight was his gift from the Gods, and after a century of sacrifice and denial, he was going to take full advantage of his reward.

⚜

MORGANA HAD FELT the Berserker awaken, could sense him even in darkness. But she'd been unaware that he'd moved until he'd snatched her from her bath and lay claim to her mouth.

Now she lay beneath this fiercely masculine creature, his pulsating erection hot and hard against her belly, her knees clutching at his flanks as though inviting him inside her.

She was aware of the danger of their precarious position, but couldn't seem to tear her mouth away from those magical lips of his. It wasn't their contrast to the unmitigated hardness of the rest of him, nor was it the arousal that flooded her the moment their flesh had connected.

Not entirely, anyway.

What kept her latched to him was the pure and raw emotion emitting from his every pore. She'd fallaciously assumed he was a beast of rage, need, and impulse. But the signature his aura blanketed about them proved her wrong. He bled a lonely sort of anger that hid within it a longing born of deprivation.

Morgana had never before touched someone so—alone. She could read his almost reverent awe as he explored her. Was charmed by his elated joy when she'd wrapped her legs around him. And was seduced by the dominant strength of his arousal mixed with the careful way in which he avoided using that strength to harm or subdue her.

Not that she'd *needed* to be restrained.

For some alarming reason, her body responded to him with the same kind of violent intensity. In his arms, she became a creature of primeval desires and pure instinct. Thoughts of consequence and reason flowed away from her like driftwood in a strong current.

He was nothing but a large mass of shadows and angles backlit by a blue moon. Some silvery light shredded against the sharp slash of his cheekbone, or caught the sheen of his dark hair, but his eyes remained a mystery to her. His expressions hidden. She didn't need to see them to understand what she needed to know.

The Berserker meant to make her his mate, in the most fundamental sense of the word.

Unless she stopped him. And she should—stop him—any moment now. There was too much she didn't know. The man drawing his lips down to worship the sensitive hollow of her neck had only just yesterday slaughtered a hundred men. He was dangerous, nay, lethal. And she couldn't afford another enemy right now. Not one as powerful as this.

But, oh, those lips. Those wicked, mesmerizing lips. How could she stop them when they left a trail of devastating desire in their wake? Every inch of skin he explored came alive as if for the first time.

His hands didn't remain passive, either. They spanned her naked flesh with the exuberance of a novice and the skill of an incubus, summoning storms that drenched her with desire and drowned her in sensation.

Feminine muscles clenched as long, venturing fingers reached between their bodies and stroked along the sensitive flesh of her inner thigh. Thrills danced along her nerves and jolted up her legs to settle into moist folds of her sex.

Morgana had been aroused before. Had explored her passions with bold lads in her highland clan, but never had the threat of a touch affected her so intensely. Her blood sang for it. Her body vibrated with need. Her skin flushed with anticipation.

A sound of pure masculine delight rumbled from his throat as his probing fingers slid through the slick cleft of her sex to brush along the quivering place that shot pure bliss to the most miniscule fibers that comprised her very being.

Her arousal was such that he didn't even need to manipulate

the soft aperture of flesh to elicit pleasure. But he did. With a possessive nibble at her shoulder, he worked his strong fingers in a circular motion, his lips branding their way down her chest to nuzzle at her trembling breasts.

Morgana's breath ebbed and flowed with the sure movements of his hand. Her beast touched her as though he found as much pleasure in the act as she. His cock became hotter and fuller against her thigh, but he didn't move to claim her, seeming content in the slick unhurried movements of his strong fingers against her.

Pressure built quickly, and her hips jerked and bucked beneath him. That pressure dissolving into a pleasure so intense, she couldn't hold in her panting cries of release as it crested and crashed like the tidal waves of a gale storm. When Morgana wound so tight she thought she might break, the Berserker slid a finger inside her, his thumb remaining to thrum at the nub of pliant flesh.

Stars exploded behind her closed eyes. The intrusion was just a finger, but his hand was big, his fingers long. She climaxed on a pulsating quiver that caused her legs to clench around his hips as though to imprison her to him. Her cries must have rung through the night and scared any lurking creatures away, so transcendent was the sensation.

"Yes," she gasped in a strained whisper, feeling the sensations begin to ebb, not ready to be through with it yet. "Don't stop! Don't ever stop," she begged.

He stopped. Rearing back as though she attacked him, his shadow loomed over her like the devil's own angel of wrath.

"*Hvorfor snakker du i den engelske tungen?*" he demanded in a voice as sharp as the blades of his axe.

Perplexed and drugged soporific by the pleasure he'd just given her, she could only stare up at his shadow in puzzlement. How could she answer him in a language she'd never learned? Oh dear, this just became way more complicated. What did he want? What had angered him?

"I'm sorry, warrior," she ventured, her chest fluttering with panting breaths. "Do you not speak English?" It was almost certain he didn't speak in her native Gaelic tongue.

"This heaven is for the Northmen," he growled back at her in perfect English. "You sound like a Pict and speak in the English tongue."

Brows drawing together, she lifted herself up on her elbows. "I *am* a Pict," she confirmed. "And, while Yorkshire is a lovely place, I'd hardly call it *heaven*."

"Yorkshire." He tested the word as though it were alien to him. Then sprang off her with a feral curse, and snatched up his axe and swung it toward her. The blade came to a halt in the valley between her breasts, kissing her sternum but not breaking the skin.

"What are you?" he demanded. "And if you lie to me, I'll spill your blood."

"You can't spill my blood, Berserker." Morgana said calmly, trying to maintain composure while she gathered her wits and clenched her thighs together. "I am your mate."

CHAPTER 5

"*N ie*," Bael's nostrils flared on a breath of pure desolation. "I'll *not* do this again," he snarled, tempted to press the axe deeper into the quivering flesh of the temptress sprawled on the moss, and end them both. This wasn't happening. He was supposed to be dead. He'd *earned* it.

"What do you mean, again?" she asked softly. "We've not met before this day."

Bael's eyes widened. He'd heard that voice before. He *knew* that face. Would kill for it. Die for it. For *her*. He'd left his army behind for her, and they'd likely been slaughtered by the Saxons and claimed their reward in the afterlife.

"Nie!" he groaned, flinging his axe to the ground. "Nie, Nie, *Nie!*" Bael's punch felled a tree, and the woman leapt to her feet, blindly trying to find him in the dark.

"Please, don't be upset," she begged. "I didn't *mean* to kiss you. It's just that—you were dying, you see, and my hands were bound so the only way I could save your life was to breathe magick into your lungs. I had no *idea* at the time you were a Berserker."

"You had no right!" Bael roared, furious enough to shake the woman. Rattle her teeth. He dare not touch her, though. He wouldn't be responsible for his actions if he caught sight of those tempting breasts bouncing with movement. "My life was not your responsibility to save. There is glory in death. *Release.* You have stolen that from me, *witch*." He thrust his finger at her.

"We prefer the term *Druid*," she corrected, then squeaked when irritation flared and he took a threatening step toward her. Covering the noise with false bravado, she distracted him by planting her hands on those generous hips. "And do forgive me for *saving your life*." Her sweet voice dripped with sarcasm. "But I needed you."

Of course that was why. This wasn't even a misguided attempt at kindness, she was just another woman wanting to use him, make demands of him.

Bael hated that he couldn't stop drinking in the sight of her like a doomed man drank mead. She would be just as honey-sweet on his tongue. "What do you want from me?" he couldn't stop himself from asking.

"I need your help... saving the world," she ventured.

Bael retrieved his axe. "Did you not hear me, Woman? I am *done* with this world!" He thrust his axe into her hand and used his own to shackle her fingers around it before pressing the blade against his skin. "This is your mistake, now fix it."

"What do you mean?" she eyed the weapon skeptically.

"I was dying when you found me. Send me to Valhalla."

"Nay!" she cried, struggling in vain to break his grip.

"Do it!" he goaded through clenched teeth, desperate to be free of yet another hellish lifetime of loneliness and rejection. He couldn't face it, not again. "Do not shackle me to you. It is too cruel."

Hurt flared in her wide, clear eyes and anger followed it. "You seemed to want me plenty only moments ago, and after I healed you."

Memory returned to him as his beast rippled beneath his skin, closer to the surface now. He'd been mated. That first kiss, the one that had breathed life back into his body had bound him to her for the entirety of her life. Bael shuddered. There was nothing in the world as sweet as her lips. He still wanted her plenty. So much it was physically painful. "That wasn't me," he said irritably, trying to push the memory out of his mind. "I mean—it was—my Berserker beast."

The witch didn't stop her struggling against his grip. "I rather liked *him*," she muttered.

He'd liked her too, Bael thought bitterly. Liked her enough to mate with her.

Gods be damned.

"Hold still, witch," he said more gently.

"Druid," she corrected again, still tugging against his hold.

"Listen to me," he demanded. And she paused, blinking up at him. "I am old—"

"Oh, you can't be more than forty," she interrupted him.

He tossed her an irate glare of warning before realizing she likely couldn't see him very well in the dark, despite the moonlight. "I have raided and warred for more than a century. I'm done. And this world is well rid of me. I think you are a woman with a gentle heart. I beg you, end my life. Send me to my reward. The Gods know I've earned it."

Her eyes softened, mirroring an alarming amount of his own bleak emotion back at him.

"I-I can't," she whispered, her chin wobbling precariously. "I'm sorry, warrior."

"You *can*." he stepped into the blade, shoving it beneath his neck. "It's sharp, and if you strike fast, I'll feel no pain."

"You don't understand." She shook her head side to side in little horrified jerks.

"No *you* don't understand," he gritted out. "You don't understand what it's like to be tied to a woman who doesn't want you. You don't understand what it's like to have no other purpose than to spill blood and take life. You can't know how many terrified screams echo in my head on a silent night like this. Men. Women—"

"Stop!" she cried. Pulling at the axe with enough strength to startle him into letting it go. It fell to the moss with a great *whump*. The witch brought her hands up against her heart, and clutched at her chest as though it was breaking. "Stop remembering," she begged, sudden tears staining her face. "I can feel your pain. It's tearing me apart. *Please*!"

Stabbed with a dagger of guilt, Bael reached for her and she jerked away from him.

"I'm empathic," she moaned, wrapping her arms around her naked waist and bending beneath the hurt. "I *do* understand."

Bael had been carrying this weight with him for so long, he'd adjusted to it. If his broad shoulders still felt like bowing beneath it, he could only imagine how it could crush a soft creature like her. With great effort, he thrust it down in that deep, dark place within himself where it resided, knowing it wouldn't stay locked away for long.

"Do you see now?" he murmured. "It would be better for us both if you ended it. I cannot do it myself. Such a dishonor would keep me from the halls of Freya."

She straightened and nodded, wiping the tears from her cheeks with the back of her hand. "I am an Autumn Druid," she said tearfully. "My element is *water*. Blood is comprised mostly of water, and blood magick is strong and dark in the hands of one with my power." Her eyes were earnest pools in her luminous face. "So you see, warrior, I have taken a vow never to spill even one drop of another's blood. Not by weapon or with my magick."

Bael's shoulders fell. "Then I will go back to the Saxons, and take as many of them to the afterlife with me as I can."

Her eyes suddenly brightened as though she had an idea. "Or, perhaps you can take me home to Loch Fyne. My brother, Malcolm, *hates* Vikings. He'd probably kill you soon as look at you. Especially if I tell him that we've...that we're... What we did just now." Even in the near-darkness, her eyes flickered down toward the mossy earth.

Bael longed for the pleasant illusion of before. More than tempted to pull that lush, naked body close and drag her back to the moss beneath him, he clenched his fists at his sides as recognition jolted through him.

"You are a Pict." He took a step toward her, repeating her last words. "Your brother is named Malcolm." She retreated from his next step. "And you hie from Loch Fyne."

"Aye," she nodded, wrapping her arms around herself and shivering in the chilly autumn night.

Bael snarled, trying to ignore his instinct to warm her. "Is your brother not the prodigal King of the Picts, Malcolm, The Mormaer of Moray? The last of the Highland Druids?"

His little mate snorted and tossed her head, her eyes flashing with their first bit of temper. "He was never prodigal, our father, Duncan, was betrayed and Malcolm was taken captive. And, I'll have you know, Malcolm is most definitely not the last of the Druids, there are three of us in the de Moray family alone." Her imperious posture was a bit ruined by her nudity. "And yes, while he is one of last *male* Druids left on this earth; there are more than a few females left. Though our numbers are quickly dwindling."

"You mean to tell me you're a Pictish Princess?"

"A bit," she winced, obviously correctly reading the disapproval in his voice. "I am Morgana de Moray. Malcolm is my older brother." She dipped her head in a polite gesture, as though from habit.

"Everyone knows only men of your people are Druids." Bael crossed his arms over his chest.

She scoffed again, flipping her hair over one shoulder uncovering a globe of pink-tipped perfection, obviously unaware that he could see her.

Bael's mouth watered at the memory of her breast in his mouth and bit back a frustrated groan at the unfairness of it all.

"Everyone *knows* that because it is what the Druid men *wanted* everyone to think. It is how they protected the Druid women from the Romans and the Vikings." She glanced up at him, though Bael knew she only saw shadows. "When Malcolm was captured, my cousin Kenna and I were protected no longer, and that is how I find myself so far from Loch Fyne. That is why I saved you, warrior, because I knew when I saw you take that bridge on your own, that you were the only man alive who could get me home."

"You were wrong." Bael informed her, stooping to gather his axe and looking around for his trews. He found them stretched out by the river, clean and dry.

Just how long *had* he been asleep? He went to them, turning his back on the woman whose glowing nakedness was becoming more and more difficult to ignore. "Put some fucking clothes on," he ordered.

"But... it's dark," she pointed out needlessly. "Why does it matter?"

"I can *see* in the dark," he growled. "I can see *everything*."

"Oh," she gasped, sounding less distressed than she should. "Oh my."

Bael heard her soft foot falls as she tiptoed next to him and snatched her shift and kirtle from the moss. Shaking it out, she pulled it over her head in an adorable sort of hurry.

My mate.

Bael shook his head, helpless frustration gathering in his soul. *No.* Never again. He'd been cursed with a mate before. And she'd made the second half of his life more miserable than the first.

There was only one way to free himself from this damnable curse.

And that was to die.

CHAPTER 6

T he three Wyrd Sisters huddled around their cauldron in a dank Highland cave of black stone. The cauldron's fire illuminated a still grotto, but the sound of roiling ocean echoed off the narrow, high walls.

"Thrice the raven hath devoured his mate." The first witch, Badb, tossed in a disembodied raven's wing.

"Thrice the dead tree bloom'd 'neath a blood moon." The second witch, Macha, stirred the brew with an unnaturally gnarled branch.

"Because there are four, Death must rise soon." The third witch, Nemain, passed a hand over the cauldron and the unmentionable putridity coalesced.

They chanted together:
"Awaken the demon of lust and blood.
And the world will end in fire and flood."

BADB PULLED a claw from her decrepit robes, her crone's voice rasping off the smooth stone walls.

"Edward the Confessor died, and his throne is cold.
A foot of crow to ensure King Harold won't grow old."

. . .

ALL CHANTED:
>   *"Awaken the demon of lust and blood.*
>   *And the world will end in fire and flood."*

MACHA PRODUCED what looked like a small piece of raw meat from the pouch hanging from her generous hips.
>   *"The Norman Bastard William sails in two weeks time.*
>   *The liver of this fen rat to ensure his troops do fine."*

ALL CHANTED:
>   *"Awaken the demon of lust and blood.*
>   *And the world will end in fire and flood."*

NEMAIN LIFTED a bundle above her head, and pulled a knife from beneath her flowing blue gown. Her young, angelic face twisted with triumph and malice.
>   *"We gave the Pict throne to Macbeth, but thereon he was slain.*
>   *The blood of this stillborn druid babe will make it ours again."*

MORGANA LET the pool of water—through which she watched her enemies—stream through her fingers with a cry of distress. She couldn't bear to see. Her empty stomach churned and she gagged.

Blood magick. The Wyrd sisters were using whatever Druid blood they could find to regain their power. They *had* to be stopped. She met the gaze of the Berserker, who crouched beside where she knelt next to the stream. The whites if his eyes gleamed in the bright moonlight, though she couldn't make out the color of the irises. She could, however, feel his disgust mirroring hers, and from that she took hope.

"You see what manner of evil I'm up against, warrior? None

of us can stop them on our own. I need to return to my brother, and find my cousin, Kenna, or all is lost." She felt his hesitation underscored with curiosity. "This is why I need you."

"I was told Druids do not have magick as powerful as this." He gestured to her hands which she had cupped to create a seeing pool. "I thought they were alchemists and astronomers with simple magicks drawn from the earth and elements."

"That is true of most Druids," she explained. "But in every generation, there are three born to the Druids of Moray who are granted great powers by the creator, the Goddess. They are guardians of the earth and elements, protectors of the people, and keepers of the sacred Doomsday Grimoire."

"And you are one of the three?"

"Aye." Morgana scooted closer to him, not missing the way he tensed. "Like I said before, I'm the Autumn Druid. My element is water. Then there's my brother, Malcolm, he's the Spring Druid, his element is earth. And my cousin, Kenna, she's the Summer Druid, her element is fire."

The Berserker was silent a moment before asking, "What about winter? What about air?"

A familiar pang of fear sliced through her as she thought of the three Wyrd sisters who'd once been ancestors, but had become their enemies. "It is said that the Gods believed that all four Druids with magick such as ours would be too much power for us mortals to wield all at once. And so there have only ever been three, with a season rotated out of commission from each generation. You see, the Doomsday Grimoire prophesies that when all four seasons and elements are represented on the earth at once, then the end must surely follow."

"The end of what?"

Morgana swallowed around a lump in her throat. "Of *every-thing*. The end of days."

The direness was apparently lost on him, as he just lifted the shadows of his wide shoulders in a careless shrug. "And now there are four?"

"*Yes.*" She held up her hands, as though the pool was still there. "These women, they call themselves the Wyrd sisters. Malcolm and Kenna found a record of them in the Moray archives. They were supposed to have *died* two hundred years ago. They are of a generation long past. And Badb, the crone, *she* is a winter witch. Her element is air. So like they said, now there are four. According to the prophecy, this will bring about the end. All they need is the Grimoire."

"Why not just keep the Grimoire from them?"

"We've been trying, but the Wyrd sisters are powerful adversaries."

The Berserker scoffed, "They did not seem so frightening."

"Do not underestimate them," Morgana warned. "They are the reason this isle is in turmoil. They brought about the deaths of Edward the Confessor. It is because of them King Harold and his brother, Jarl Tostig are fighting on opposite sides. In my Kingdom in the North, they prompted Macbeth to kill my father, King Duncan, and while the usurper Macbeth sat on the throne, he banished us all and tried to assassinate my brother. I was sent to the Saxon King Harold and Kenna escaped with the book. No one knows where she's gone."

"Can't you see her in the water?" The Berserker motioned to the stream.

Morgana shook her head. "Nay, I've tried. She's hidden herself, somehow. And while that protects her from the Wyrd Sisters, it also conceals her from me."

He was silent a long time as he stared at the brook which bubbled happily over stones, the sound incongruous with the ominous moment. The moon cast his brutal profile in shadow, and Morgana was again impressed by the sheer size and strength of him. He really was a magnificently rendered warrior, if a bit suicidal. If only she could convince him to help her.

"What else can you see in the water?" he asked finally, remaining utterly motionless. "Can you predict the future? Could you—foresee my death?"

"You're rather preoccupied with dying, aren't you?" she snapped, irritated that he still didn't seem to grasp the gravity of the circumstances. Just her luck that she would be stuck trying to avoid the Apocalypse with one of the only people alive who couldn't care less.

He didn't answer her question, and so Morgana answered his on a beleaguered sigh. "I can see the past in a mirror pool. I can see what has transpired and what is transpiring at this very moment. Kenna, only *she* can see what is to come in the flames. Though, that power is less definite."

He grunted and stood, securing his axe to the leather strap on his back.

"Where are you going?" Morgana demanded pushing herself up and following him toward the trees.

Again he didn't answer, but she could read a conflict inside him. Anger, need and loneliness amalgamated with arousal, awe, and something she couldn't quite define.

"I'm your *mate*," she called to his retreating back, fighting an incredible surge of desperation. "Aren't you supposed to, I don't know, protect me, or love me—or something?"

He froze, but didn't turn around.

Oh, drat. The anger she'd read spiked within him, under-scored by a cavernous pain so intense it took her breath away. Morgana knew she'd said the absolute worst thing possible. "I'm sorry," she whispered. "Don't leave. You're my only hope."

His head turned to the side, and she could again make out the profile of his brutal features in the moonlight. "It is I who am sorry, *Princess*," he sneered. "For if that is the case, then all hope is lost."

Morgana opened her mouth to beg, to berate, to *seduce* him into action if she had to. But all that escaped her was a gasp of shock and pain as an arrow whistled through the darkness and lodged itself in her shoulder.

CHAPTER 7

The force of the impact drove Morgana to her knees and she fought to regain the breath that had been knocked out of her with desperate but fruitless gulps of air. The fear that another arrow would find more dangerous purchase seized her, and she fought harder to regain control of her lungs and her body.

She looked down at the weapon protruding from her shoulder. Three swan feathers bedecked a willow shaft. This was a Saxon arrow.

How had the Saxons found them so soon?

Another whistle screamed through the silence of the night, and Morgana looked up just in time to see the warrior reach out and pluck the arrow from the air, snap it with his fingers, and fling it to the ground.

Then he was gone. Without a single word or a glance back at her.

Had the warrior saved her life only to leave her here, wounded and alone, with naught but shadows and blood to keep her company?

The thought frightened and galvanized Morgana at the same time. She may be alone, but she was *not* defenseless. As long as there was water, there was a weapon. And, though she couldn't take a life, she could certainly incapacitate an assailant or two long enough to get away.

She hoped.

Fighting a rush of dizziness as she stood, Morgana stumbled back toward the river, cradling her wounded shoulder with her good arm. The pain pierced and burned at the same time, and she knew that in order to heal the wound, she must first remove the arrow.

The kiss of a breeze preceded the tickle of another feather against her cheek as it whizzed past. Morgana dropped to the ground again, hissing as the movement burned through her shoulder like a cruel brand. She didn't allow herself to contemplate the inches she'd just come from the end.

She was about to crawl through the moss to get to the brook, when the unmistakable sound of a death cry followed by a very final sounding *crunch* echoed through her little grove. The succession of rustles, growls, screams, and wet, sickening sounds made Morgana want to cover her ears, but she didn't.

Because she knew who stalked the darkness.

She should have guessed that *he* wouldn't have left her, even if his counterpart wanted to.

When the struggles in the foliage abated, the warrior stepped from the trees looking like a shadowed wraith of fury and muscle.

Morgana didn't have to see the obsidian eyes and bestial snarl to know that the Berserker beast had returned, and he brought the wrath of the Viking war gods with him. When he sighted her, he made a sound that vibrated through her bones, something between a purr and a snarl.

Before she could call out to him, she was gathered into his arms, again cradled against a chest as smooth and hard as tempered steel.

"It's *you*," Morgana murmured to the beast. It surprised her how glad she was to see him, this blood-thirsty creature. To her, he was a rather tender monster, and much more preferable than the grim, suicidal Viking.

Gingerly, he tucked her injured arm against her chest and held it there, making more a sound of distress than she did. His concern for her and the pleasure he felt at torturously killing those who dared to wound her radiated from his feral emotions.

Finding herself oddly touched, Morgana rested her head against his shoulder. "I can heal it," she reassured him through teeth clenched against the pain. "But first we must go, in case there are more."

He grunted in denial, the instinct to kill still surging within him and reaching out to her.

"Please... take me home," she whispered softly, lifting her good hand to his cheek and ignoring the slickness she knew to be blood. "There will be much more blood to shed before this is over, I fear. But for now, I think it's best that we run."

And so he ran.

Morgana had a sense of trees bending past them, of black and blue hills giving way to flat swathes of dark pastures. The Berserker's legs devoured distances with a speed that exhilarated and terrified her. It felt like they were flying. Morgana could sense the care he took not to jostle her, and as dawn turned the sky behind them a brilliant pink, her lids drooped despite herself. She knew she should ask him to stop. That she should see to her wound, but the bleeding wasn't much. She could just rest for a few moments while she and her warrior flew away from their enemies. And those few moments became oblivion.

Frigid water startled Morgana from slumber, and she awoke submerged to the neck in a still pond. Her dark Berserker still cradled her against him as a sky flushed with fire by the setting sun backlit his ebony hair and obsidian eyes. Hadn't it been dawn when they'd left Yorkshire? Had she slept all this time?

Morgana gasped as her shoulder throbbed with intense pain, and the beast made a harsh noise as he gestured toward it.

"I need you to snap off the shaft here," she pointed with her good hand to the wood between her shoulder and the feathers. "Then I'll need you to pull it through as swiftly as you can."

The Berserker nodded, though his features conveyed reluctance.

"I'll be alright," she assured him.

He released her, allowing her to stand in the chest-high water, and held her gaze as he reached for the weapon, a dark wrath swirling in his fathomless eyes.

And then the arrow was gone. She'd barely seen him move, barely even registered the sharp burn as he broke the protruding arrow and yanked it from her body.

Unable to withstand the excruciating pain, Morgana sank to her neck in the pond and closed her eyes, whispering the self-same spell she'd used to knit his wounds the evening before. The sensation of her flesh, connective tissue, and veins knitting together wasn't pleasant in the least, but it was a relief, and after a few gasping moments, her shoulder was as good as new.

Gaining her bearings, she tried to ascertain their whereabouts. The Yorkshire hills no longer rose against the sky in dark green and black ribbons of sloping movement. Flat, wide squares of land dotted with tree-lined brooks and stone walls or wooden fences partitioned fields recently harvested. To the west, a dark forest bracketed the small loch in which they now stood. He'd had to have taken her fifty or so miles by her estimation. And that should afford them a luxuriant head start should King Harold send anyone after them.

"Thank you, warrior," she sighed and stood, slicking her water-soaked hair away from her face.

He regarded her with a bestial astonishment, cocking his head to the side like an enormous Cerberus. Without warning, he seized upon her blood-soiled dress and ripped the bodice open to the navel causing her breasts to spill out.

"Do you mind?" she huffed, swatting at him ineffectually as he used those soulless eyes and strong hands to examine her newly mended shoulder with the thoroughness of an alchemist. "I told you it was healed, now unhand me if you please!"

He looked like he was about to, when the gentle bob of her breasts above the water arrested his unnatural attention.

Morgana fought a blush as his grip on her shoulders intensified and his features tightened with naked hunger. Those lush lips parted on a hushed, yearning moan. His eyes lifted hers, ensnaring her within the voids of black she'd thought were empty, but instead held a bottomless well of unfulfilled desire as his head lowered and his lips inched toward her in infinitesimal degrees.

If she'd read dominance, expectation, or superiority in his emotional signature, she would have frozen him in a block of ice and left him to melt. But the dichotomy of the soft emotions emanating from such a hard man reached past her defenses and touched her gentle soul.

His heart, wounded and broken and atrophied from disuse, ached with wanting. Her nearness caused him pain—no—fear. She could feel his need to touch, to connect. Could sense the desolate isolation lurking within such a primal creature. It was as unnatural for a Berserker to be alone as it was for any human. Every man lived in fear of rejection. Somehow Morgana could feel that for a Berserker, it was a sentence worse than death, something to be terrified of.

And this beast, this lethal, predatory killer, who'd slaughtered more than a hundred men in the last twenty four hours was afraid of her. And not her magic.

In that moment, surrounded by still, calm water and the vibrant colors of a fading day, Morgana surrendered to her impetuous nature. Tilting her head back, she opened her lips with invitation.

And it was all the beast needed to stake his claim.

CHAPTER 8

I f Morgana lived through all this, she planned to encase those magical lips of his in bronze and display them as gloriously as she dare on her mantle. Words most men would eschew coalesced in her mind as she and her Berserker savior devoured each other in a kiss that should have set their cool lake aflame. Luscious. Uncomprehendingly sweet. Wet, warm, and seductive. All descriptions she would have pegged as feminine, and yet they applied to this warrior, but *only* to his unparalleled mouth.

Theirs was a kiss for the ages. Full of wordless promises and new, untried emotions. Morgana didn't dare allow herself time to examine them; only let them wash over her like the incoming tide and pull her back toward their depths.

The hot stroke of his tongue destroyed all resistance. At the animal sound of pleasure he produced in his throat, she forgot all about things like magic, duty, and foreboding prophecies, replacing them with temptation, instinct, and lust. Crashing over her like a storm surge, Morgana couldn't tell if the genesis for this overwhelming desire was him or her, but she couldn't bring herself to care. All she wanted was his warm hands on her cool flesh. She wanted to finish what they'd started in that mossy grove in Yorkshire. Now that she'd had a taste of the pleasure his hands could provide, she wanted to experience all of him.

Most especially that sinful mouth.

A part of her knew that once he returned to himself, however that was possible, there would be consequences to this wanton behavior. But for now she was in the clutches of the beast, surrounded by her element, and entirely absorbed by the wicked impulses they created together.

She closed her eyes, focusing all her being on where they connected.

Their lips.

His hands, which finally ventured from her shoulders to explore the parts of her submerged in the crystalline water, were rough, yet careful.

She didn't dare move, for fear she would break this spell not of her casting, but one woven by a force stronger than she could ever hope to be. Fate? Destiny? She didn't believe in these things, did she? Though, as his fingertips spread wellsprings of desire wherever they endeavored, she somehow knew this connection was more than magic. More than a mating. Just...more.

She expected him to drag her against his hard body. To clutch and paw at her in accordance with the desperate surges of primal lust she could feel tearing through him. And, yet again, he surprised her.

When his hands encountered the ripped dress hanging off her elbows, he finally broke the contact of their mouths as he used the buoyancy of the water to gently relieve her of her soiled garments.

He didn't let her sink into the obscuring depths of the lake again. Instead, he lifted her body so she floated on her back, her entire pale, wet length exposed to his demon-black stare.

The absolute worship she read on his face infused her with a current of desire and power and Morgana could swear that the water heated around them. His eyes devoured her as hungrily as his lips had, touching on the rivulets of water finding intimate crevices to escape back into the loch. The caverns beneath her breasts, the creases of her hips, the hollow of her neck. When his eyes found the nest of dark curls between her thighs, his tongue reached out to wet his full lower lip, and the motion sent slick desire rushing from her body.

Feeling mischievous, Morgana parted her legs and opened her arms, but only to prepare for a strong stroke through the water, surging her away from him.

But the beast was too fast. His hand lashed out and caught her ankle in an iron grip, dragging her through the water back toward where it lapped at the wide swells of his shoulders. Without preliminaries, he hooked her legs over his shoulders and imprisoned her thighs open with his big hands, utterly exposing her.

Morgana felt like she should struggle, that she should give some maidenly protestation to his bold treatment, but the pure awe affixed to his brutal features gave her pause. He looked at her, at that most intimate part of her body, with the eyes of a demon and the reverence of a saint. He swallowed once. Twice. And then licked his lips again with an anticipatory noise that reverberated through her like the roar of thunder.

A deep tremor overtook him, as though his barely leashed beast was about to be splintered by desire. His hands felt heavy against the tender skin and muscle of her inner thighs as he turned his head to press a kiss against the sensitive flesh above her knee.

Morgana's ears echoed with the beats of her heart as she watched the last vestiges of evening light slide along the wet layers of his dark hair when he bent his head. His mouth drifted to the inside of her thigh, pulling her toward him in dangerous increments, his hands moving to make way for his venturing lips.

Her breath caught at another kiss, higher this time, where the skin was sensitive and thin, where blood and nerves scattered incomprehensible sensations through her entire body.

Morgana spread her arms to keep her upper half afloat, feeling as though she watched his ministrations from far away, but felt them through her whole being. Her skin felt both scorching and freezing all at once, gooseflesh blooming and tightening her already aching nipples as her heavy breasts bobbed weightless atop the water.

She gasped as his rough palms began to explore her hips with excruciating slowness. A shuddering weakness stole her ability to move. Paralyzed by desire, she allowed him to push her legs wider and secure her hips above the waterline.

A hot current of longing escaped the place that now quivered for his touch. For his mouth. Her bones felt as though they might melt like steel in a forge. A liquid fire snaked through her, followed by moist and languorous pulses of need.

Finally his hands spanned the place where her hips met her sex. His thumbs stroked through her fine hair, parting the folds of humid flesh.

A sob ripped from her throat as the heat of his reverent exhale caressed her, followed by the pressure of his lips. A soft lick was followed by a gentle tug at just the correct spot, and the throbbing need she'd felt instantaneously released into a flood of searing, luxuriant pleasure. His tongue was silk against the satin of her body, slipping playfully among her intimate flesh, finding places that made her buck and caused her feminine muscles to clench around emptiness, demanding to be filled.

He tested the entry to her body with his tongue, then split her with a sinuous lick, latching on to the exposed nub of pure sensation, abrading it gently as his long, curious finger replaced his mouth. She was so wet, so incredibly slick, that he glided in with no resistance. This seemed to further excite and encourage him. He withdrew, and his second finger joined the first, stretching her body in a pleasurable test.

The growl of approval he gave propelled her to a screaming climax. Morgana bowed back, submerging her head under the water and released her scream in an explosion of bubbles. It was impossible for her to drown, and so she just allowed the water to assist the unparalleled bliss to flow in, through, and around her. It was a flash flood powerful enough to shatter dams and over-flow the banks created by the mere encasement of her sinew and skin. Pleasure came in wave after title wave of ecstatic sensation, and her Berserker's worshiping mouth stayed with her until he'd wrung every last shuddering drop of bliss from her bones.

Her Berserker.

She floated back to the surface boneless and unhurried, enjoying the little pulsating aftershocks of pleasure vibrating in her core. What she saw when she broke the surface stole all sense of reason.

Hunger. Possession. Dominance. All the things she'd wanted to avoid before because of the answering intensity they released within herself.

He split her legs even farther apart and eased them down his wide shoulders, sliding her body down his torso with a diabolical slowness that both aroused and unsettled her. Once his mouth could reach her breasts, he bent his dark head to them, impris-oning her ribcage with his rough hands. Taking the tip in his mouth, he held the wet and chilly nipple in his teeth and stroked it with his tongue, again asserting just the right pressure to make her arch in ecstatic response.

She clutched at his arms, his shoulders, and finally plunged restless fingers into his length of thick hair, holding his scalp in a wordless demand. Needing the feel of his skin against her, she wrapped her legs around his hard, naked torso, surprised to feel that he must have shucked his trews before walking into the loch.

She was going to take him, or he would take her. Either way, Morgana knew that their bodies needed to join, that she needed him to fill her, to flow within her, to connect them as one. Drifting down his muscled body, she didn't stop until the hot brand of his cock rested against her cleft.

He sealed his mouth to her once again. His kisses both rough and sweet. And she felt lost in a sea of sensation, like a vessel with no oars, adrift and out of control. Their mouths fused with a sort of ravenous compulsion, refusing to separate. Her exhale became his next breath. His groans of need suffused her lungs with life.

She let a hand drift down his chest to the obdurate muscles of his stomach, meaning to guide him exactly where she wanted him.

As usual he was faster, caressing up her thighs and then parting her slick folds beneath the water.

She gasped as he tested the clenching, demanding muscles of her sex. She writhed against him, hitching toward the hard shaft of flesh pulsing hot beneath the cool water.

"Now." She'd meant to command, but the word escaped against his lips sounding like a plea.

He slid into her with a slow, heavy movement, his gaze alert, concerned, and amazed. Her eyes widened as he stretched her to the limit, and he withdrew at her first grimace of discomfort, only to start again, gaining a little more ground with each careful thrust.

It wasn't the discomfort that brought a tear to Morgana's eye, but the infinite care and restraint the Berserker showed for her. His every muscle wound tighter than a bowstring, his body trembling with the force of the bestial need surging through his veins. She could feel it, was consumed by it, and yet, the predator inside him was overcome by an awe-struck tenderness, a paradoxical sense of humble concern that she didn't need to read his emotions to find. It shown in the brutal planes of his face, in the softness of his drugging kisses, and in the supportive, yet gentle hold as he pressed himself farther and farther into her body.

Suddenly her tense muscles released, taking him fully, and Morgana let her head fall back in pure, blissful relief.

He kissed her throat, his breath hot against the cool skin, as he slowly moved inside of her.

Gasping, she pulled and grasped at him in a wordless plea for more. His skin was smooth, roughened in some places by hair or by chill bumps. But he would not heed her inarticulate demands as he pushed into and pulled out of her body with infuriating slowness. She couldn't put into words what she needed from him, what her body demanded. More? Faster? Harder? She wanted that, and yet, she wanted him to do exactly what he was doing.

She squirmed, arched, and clutched at him, the noises she made sounding like they were ripped from a torture victim rather than a lover. Her soft inner muscles clenched around his invading hardness, drawing his own tortured groans from his throat, and still he kept his rhythmic thrusts slow and methodical. Regardless of her powers over water, it was impossible to find purchase in the loch unless she had her feet on the ground. He had complete control, and he wielded it with complete discipline.

The feel of him inside her was delicious, voluptuous even, his hard body molding against her soft one. The loch stole away any traces of blood or violence, letting the water become their haven.

Morgana smoothed her hands up the swells of her Berserker's arms, and wound them behind his back, displacing the water between them to wrap herself around him in the most intimate of embraces. She didn't even know his name, but she could feel a century's worth of loneliness contained in the way his arms held her and it seduced her like nothing else ever had.

Each stroke of his strong hips told her a little more about him. Every soft nip of his teeth on her shoulder, nuzzle of her neck, or exploring caress of her spine with long, careful fingers conveyed a piece of his soul. Morgana understood that men, like beasts, communicated in such ways.

It was easier to settle disputes with fists rather than words, and easier to claim a woman with brute strength than with poetry. But this man could use his gifted mouth for something other than words. In fact, it didn't seem like the Berserker beast had the ability to vocalize anything. And he didn't need to, because Morgana understood everything he felt. Every impulse he had. And while in this... form, for lack of a better word, his entire being seemed to be focused on her. Her needs. Her safety. Her pleasure.

Still refusing to quicken his pace, he gripped her ass in his hands and angled her in such a way that his every stroke glided along nerves she wasn't aware she possessed. She could feel every hot inch of his cock abrading inside her with aching precision, learning what made her moan and repeating it until she cried out. Those cries eventually became screams of unadulterated rapture. Her second climax built within her thrust upon thrust until it eclipsed the first and climbed higher still. Her every muscle spasmed, her jaw locked with helpless pressure, and her hands clutched at his hair, pulling it with desperate strength and eliciting a growl of delight in response.

His great, heavy body shuddered in her embrace and his groan was a soft breath against her ear that contained too much. It was a sound of relief, pleasure, pain, and joy, the force of which sang through her as her body milked him toward release. He swelled within her, stretching her further, his arms tightening their hold and his hand cupping the back of her head with infinite tenderness even through the most gripping surges of his endless climax.

Morgana remained locked around him like a barnacle. Her ankles hooked at his hips and her arms around his neck while her face nuzzled into the length of the soft beard at his jaw. This beast had changed everything. She'd always wanted to do her duty, to protect the world from evil. But now she wanted it for a different reason. A gift. For her Berserker. She wanted to save the world for him, and then convince him of its worth.

Resolved, she placed a kiss on his neck, nibbled at his ear, and smoothed the wet hair down his back. She didn't care how long it took to fill his empty heart; she'd show him the meaning of life.

Even if it took a lifetime.

❀

IT WAS ALWAYS such a concentrated effort for Bael to beat the beast back into remission. He knew Berserkers who returned to themselves the moment blood was washed away from their vision. Others could sometimes control it in the heat of battle.

Not him, though. Once his Berserker beast took over, the damnable creature wrung every last moment of violent freedom before Bael could wrestle him back into his cage of rib and flesh.

Reason and consciousness turned the Berserker's growl of pleasure at the tiny nip on his earlobe to Bael's growl of fury. He awoke, for lack of a better word, *inside* the tight flesh of a woman.

His woman.

"Nie!" Chest burning with betrayal, he jerked out of and away from her. The water resisted his movement as he threw her as far from him as he could, ignoring her shocked little squeak.

Turning from her, he hid the shudder that resounded through his bones. Little aftershocks of a release so intense his body still sang with bliss. Bael tried not to think of how warm it had been inside of her. How soft and wet and inviting.

A furious sound exploded from his chest, and he stormed through the water toward the shore trying to wipe the intoxicating taste of her from his mouth.

"Stop. Wait!"

He ignored her breathy, desperate orders, closing his heart.

The mud grabbed his foot. No, not mud, too chilly for that.

Ice. It crawled up his calves, imprisoning them to the bottom of the loch. With a surge of strength, Bael broke through one of the ice bindings, gaining a step. But the other one thickened with alarming speed, and held him to the ground as the free foot again became entrenched within a block of solid water. Bael struggled as it crawled up his thighs, and encased his hips, blessedly leaving his manhood unfrozen.

The loch carried his mate to him, without her making one move to swim.

"Release me, witch!" he snarled, doing his level best not to look at the pink blotches of skin where his beard had abraded her cheek. Her neck. Even her lips were swollen. Bael slammed his eyes shut, willing the twitching heat in his cock to abate.

A hand caressed his cheek. He couldn't be more startled if she'd decapitated him with his own axe.

He still refused to look at her, this time because he couldn't reveal whatever strange and vulnerable emotion she'd just dredged from the black depths of his heart with her touch.

"I'm not finished with you, Berserker," she murmured in a voice husky with pleasure and sex.

Her words, obviously meant to seduce, encased his heart with ice. She may not be finished with him now, but she would be. Eventually. He'd serve his purpose to her and she'd toss him aside like so much unwanted rubbish.

They always did.

In that moment Bael hated her. Hated the sweetness of her sex still lingering like a tempting nectar on his tongue. Hated the memory of pleasure too intense to be real sweeping through him and his beast, simultaneously, as he spilled himself inside of her. Hated the way his skin seemed to ache for the tenderness of her embrace.

Hated the Gods for binding their Berserker creations to a mate. The promise of heaven twice denied was the worst form of torturous hell.

"Let. Me. *Go*," he ordered in a low voice, opening his eyes, but refusing to look at her.

She pulled her hand away from his face. The water froze even stronger around his muscles, and a shudder borne of cold rippled through him.

"And if I do, what then? You'll abandon me, your mate, here in the middle of nowhere and toddle off to get yourself killed?"

"Probably," he clipped, knowing he lied to them both.

"You would leave me here alone and pursued by my enemies?" She sounded aghast.

Never. "Yes," he gritted. "It's not as though you're helpless." He gestured to his imprisoned lower half.

"Let me warn you, sir, that if anyone is going to abandon anyone here, *I* will be leaving *you*." The water around him stirred with indignant ripples. "You'll not thaw until spring, which will give you plenty of time to come to your senses."

His senses were the problem. They honed in on the fresh scent of her warm skin, the lilting brogue of her voice, spinning him about and tempting him to abandon all reason instead of her.

He met her swirling blue eyes with the hardest, coldest stare he could muster. "Do what you will," he challenged. Better that she leave him here to freeze to death than make him care anymore than he already did.

She crossed defensive arms beneath the water pushing glossy cleavage together for his eyes to feast upon. "Bring him back," she ordered.

Bael knew she was referring to his Berserker. "Why, so he'll do your bidding?"

"Nay," she mulishly denied. "Well—yes, but it's very important bidding. And *he* doesn't seem to mind."

"*I* mind!" Bael roared, swiping for her and falling short as the water carried her out of his reach. "This body is *mine*. How dare you beguile my beast with your magick and take me against my will."

The ice climbed his torso, threatening to squeeze the air from him.

"How dare *you* accuse me of using my magick to seduce you? I did *no* such thing!" she sputtered indignantly. "You ripped the dress from my body, you kissed me, and *you* threw my legs over your shoulders and had your way with me. I had *nothing* to do with that."

"Horseshit. That wasn't me, and you know it. I wasn't in a place to deny you. You used my beast to bring you here."

"I said *please!*" she spat. "And you—*he*— seemed more than happy to oblige. And don't for one moment think that you can make me feel like I took advantage of you. Do you really mean to convince me that you *or* your Berserker beast, possibly one of the most lethal creatures in existence, is vulnerable to the likes of me?"

That was exactly what he meant, but hated the way her words made it sound. "Isn't everyone vulnerable to magick?" he volleyed back.

In a fit of incense, she splashed him, and the cold lake water felt like a thousand tiny needles of feminine ire against his skin heated by lust and anger.

"You *dare* insinuate that I used my magic to force you against your will? I am a Druid of Moray. I stand for all that is good and light in this world. I would *never*—"

"Never. What?" he interrupted, motioning to his prison of ice.

Her lovely eyes widened as she flushed a tempting color of pink. "That's different... I...You... Ugh!" Throwing her hands up with a noise of sheer frustration, she turned from him and threw out her fingers, whispering a few words that brought her torn, soaked dress to her from where it had been floating in a sodden heap on the still water.

As she stalked toward the shore, Bael couldn't stop himself from savoring every inch of pale skin revealed by the retreating loch surface. Her long, mahogany hair, glistening with water. The drastic indent of her waist. The dramatic flair of her hips. The lush globes of her round ass swaying over soft, sloping thighs and tempting, dimpled knees.

He clenched his fists below the water, realizing that all the ice in the world couldn't cool the inferno of lust she evoked within him.

She used some kind of witchcraft to draw all the moisture from the fabric of her dress with irate movements. Bael had the impression that anger didn't come often or easily to her.

What would it be like to be a creature of serenity, as still and tranquil as the glassy pond in which he stood? Ponderously, he brought a palm to the surface of the water, letting it flow through his fingers and ripple over his skin.

No tangible element existed as soft and malleable as water. It sustained life, made that which was heavy more buoyant, and cleaned away rot and blood. Bael's eyes flicked back to the witch —er—druid as she yanked her dry, worn garment over her head and clutched at the ripped bodice, grumbling to herself.

And yet, he thought with a wry smirk, who could withstand the force of a flood? The sheer strength of a tidal wave? The raw power of a sea gale? He pictured the mountains and canyons of his homeland, carved by colossal glaciers. Of the fjords that shaped the landscape over untold millennia. Water did all that, sometimes with the patience of the ages, and sometimes with the immediacy of devastation.

If he was a mountain of a man, Morgana de Moray was the river that could carve through his defenses, shape the very essence of his being, and flow through the heart he'd carved of stone, chipping away at his soul drop by relentless drop.

That made her unspeakably dangerous.

Struggling and fighting against his frigid bonds, Bael strained this way and that, flexing his muscle and surging against ice as unyielding as rock.

A crack in the ice encasing one of his legs caused a flicker of victory that was quickly extinguished as he realized Morgana was standing over him, *on top of the water*, her dress lifted away from the moisture revealing her shapely ankles at nearly eye-level.

She didn't give him time to ponder why the view of that ankle was more arousing than a thousand naked women. Instead, she held out her palm, and regarded him with the most serious expression he could imagine on a sweet face like hers.

"I've come to strike a bargain with you, Berserker," she said with mysterious stoicism. "Take me home to Dun Moray, and I vow on the Goddess that if you still want to die in battle, my brother, Malcolm will gladly put you in the ground."

CHAPTER 9

M organa could think of nothing more exhilarating than traveling in the arms of a sprinting Berserker. It truly did resemble flying. By the time the sun disappeared, they'd reached Hadrian's Wall.

"I'd thought we'd traveled forty miles or so at most," Morgana marveled. "You had to have taken me at least a hundred and forty since Yorkshire in one night."

"At least," he mumbled, as they ventured into the wilderness beyond the wall.

Now, hours later, stars pricked the sky with pinpoints of light. Clouds gathered in the distance to the west, rolling with an approaching thunderstorm, and the moon glowed as a waning orb in the east.

"At this speed, you could have me to Loch Fyne by tomorrow night," she calculated, enjoying the moist, chilly air contrasting with the warmth of his chest against her body.

"I will have to stop and rest, eventually."

"Of course," she said quickly, feeling a little foolish that she hadn't really considered the mythical Berserker to be a beast of finite stamina. "How long can one such as you run?"

Her curiosity seemed to irritate him. "I told you I'd get you home as fast as I can. I'll only stop long enough to eat and regain my strength."

They'd had speared fish before leaving the side of the loch where they'd made love. Morgana looked up at the hard jaw of the man who carried her through the night. He'd been inside her only hours ago, caressing her skin as though it was the most precious thing he'd ever put his hands on. She wanted that back. Gods help her, now was not the time for such concerns, not with so much hanging in the balance, but all she seemed to be able to think about was the possessive worship in the Berserker's eyes. And the steely disdain in the eyes of the man now carrying her toward home.

"I wasn't questioning your word," she clarified gently, though she had to speak with a little more force to counteract the rush of the air around them. "I'm merely curious. Exactly how fast and far can Berserkers run? I can't say I've met one before."

Her words seemed to mollify him enough to answer her question. "Most Berserkers move with supernatural speed, but usually in short bursts for battle or pursuit. We all have a specific strength that sets us apart from the others. Mine is speed and endurance."

"Luckily for me." Morgana beamed up at him with her most charming smile.

He didn't answer.

Sighing, Morgana burrowed a little deeper into the warmth of his chest. She thought she felt a tightening of his hold around her legs and ribs, but wondered if she only imagined it. He was too surly a man to be the cuddling kind.

"For what it's worth, I wanted to thank you for taking me home," she offered, hoping to warm the ever-present chill of his company.

"I didn't have much of a choice," he mumbled.

"I suppose not," she conceded. "But it's important that you know I appreciate it, all the same."

He didn't look down at her, keeping his eyes affixed on some distant point in the darkness that only he could see, but she had the sense that she'd surprised him. No. Astonished him was more like it.

What a curious creature he was, to say nothing of the gentle, deadly beast that lived inside him. He was her lover. Her mate. And yet Morgana realized she knew nothing about him.

"What is your name, warrior?"

"Bael. Bael Bloodborn."

"Bloodborn," she echoed. "A...Berserker family name?"

He shook his head, leaping over a fallen tree and jarring her a bit with the landing. "Nie," he answered. "I am the Bastard of Sigard Fjordson and his Persian slave. At the temple of Freya, we bastards have to earn our names through our deeds."

"Bloodborn," she whispered again, the name holding a more sinister meaning now. "I like the name Bael. It's strong and bold. It suits you."

"It'd be my name whether it suited me or not," he said gruffly, but a small prick of awareness skittered along the fine hairs of her skin, telling her she'd alternately pleased and discomfited him.

"I think I like the name Bloodborn better than Fjordson," she continued, enjoying the bit of warmth flowing between them. "It's more, um, evocative, surely. And, er, I'm certain well-deserved. Also, there's something to be said about being the first of your name, isn't there? For example, you can forge your own legacy, that is, if you wanted to live long enough to do such a thing." Morgana furrowed her brow, she'd taken a conversational turn there she hadn't meant to.

"Bastards don't leave legacies."

"I don't know about that," she gently argued. "There's a rather dangerous one bearing down on England as we speak." She, of course, referred to William the Bastard, of Normandy.

He grunted, and Morgana decided to take that as a concession of her point. She was studying his jaw again, the way it connected to the sinew of his neck, tightening beneath her weight, but not straining.

A Persian mother? She could see it now. The dominance of his sharp nose in his otherwise aquiline features. The dangerous angle of his jaw where his Northman blood would want it to be square. The fullness of his lips. The blue cast when the moonlight glinted off his ebony hair. He wasn't dark enough to be exotic, but neither was he cast from the same grey skies and long winters of the people of the north and west. His ancestors were kissed by the sun, and the burnished bronze of his skin likely retained that kiss year-round.

She'd certainly like to find out.

"Where are your mother and father now?" she queried, trying to imagine them waiting at home for him to return from raiding the Saxons.

"Dead."

"Oh, I'm sorry." It sounded insufficient, even to her.

"Don't be," he droned tonelessly. "I'm not."

That saddened her. She'd loved her parents dearly. Their loss was a constant ache, most especially since they were taken from her too soon by Macbeth.

More indirectly, by the Wyrd sisters.

"What about siblings?" she asked.

"What about them?"

"Do you *have* any?" He was being obtuse on purpose. Likely because he wanted her to be quiet. Well, it had never worked with Malcolm, she wasn't about to let it work now.

"I am alone in this world, *witch*, is that what you wish to know?"

"Druid," she corrected, automatically. "But I, too, have a name. It's Morgana, and you can address me as such." She gentled her voice, trying to be conciliatory. "I wasn't trying to ask you painful questions. I was just trying to get better acquainted with you."

"Well, don't," he barked. "There is nothing to acquaint yourself with. I kill people. That is who I am, that is what I do. Sometimes for money. Sometimes for survival. I go to war. I go to sleep. That is my life. I spill so much blood I bathe in it. I see it when I close my eyes. I took my first life the moment I came into this world, and I haven't stopped since."

"Your mother?" Morgana ventured.

The tightening of his jaw could have been a nod. It was too dark to be sure. Morgana was silent a moment, her heart bleeding over the emptiness emanating from him. It wasn't pain. It wasn't rage. It was... nothing. A fathomless, bleak, and yawning chasm devoid of all but a century of blood and loneliness.

Was it possible for someone to be *full* of emptiness?

"Bael, I—"

"Don't." With a burst of speed, he made it impossible for them to talk as he barreled into the Lowlands of Scotland at an incomprehensible pace.

They didn't stop until they'd chased down a sea storm. Lightning boiled the clouds building over a distant peak, smelling of brine and heather and something like singed darkness.

"I see a loch with a thick tree line." He spoke for what seemed like the first time in ages. "We should rest there until we know what those clouds are going to do."

Morgana wondered which loch he referred to, but she couldn't see a blasted thing with the clouds covering the moon. Though, something told her dawn would be upon them any moment. She could feel it in the mists, in the condensation of water on the blades of long grass. It smelled like home.

Like the Highlands.

He set her on her feet and she gripped his powerful arms in order to steady herself while she gained her bearings.

"Stay here, I'm going to hunt," Bael ordered.

"Don't leave," she pressed fretfully, worried that she'd angered him enough that he might not come back.

"I can't run like that another day without food," he said. "I'll start a fire." He left her, rustling around in the darkness for a time and then returning to where she stood, blindly following his movements with her hearing.

"What do you have to start a fire with?" she asked, wishing she wasn't so ineffectual with nothing on her person but a torn dress and a pair of ill-fitting boots.

"You're not the only one with magic, Princess." *Princess?* Well, it was a good deal better than *witch*. She decided it was progress.

A pyramid of logs flared and leapt with light, throwing deep shadows against the Berserker's dark eyes and painting the chiseled planes of his figure in stark relief.

Bemused, Morgana wandered toward the warmth of the flames blinking her surprise. "I had no idea you had fire magic," she exclaimed, quite breathless. "What else can you do?"

"This is the extent of it." he motioned to the stack of wood. "We can create and extinguish a moderate flame, but rarely can a Berserker wield fire."

"What about water?" she asked, motioning to the loch, still a swath of darkness beyond the bank.

He shrugged. "I know a Berserker or two who can summon mists, or work curses. But our magicks are more for survival and combat than anything."

"Fascinating!" Morgana exclaimed, lowering herself by the fire and resisting the temptation to take her hands from where they held her bodice together to hold out to the enticing warmth. "Tell me everything."

He looked at her askance, which she was pretty certain he'd been avoiding since their little interlude by the other loch, both mile and hours past. His eyes skittered away from her, then back.

"My cousin, Kenna, can wield fire, but not ignite it," she mused. "How incredibly useful a Berserker would be to her."

She'd said the wrong thing. Again. She caught the distinct chill in his eyes before he turned away from her. "I'm going to get food," he informed her.

"But, I can call fish from the loch," she protested.

He was gone.

Berating herself, Morgana padded to the water's edge and crouched down, meaning to pull some fish with her magic, just in the unlikely event that Bael's hunt was unsuccessful. The glint of the firelight danced off the still loch, and the past called to Morgana like a wayward siren.

It seemed like an invasion of privacy, somehow, but as she cupped her hand in the water and held it up to the light, she knew that what she would see in this pool would give her the key to unlocking the Berserker's heart.

A WOMAN with hair the color of a spring poppy wove a tapestry in a longhouse adorned with scroll work and animal furs. She hummed to herself a lovely tune while motes of dust and wool glinted in the late-afternoon sun. Her tranquility never faltered even as a giant warrior, his tattoos glowing from skin the color of burnished copper, ducked inside and stalked to her, hauling her to stand and pressing her against him.

"Accept me, woman," he crooned against the hollow of her neck, pausing to press a playful kiss on her rosebud mouth. "Or must I spend another night persuading the words from your lips on sighs and screams?"

"Bael," the woman laughed, glancing surreptitiously around the longhouse, as though checking if they were alone. "What are you doing here in the middle of a training day?"

"What do you think I'm doing?" Bael's shoulder flexed with a movement of his hand, and the woman's bodice was untied. "I am seducing my mate."

She pushed at him, ineffectually. "Won't they miss you at the temple?"

Bael paused in his passionate exploration of her clavicle to pull back and look at her. "What do they have left to teach me at the temple? I'm their fastest warrior. One of their deadliest. They would rather I focus on claiming my mate. It makes me less of a liability."

"About that." She reached up and pulled her bodice together fingers

stuttering as she worked to retie it. "I don't think we should be together during the day like this, someone might see."

Bael's dark eyes lit with suspicion, and beneath that, fear. "My Berserker accepted you as his mate last night," he said more seriously. "Once you accept me, you'll live in my house, sleep in my bed, bear my children. Who cares if anyone sees us? Let them stare."

She turned back to her weave, strumming lines of wool. "Our children," she murmured. "Won't they be dark, like you?"

Bael crossed thick arms over his chest. "Does that matter?"

"Of course it matters. Do you want your children to be laughed at? Do you want them to be outcasts—Persians— like you are?"

"I'm a bastard, not an outcast, Heida. And I'm only half Persian."

She didn't look at him as she said the words that distinguished the light in his eyes. "Do you think someone... like you should be having children? Should even be mated at all?"

Bael seized her arm, forcing her to meet his dead gaze. "I am mated. To you. Or don't you remember begging me to pledge my life to yours last night as I fucked you into oblivion?"

"I wasn't thinking," Heida's fingers blithely worked on her weaving, and she lost herself to the project, effectively shutting Bael out. "And truly, you should have known that a daughter of Jarl Thorsen would never be allowed to mate with a Bastard. Berserker or no Berserker."

Bael's eyes widened with panic and rage. "You don't know what you're doing," he grit out. "I'm bound to you. For the rest of your life. There can be no others for me. Only you, until you die, or I do. Do you understand what that means?"

"I understand that you can prolong my life exponentially," Heida postulated.

"It means that if you do not accept me—"

Placing a finger over Bael's mouth, the woman managed to look both condescending and cold with a tinge of regret for show. "Maybe that's for the best. You can devote yourself to the temple, and visit me from time to time should you like to lie together. But when I marry, it will be to someone worthy of a daughter of Thorsen. I have heard today that

*Prince Bjorn of the Vale is looking for a wife, and may ask me to be his.
Which would make me—"*

MORGANA CRIED out as her hands were seized in an iron grip,
the water showering everywhere with the force of the movement. Bael's lip curled into a snarl as he finished the cruel, selfish
woman's words. "A *Princess*."

Sensing somehow that a struggle would only incite him
further, Morgana curled her hands into fists. "I'm not like her,"
she declared.

"You're more like her than you think," he growled. "You
bound me to you against my will. You manipulate me to do what
you want."

She jerked ineffectually, trying to free herself from his
unyielding grip. "I may be a Princess, but I don't care about your
parentage."

It was clear from the look on his face that he didn't believe
her. "Your brother would. Your father would have. And you
would bend to their will once they found you a lordly husband
with overflowing coffers and pretty manners."

"You obviously don't know me very well." Morgana rolled her
eyes. "I find pretty manners boring."

His eyes flared in the firelight. "You would rather me treat
you like the barbarian I am? Because let me warn you, *Princess*, I
doubt you could handle the demands I'd make of you."

Impulsively, Morgana lifted to her toes, bringing her lips as
close to his as she could, letting the tips of her breasts, bared by
the torn dress, tease the smooth flesh of his chest. "Try me," she
challenged in a throaty whisper as her heart rate spiked in
tandem with his.

She didn't miss his intake of breath, nor could she ignore the
violent response of his body to the nearness of hers.

"You're toying with a dangerous beast," he warned.

KERRIGAN BYRNE

"I've already tamed the beast," she shot back. "Now I just need to persuade the man."

"*Never*," Bael vowed before his lips took hers with quelling force.

72

CHAPTER 10

B ael's kiss quickly deepened from possessive to frantic. Though her body tensed in shock, her mouth melted against his.

Her words had released something more frightening than a beast inside him. More like a devil. He twisted his mouth over hers, claiming entrance with his tongue from every angle he could possibly devise. Before crushing her to him, he yanked her dress from her shoulders and followed it down the curves of her lush body until it fell from her hips.

Though her fingers trembled as they clung to the nape of his neck, her mouth yielded to his demands, meeting his possession with sweetness and his dominance with a moan of submission. The kiss didn't sate his growing desire for a taste of her, as he'd hoped, but ignited a fury of desperate lust.

She'd submit to more than his tongue before he was through with her.

"Yes," she hissed against the cavern of his open mouth, as though she'd heard his dark thoughts.

That one word broke any chain that held him in check. Bael ripped his mouth away from her long enough to have her on her back, his eyes raking over her passion-flushed skin. "Remember you wanted this," he felt compelled to warn her again.

Or was it a threat?

"I do want this," she reached for him. "I want *you*."

Couldn't be. She wanted the gentle, worshiping Berserker who'd made love to her in the lake. She didn't understand, couldn't comprehend that she now faced a killer who would fuck her into the dirt.

Bael almost felt sorry for her.

Almost.

With a growl, he settled his bulk atop her and kissed her again, pouring fifty years of deprivation into her open mouth. He knew his lips were rough, demanding, and agitated. That his beard abraded her tender skin. But she made soft little mewling sounds of pleasure into his mouth that nearly drove him over the edge before he even took off his trews.

He'd never wanted anything like he craved the pale body glowing beneath him in the firelight. He couldn't remember a time he'd been so hard. So out of his mind with need. So fucking insatiable with lust.

Reaching between them, without parting their fused lips, he undid his belt and freed himself. Mounting her—heart thundering with the strength of his desire—he positioned the blunt head of his cock against her vulnerable opening.

Her sex was a moist cleft hidden by soft cinnamon curls, and she drew her knee up his waist to grant him easier entrance.

"Take me," she whispered. "I am yours."

Mine. His beast rejoiced.

"Nie," he growled between clenched teeth. "Take *me*." He surged forward until his entire length was buried in the succulent flesh of her body. "Take *all* of me."

Though her body reflexively clamped down on his intrusion, a rush of moisture eased his way as her hands threaded through his hair at the temples, tightening the tattooed skin there.

"I will," she gasped, lifting her hips to meet his. "I do."

He couldn't stop to consider the full extent of the meaning in his words to her. Take me. Take my cock. Take my seed. Take my heart, my soul, my needs, my emptiness.

Take all of me.

It was too much for any one woman to hold.

But she did. She held him so sweetly in the cradle of her thighs he thought he might expire from the bliss of it.

And wasn't that what he wanted?

"Nie," he said again.

Bael forced his mind to be dark and quiet, to focus on the tight sheath of her flesh already pulling little tremors of pleasure from the base of his spine.

With a savage groan he slid his hand beneath her ass and set a punishing rhythm, pulling back to watch her breasts bounce with each brutal stroke.

His mate's lips were parted, teeth bared like a lioness in a face glowing with an answering lust that shocked him.

"*Yes,*" she countered with a hiss, and thrust her hips up to meet his with such force that she nearly lifted his heavy body.

The contact was like the bolt of lightning that touched down in the distance. Sensations exploded within him that he had no name for and had never before encountered in his long life. Instead of holding her down and fucking her into oblivion as he'd planned to do, Bael burrowed his arms beneath her and pulled her to him, falling back onto his knees and holding her against him as he plowed her again and again.

She wrapped her arms around his back anchoring herself to him as his every powerful thrust jolted her upward. Their hips connected with starting force, and she made a sound of such wicked encouragement each time that drove him out of his mind.

She screamed her pleasure with astonishing quickness, her body clenched in an endless shudder of ecstatic release. The sublime contractions of her gripping sex pulled a violent answer from his own. He crested on a spiraling cataclysm of sensation, undulating outward like the ripples of a pool until his entire body was locked by crippling pleasure.

He bit down on the delicate sinew where her shoulder met her neck, marking her. Claiming her. Sending her over the edge once more with a feminine cry of surprise and delight as she pulled at his hair in pulsating fistfuls.

Thunder rumbled in answer to their cries, and the electric build of the storm that accumulated over the sea held the whisper of danger on the wind. Though as Bael watched the siren he'd mated come apart in his arms, he could think of nothing as dangerous as her.

BAEL WOKE to the sound of a scream. Not a scream of fear, nor one of surprise. This scream carried with it a particular note of gleeful, victorious evil. Bolting upright, he reached for his mate, and barely held her from where she tried to jump out of his arms toward the water.

"Let me go," she hissed. "The Wyrd Sisters. They found us!"

A specter rose from the water in the shape of a voluptuous woman, she threw out her hand, flinging lethally sharp shards of ice at his mate.

Morgana leapt away, slicing through the water with her own blades of ice conjured with a flick of her wrist. But it only had a momentary effect, each projectile shattering against the other's with supernatural precision. The specter's shards seemed to be garnering help and velocity from a gathering tornado reaching down to the Loch from dark and angry clouds.

The women spoke in a Gaelic tongue he didn't understand. Incantations, threats, spells, or vows of retribution. It didn't matter; all that mattered was getting Morgana out of danger.

Bael grabbed for his axe, which was never out of reach, and hissed as his hand came away singed.

In the pit of fire he'd built, standing on the bones of their supper, another specter dominated the flames. A slight girl. Her eyes glowed with an even brighter light than the flames comprising her body. She held his axe in her fiery grip, heating the metal to a molten orange. "Touch it," she taunted in the voice of a child. "Take it from me, I dare you."

Snarling, Bael gritted his teeth in preparation for his torment, then he roared as he plucked his weapon from the ground and leapt for Morgana.

Though he gripped the leather-wrapped part of his axe, the heat of the metal bled through, blistering his hands. He didn't care. He'd survived worse. All he felt was his blood pounding to reach his mate. His entire being focused on her.

Just as a sickle of ice flew toward her heart, Bael swung his axe with all the speed he could muster and scattering shards to the gathering wind. But he didn't stop there. Thrusting Morgana behind him, he flailed at the specter of water with such whirring speed, he turned her to steam with his glowing blade.

The wind screamed that bone-chilling evil sound and the brewing storm unleashed its rage upon them.

Scooping Morgana into his arms, Bael ignored the intense burning in his palms and the stinging lash of the deluge as he bolted into the trees. Never in his life has he run from a battle, but these spectral witches had no blood with which to spill. No bones to break. No hearts to stop.

Just elements.

And blood magick. The darkest and most potent kind.

We're coming for you. A crone's whisper drifted through the scream of the wind, kissing his spine with ice and dread, though he knew the threat was directed less at him and more at the precious woman he carried in his arms. *We're coming for the Grimoire.*

Prepare for the end.

The last word fractured against dying branches and echoed about the forest with eerie force as though coming from everywhere and nowhere at once.

"Babd," Morgana's frightened exclamation vibrated against his skin. "She's air. There's no escaping her!"

"She won't get to you," Bael vowed, and doubled his speed, careful to keep his mate's limbs from finding an errant branch as he plowed through the forest, desperately forming a plan of action.

A tree root nearly tripped him, and Bael could have sworn he'd seen it lift. Taking more care with his footing, he noticed the ground beneath his boots growing softer as the wind began to die away. More roots and tree limbs conspired to steal his footing, though the ground seemed to want to hold him into one place.

What fresh sorcery was this?

In three more steps Bael struggled against roots, vines and branches. For each one he broke, two took their place, latching to his limbs and locking them down. His axe was stolen from his back, his neck lashed with willow cords.

He fought them, clenching his little mate tighter, his enraged roars drowning her protestations.

A blade nicked the nape of his neck from behind, all flora tightening enough to choke his very bones.

The dark voice that pierced the forest resembled nothing of the three Wyrd sisters from which they fled, but was masculine and heavily accented even though every word was annunciated with lethal clarity.

"Take. Yer filthy. *Viking* hands. *Off* my sister."

CHAPTER 11

"W here is he?" Morgana demanded, blocking the Pictish King, Malcolm de Moray's intent scrutiny of the blaze illuminating Moray Castle's great hall.

Her brother's cold green eyes slid to her, and a flicker of what might have been affection touched them. "If ye're referring to yer Berserker, he's in the dungeon."

"Don't let him fool you," she cautioned. "Berserkers cannot be bound by chains."

"I reinforced the chains with magic, until I can figure out how best to kill him."

Morgana gasped, fighting the childish urge to yank on his wildly auburn hair, the exact same shade as hers. "You'll do no such thing!" She wagged a finger at him. "I forbid it."

"Ye forbid yer king?" A russet eyebrow crawled up his broad, noble forehead toward a crown of gold shaped with short spikes fashioned to look like young Elk antlers.

"You're not my king, you're my brother," she snapped.

That produced a short sound of amusement from her other-wise stoic brother's throat. "He seemed to be under the impression that I was duty bound to end his life," Malcolm observed, leaning forward in his throne until his royal robe fell from his wide shoulders. "Really, sister, warn a fellow before pledging my hand at murder next time. And be happy I allowed ye to waste yer magic healing his burned hands before we arrived home."

"He used those hands to save my life." Morgana studied her brother, worrying the skirts of her clean frock, wondering at the change in him. He'd been a handsome, sparkly-eyed youth with a quick temper and an even quicker wit. His hair had been wild and wind-blown like hers instead of slicked back into this tight queue. She'd liked the way his smile smoothed the calculating sharpness of his features and made him seem so young.

That was before Macbeth. Before they'd been taken prisoner and banished from their father's kingdom. Before the battle Malcolm had waged to win his throne back.

Before Kenna disappeared.

He didn't look so young anymore. He looked like a dominant man who carried more weight than even a Berserker could hold. Malcolm de Moray wielded unimaginable power, and yet something about him was broken.

Morgana was starting to think that she'd gotten the better bargain in her exile with the English King. Something had happened to Malcolm. Macbeth and his insane bitch of a wife had irrevocably harmed him, somehow.

She'd find out just as soon as they addressed the trouble at hand. And do what she could to heal the bleak rifts she could feel emanating from his soul.

"Any word from Kenna?" She walked away from the warmth of the fire, missing her cousin and closest friend with a physical ache.

"Nay," Malcolm sighed. "I stare into those bloody flames for hours every day searching for a message. But I know she's alive."

"The Wyrd Sister's storm is gathering closer," Morgana observed from the casement, watching lightning branch from the angry sky to the south. "What should we do?"

"Let them come," he rumbled. Standing, he gathered his

black robe about him, his crown gleaming in the flames, and held out a hand to Morgana. "We'll fight them together."

She went to her brother, his emotions as cold as the grey stones of Castle Moray. Wasn't he frightened? Wasn't he angry? "But, Colm, we are only two, we haven't a third. If we can't cast a circle, how can we protect the Grimoire?"

"I doona think we can," he said after a long pause. "But it is our duty to try."

They both walked to the dais in the middle of the throne room. Upon the pillar of stone lay a thick volume bound in an almost blonde leather. Blue tattooed runes adorned the corners and stretched toward the center of the title. Wards of protection surrounding a word spelled in a language not meant to be spoken.

As Morgana neared it, she felt the little thrill of danger that always jolted through her when in the presence of the Grimoire. Though, it didn't look as ancient as she remembered, it also didn't pulse with the same mysterious call she'd felt as a girl when sitting at her father's feet in this very throne room.

She was grown now, a Druid in her own right, and after all they'd been through, nothing ever held the mystery or magic it had seemed to all those years ago.

Wooden shutters began to rattle; the storm had truly finished brewing and now became the harbinger of evil intent. It battered against the heavy wooden door of the throne room, chilling the air and carrying with it whispers, threats, and maniacal laughter.

"Perhaps we could use Bael." She thought of her lover, her mate, locked in the dungeon by magical chains. "He could be our third. He has a little Berserker magic." Also, she wanted him here with her. Though she knew there was not much he could do against magic, his presence, his strength, made her feel safer. Made her feel more powerful.

Malcolm shook his head. "He has no Druid blood. It wouldna work."

"But couldn't we try?" she argued. "He could at least use his axe to protect us."

Her brother studied her with shrewd eyes for a moment. "A Berserker, Morgana? *This* is who ye choose after all the suitors Father paraded in front of ye?"

Morgana shrugged. "I didn't *choose* him, exactly. I saved him and he sort of ran off with me."

"Ye care for him."

"Inexorably."

Somewhere in the castle a window broke. Lightning lashed about the stones in unnatural strikes.

"But—a *Berserker*," he repeated the word like it tasted foul. "They're so proprietary. They tend to be a violent, jealous, barbaric lot with no morals and even fewer scruples. Ye're not only a Princess, Morgana, ye are a Druid. One of the Sacred Triad."

"Really, Malcolm, you want to have this conversation *now?*" She gestured to the forces rattling the door, to the smoke beginning to curl beneath it. "Don't you think we have more pressing problems to focus on?" Malcolm and Morgana clasped hands over the book.

"I'm just saying," he continued as though having an argument over an evening ale. "Ye deserve better than a Viking—"

"There *is* no better, Malcolm," she hissed. "Or don't you remember, I can feel what he's feeling. That man you call a *barbarian* has been alive and *alone* longer than you four fold. His emotions run deep as the ocean, and he's never had anyone upon which to shower them. Why do you think he's given up? Because a man who feels that much, can't survive so many rejections. Cannot thrive in solitude. He wasn't made for that."

"But, Morgana —"

She silenced her brother with a look. "I know Bael can be a bit vicious and maybe even something of a savage, but he's *my* savage, Malcolm de Moray, and I accept him as he is, as *mine*, so you must as well. I knew the moment we kissed that he was somehow meant for me, so don't try to talk me out of it. You know it won't work."

"But—"

"Now we have a protection spell to work, and not enough time to work it in. Chant with me, brother." Morgana was amazed that Malcolm didn't seem more worried. That there wasn't sage burning in the corners of the throne room or Ash leaves in the windows. Where were the wards drawn with crushed burdock, black cohosh, frankincense, and heather? "If we survive this, I'm going to have a discussion with you regarding your lapse in protection."

He merely lifted another eyebrow at her, and Morgana decided she was beginning to hate that eyebrow.

Morgana began the protection chant. "*I am protected by your might, O infinite Goddess of the night.*" Malcolm joined her the second time, their voices truly melding by the third.

The flames in the fireplace flared to an inferno. The stone of the altar upon which the book stood vibrated and those vibrations reverberated through the stones at their feet. The storm raged, hurled, and concentrated on the door until the hinges burst and the heavy oak crashed to the stones.

The flames that had weakened it were extinguished by the tumultuous downpour as lightening illuminated three figures in the arched doorway.

The Wyrd Sisters.

They manifest as maiden, mother, and crone, a blasphemy of the sacred Goddess from whom they drew their power and then twisted it into something dark and self-serving.

They, too, were chanting as they slinked in oily progression toward Malcolm and Morgana. Their language was older, their spells more ancient, yet so far, their powers clashed against the Moray Druids like the waves against a cliff.

"Give us what is ours," Badb, the crone, lifted a gnarly finger from beneath black robes, indicating the Grimoire. At her gesture, the book slammed open, its pages flipping in the wind with startling speed before landing onto the most dangerous ritual in history.

The Curse of Four: The seven seals.

The ritual that would bring about the Apocalypse.

"Nay," Morgana yelled. "It was *never* yours. It will never *be* yours."

The girl stepped forward, more than a child, not yet a woman. *Nemain.* Her angelic face and golden hair made all the more horrifying by the sacrosanct lust in her eyes as she stared at the book. "The Grimoire belonged to *us* centuries before it came into the hands of you Highland Picts," she informed them condescendingly.

Macha advanced, her body sheathed in a form-fitting gown made of all curves and womanly seduction. "We are the Moray's of Eyre, and it is our right to enact the Curse of Four and awaken the Horsemen."

"Why?" Morgana demanded. "Why would you do such a thing? Why end the earth upon which you live?"

"With destruction comes rebirth." The crone said cryptically, and a chill of terror kissed Morgana's spine at the vacant darkness in her silvery eyes. "With rebirth comes a realignment of power."

"It is *not* yer right," Malcolm insisted, never breaking contact with Morgana. "It is not the time. The earth is not done with her cycle. This I know, she has told me."

"It is not only our right, it is our destiny!" Nemain drew fire from the inferno in the fireplace and snaked it toward Malcolm, igniting his robes.

Morgana broke the contact of their hands to reach out to the rain, drawing the deluge toward them and drenching her brother until only steam rose from his scorched and tattered robes.

"Fool!" Badb pushed the girl, Nemain, behind her. "The prophecy says there has to be four Druids. Four Elements. We need *him*."

Macha, the mother, stepped forward and thrust her hand

toward Morgana. A dread stole through Morgana's veins, as did the woman's dark water magic. Her blood was no longer hers. It belonged to the evil woman with mirroring powers. Macha froze her in place, slowed the flow of her life until she could barely stand. Barely breathe.

Malcolm drew a heavy stone from the ground and hurled it, but the crone knocked it away in a powerful gust of wind. "Try that again, *King* Malcolm, and we'll stop your dear sister's heart forever." Badb approached Malcom, her rheumy eyes glowing with malevolence. "You see, she is expendable. We have our own Water Druid." She motioned to Macha. "And we have fire and air. What we're missing... is Earth."

"Ye know I willna perform the ritual." Malcom's voice was cold as the stones beneath them.

"Not even for her?" Badb drew a long, jagged fingernail across Morgana's throat.

Malcolm's gaze locked with hers, and Morgana put all her words into her eyes. *Don't you dare,* they screamed at him. *Just let them kill me.*

"You *know* how persuasive we can be." The old woman cackled as Malcolm's face drained of color, but he stood his ground.

"Never," he vowed, in a voice so dark, Morgana didn't even recognize it.

"That remains to be seen." The crone turned from him. "But for now we need the book."

"And men in hell need water."

"If you do not give..." Macha put her other elegant hand out, and Morgana fell to her knees. "We will take."

For the first time in her life, Morgana wished she could feel her heart pound with terror. Wished that she could sense the blood surge through her and heat her skin in a flush of emotion and pain. For now, facing the end, she could feel none of those things. It was as though her life slowed to a trickle. She could feel her heart struggling to find its fuel, her lungs trying to force oxygen into the almost non-existent flow. Muscle and tissue screamed for want of it. She was shriveling up from the inside. She knew she should be worried about the Grimoire. Knew she should be mourning for an earth that might never be if they failed. But all she could think about was how she'd never get to tell Bael the one thing he needed to hear before the end.

That he was worthy. That he was accepted. That he could be loved, if he'd allow it.

And now it was too late.

CHAPTER 12

Morgana's acceptance was a warm pillar of sun after a century of storm clouds. Bael felt it flow through him with a surge of light and power unlike anything he'd ever imagined.

Locked in the de Moray's dungeon, he'd listened to the storm raging outside and wished he was out in it, so it could clean away the bereft agony of being separated from his mate.

A mate he'd told he didn't want. A mate he'd made promise to have her brother kill him.

Instead, she'd accepted him, with barely a kind word spoken between them.

Why?

Testing the reinforced chains with his new strength, they felt more flimsy to him. Breakable.

Ha. Let the Druid King try to keep him from his mate, *now.*

A great crash reverberated through the castle, and a cold wash of dread vibrated in his bones.

Morgana, she was dying. He could feel it in the dimming of his soul.

How cruel could the fates be to lead him to her and then allow her to be taken? He wouldn't allow it. Not this time. He strained against his bonds, sweat breaking out over his skin though he felt colder than the glaciers of his homeland.

This was his fault. He'd allowed *himself* to be taken. He'd spent moments of unmeasured bliss in Morgana's arms and then slinked away to the dungeon to face his end rather than risk her possible rejection of him. He was such a fool. He should have fought for her.

He'd fight for her now. Fight for the life she'd infused within him, regardless of his resistance to it.

With a roar born of rage, he tensed against the chains, then strained, cording his muscles and calling forth his beast.

For the first time without the invocation of blood, the world faded to shades of grey. Every sound differentiated into an echo, every sight detailed with the precision of a blade. His beast surged within him and so did a new and powerful magic.

The chains shattered.

Though Bael knew nothing of the layout of the keep, he was spurred into action by the inexorable link he'd just formed with his mate. He stormed up stairs and through the halls of the castle, passing tapestries and busts that must have dated back to the Roman times. Libraries, chambers, a solarium, some of which hid cowering castle staff, but none of which contained the woman he yearned for.

His woman.

It shocked him that he allowed the people to live. That his Berserker beast didn't claim the blood that was generally his due.

Was it because of his mate? Because of her acceptance?

Morgana. Where was she?

A hiss and whistle of wind drafted though one hall, and as he followed it, it built to a scream. Voices echoed off the stones.

Bael heard his mate, his sweet, yet strong-willed woman, her voice filled with defiance, and then fear.

With no thought for tactics or strategy, he burst into the throne room intent on killing whomever was not Morgana and sorting it all out later.

He was behind his mate who'd sunk to her knees, struggling for life. Three witches turned to look at him in eerie unison. They were his enemies. They'd hurt Morgana. He'd kill them all with his bare hands.

He knew what they saw as he moved. A blur. A rush of air. And then the woman who reached her arms toward Morgana was crashing through the window casement, shattering the wood, and collapsing, broken, to the ground outside.

The sinister girl who'd taunted him from the flames was flesh and bone this time, and she made a satisfying crunch against the wall when he flung her with a swing of his fist.

He took a moment to check on his mate, his heart lifting to see her clutching her chest and gasping in huge lungs full of life-giving air.

That moment cost him.

The crone, screeching with shock and outrage threw out her hands and Bael was lifted from the stone floor, mid-lunge, as though his heavy frame weighed no more than a whisper by a wind funnel that whipped his hair painfully against his face and shoulders. He flailed about, desperate limbs trying to find purchase, but there was nothing but the most intangible and salient element surrounding him.

"I will end you," he roared.

"I will end *everything*," the crone hissed.

"Not today." With a flick of Malcolm's wrist, a discarded stone half the size and twice the weight of the old woman dislodged from the throne room floor. "Yer healer is gone, Badb. Will ye survive this?"

As Malcolm spoke, the girl struggled to her feet from where she'd crumpled against the wall in a pile of thin bones and pain. Blood poured from a crushed eye-socket. One arm hung limp from a shoulder that barely existed anymore, but she circled toward the Grimoire with a dragging limp and a maniacal sneer.

"Give Nemain the Grimoire, Druid King, or watch your

sister and her Berserker die in a storm of flames," the crone threatened.

"Bael," Morgana gasped, struggling to her own unsteady feet. "Release my mate." She turned on the crone.

Their eyes met, and for a moment, Bael ceased his struggles. She'd accepted him. Not to his face, not in the darkness where no one but he could hear. But to her King. To her family. Even to her enemies.

They were likely over before they began. Malcolm would crush the fire witch, and this crone would crush Bael. He could already feel her taking his breath. But he'd die with the knowledge that he'd been enough.

Enough for *her*.

Chaos erupted in a flurry of simultaneous action.

The wounded girl dove for the Grimoire, snatching it from the altar.

In a shocking move, Malcolm hurled the stone at Badb, ignoring the fire witch and freeing Bael.

The crone didn't have time to deflect the stone, so on a scream, she jerked her entire form and a circle of gale-force wind erupted from her body, throwing everyone back against the walls of the throne room. It wasn't enough to completely redirect the stone, and it glanced off her body with a bone-crunching sound.

By the time Bael gained his footing, her robes were snagging on the shattered window as she flew into the stormy night.

Which left Nemain clutching the book.

Morgana stumbled forward, desperately reaching trembling arms toward the witch. "You'll burn in hell for this."

The girl flashed a triumphant smile, made all the more sinister by the blood coloring the spaces of her teeth. "You first," she hissed, as the fire in the hearth flared around her, turning half the throne room into a furnace.

Morgana pulled the rain inside once more, but by the time the flames extinguished, there was nothing left of the girl but a scorch mark on the flagstones.

"Nay!" Morgana lurched towards the door, the black path of char leading out into the night. She staggered as though her legs were unready to carry her yet, and Bael had her in his arms before she fell.

"We must go after her!" Morgana screamed.

The King was merely surveying his throne room, rolling his wide shoulders looking nothing more than a trifle bemused and relieved.

Morgana leaned heavily into Bael, who could feel her vigor returning with every beat of her strengthening heart.

"What is the matter with you?" She demanded of her brother. "How can you just stand there? Malcolm, they have the Grimoire!"

He turned to her, a half-smile twitching across his otherwise stoic features. "Do they?"

Bael frowned as Morgana tensed. "Colm, what did you do?"

Inspecting his singed robes, he asked. "What is a book but earth and skin?"

"*Malcolm.*"

"Alchemy, my dear sister, can create any number of deceptions, not the least of which, is forgery."

"Malcolm Duncan Connor de Moray," Morgana's voice gained strength, and she pulled herself from Bael's supporting arms. "*Where* is the Doomsday Grimoire?"

The King gave a very boyish shrug. "Kenna has it."

"Kenna," she breathed, holding a disbelieving hand to her forehead. "Oh, thank the Goddess, where is she?"

A troubled frown replaced the sparkle in Malcolm's eyes. "I wasna lying when I said I doona know. But I know she is safe, and so is the Grimoire." He took off his crown and placed it on the empty altar adding, "For now, at any rate."

Morgana wasn't done with her brother, and Bael found himself thanking the Gods he'd never been the recipient of the wrath glowing on her features. He'd remember that look for the future, and mark it as a signal to retreat.

"Then, *how* could you let them go?" she cried, pushing her strapping brother in the chest to no effect. "They killed our parents. Stole your birthright. Separated us. Don't you want to take your vengeance?"

Malcolm grabbed his sister's wrists, subduing her. "Ye canna comprehend how badly I want vengeance," he said in a voice filled with secrets, and eyes haunted with darkness. "But what ye doona understand, sister, is that revenge doesna happen in the market place, or the throne room, slinging insults and elements at each other. *True* vengeance is shadow and silence. It is patience. It is flawless calculation and perfect timing."

"You're hurting me," Morgana whispered. "Malcolm let go."

Bael made a threatening noise. Brother or no, he'd crush the man if he didn't unhand his mate *immediately*.

The king blinked a few times, and seemed to return to himself, glancing at the lethal warning etched on Bael's face. The Druid let go of his sister's wrists, but Bael had the impression it wasn't because he was afraid of her new Berserker mate, but because it was what he should have done.

Bael knew little of the Pictish Druid King. But if nothing else, he loved his sister.

Malcolm swept an assessing glance at Bael, pausing at the manacles still encircling his wrists and dangling with broken chains. "How did ye escape my chains?" he asked with only mild curiosity. "Not that I'm not grateful that ye did."

Bael reached for Morgana, and couldn't deny the astonished pride he felt when she melted into his arms. "Your sister accepted me," was all he said by way of explanation.

Malcolm nodded, as though he understood the implication. Then made a sound of only half-mocking disgust. "If ye're going to be here with my sister, I suppose I doona have to tell ye that if she sheds one tear over ye I'll trap ye alive in a hollow tree and sit by and listen to ye starve to death while dozens of tiny insects feast on yer flesh."

Bael could respect the threat. "And I suppose I don't have to tell you that, though I respect that you rule this land, I do not kneel when a King asks me to kneel."

"A good King never has to ask." It was neither acceptance nor threat. But something in-between. "Though, I'd appreciate yer help with the battles yet to come. The Wyrd sisters are injured, but they aren'a defeated. Not yet."

Bael nodded, wondering how two such men would survive each other for the sake of one tiny Druid woman. He looked down into his mate's shimmering blue eyes. Smudges of exhaustion darkened the skin beneath them, and she could only summon a wan smile.

She was the most beautiful thing he'd ever laid his eyes on.

"You truly accept me?" he asked, unable to help giving her one last chance to send him away.

She reached up to his rough cheek. "You've endured a century of loneliness. Perhaps you'll allow me to fill the next century with family and all that comes with it. All the high-handed opinions, the *irritation*, and the disagreements." She glanced at her brother, but then her gaze softened. "All the pride, the strength, and support in your moments of weakness."

Her eyes were misty when they met his again. "I can't believe you've lived so long without it all. And it's a gift I want to give to you. As your mate. As your wife."

"Aren't I supposed to propose to you?"

She snorted. "This is no proposition. We're *getting* married, whether you want to or not."

"May the Goddess grant ye strength," Malcolm grumbled, curling a disgusted lip.

Bael grinned. No one had ever dared talk to him like she did. He loved it.

"I'm falling in l—"

She pressed a finger against his lips. "Those are words better suited to when I'm not recovering from near-apocalyptic experience." She lifted on her tiptoes to press her lips against his. "And also for when we're alone, because *someone* will ruin the moment." She cast a glare at her brother, who looked offended for a second and then shrugged with a nonchalant nod before returning to his imposing throne.

"Besides, I can feel what you feel," she continued. "So you don't have to say it, though it is nice to hear from time to time." She tucked her body against his, drawing him gently toward a darkened hallway that Bael hoped led to her chamber. "I'll have few words to give back to you," she murmured into his ear. "Though words are not the primary vocation I'd have for those lips of yours."

"Oh?" Intrigue and heat speared through him, along with a softer, more tender emotion. An unhurried glow that was wholly unfamiliar and paradoxically thrilling. Was this love?

"Yes," Morgana was saying, answering both his spoken and silent question. "I do not think that words will be the basis of our relationship."

"Thank the Gods," Bael said honestly. For he was more a man of action than words, and it seemed that was fine with her. A singular woman, his mate. If she already knew what he felt, he didn't have to find words he didn't possess to convey the depth of his emotion. Some men would find that an imposition, Bael found it a great relief.

"No more talk of dying then," she said seriously.

Bael paused and pulled her into his arms, pressing a kiss to her hairline. "I'll spend the rest of my long life fighting to stay by your side," he vowed into her eyes.

He couldn't believe his good fortune. She'd dragged his dying body out of a river and breathed life not only into his lungs, but into his heart. He had a purpose to fulfill. A life to live. A mate to worship. And battles left to fight.

And to a Berserker, *that* was a world very worth saving.

HIGHLAND WITCH

The Wyrd Sisters:

*"Double Double toil and trouble.
Fire burn and cauldron bubble."*

- William Shakespeare, Macbeth

CHAPTER 1

There would be no raiding in weather such as this. Niall Thorson squinted through the gloom at the glowing windows of an Abbey. Here was a good place to take sanctuary from the gathering storm. He let his hand rest on his sword hilt as his generals, Ingmar and Bulvark, crested the hill to join him in scanning the Highland mist. "It is impossible navigate these strange Highlands in such weather," he motioned toward the Abbey glowing from a shallow valley by a clear loch. "I think we should rest here and wait for the sky to clear."

"A nunnery?" Ingmar shook the rain off his head, reminding Niall of a shaggy hound, all hair and little substance, yet lethal when riled. "A Berserker and his men in a convent... what could go wrong?"

Bulvark let the rivulets stream from his impressive russet beard, remaining stone-faced and indifferent. "It will certainly have gold to plunder, and perhaps relics with precious jewels. It's worth the risk for Christian coin."

"Forget about the jewels." Ingmar clapped Bulvark on the shoulder and shook him soundly. "The nuns, man, the *nuns*! All those clean, frightened, unprotected virgins just waiting for a handsome warrior like me to plunder them." He beat his chest with his fist, and cupped himself, with a sound of predatory anticipation.

Bulvark snorted. "Waiting for you, eh? Is that why they run from you in terror and disgust as soon as look at you?"

Ingmar waved his hand, undeterred. "Only at first, and then they're screaming for a different reason, and begging me to plunder them again." He waggled cheerful eyebrows, and motioned for the dozen Vikings behind them to follow Niall down the hill.

"I do not want you touching these women without their consent," Niall ordered, eliciting a chorus of disappointed groans and muttered curses. "They are supposed to be married to their Christian Sun God. It would be like raiders taking the priest-esses of Freya. Unforgivable."

"The priestesses of Freya will *give* themselves to you," Ingmar argued, his tattooed temples wrinkling with a mulish frown. "And our laws say that if a woman cannot fight you off, then you may claim her as your own."

"Those are *our* ways," Niall reminded. "Our laws are not even accepted through all of the Northlands. Besides, these nuns, they are not taught to fight. They are only taught to pray."

"Pray to a God who will not allow you pleasure until you are dead?" Bulvark spat on the ground. "To a husband who will not protect you? Seems like a waste of a good woman to me."

"On second thought I will not touch these nuns," Ingmar decided. "They probably only marry to their God the ones who's virginity no one else wants." He took a step back when Niall frowned at him, but shrugged and smiled. "You know, the ugly ones."

"Either way, we're only taking gold," Niall ordered. "I don't want blood spilled here."

The silver, stormy daylight faded into a grey evening as Niall crept down the hillside, enjoying the banter of his two closest friends. Even as he listened to their conversation, he also kept his preternaturally sharp ears open for sounds of enemies in the cloudy swirls surrounding them. Pictish knights and warriors fought as savagely as they did, and he didn't like to face an enemy he could not see on unfamiliar ground.

His Berserker might slaughter a friend.

He led his band through well cared-for gardens and past pens of pigs and lambs to reach the walls of the Abbey. Even if someone should look from the glowing windows, they would see no gleam of sunshine off their fine weapons. Would have no warning of their advancing band of raiders. In their furs and skins, moving with the sure-footedness of Northmen, they would be nothing but large and shifting shadows in the Highland mist.

"I have no taste for soft Christian virgins," Bulvark noted solemnly as they followed the stone walls to the front of the wide Abbey, which faced the sea. "I prefer strong, solid Viking women, who would kill you soon as fuck you. They are much more exciting."

Niall didn't doubt it. Bulvark was a bulky, bear of a man, tall and round. It would take quite a woman to be able to stand against him, or lie beneath him, for that matter. Niall doubted there were many women in existence that could.

This time it was Ingmar who snorted. "What are you saying, Bulvark, that if Niall would allow it, you would still take '*nun*' of these women?" He elbowed Niall in the ribs with a chortle at his own pun.

Bulvark clenched his jaw with irritation. "Why are you talking, Ingmar? No one marks you or finds you clever."

Ingmar's lithe form all but vibrated with mirth as he held a hand to his ear in an exaggerated motion. "I cannot understand you. Could you please E'*nun*'ciate your insults better?" He barely leapt out of the way of Bulvark's hammer-sized fist, and had to dance around the giant Viking to avoid injury. "What's the matter Bulvark? You look '*nun*' too happy."

Bulvark finally caught him with a shove, bouncing Ingmar off the stone walls of the Abbey and caught him in a choking grip.

"Everyone tires of your nonsense," he growled to the younger, slighter man.

"Don't you mean, '*nun*'sense?" Ingmar squirmed in the war-honed general's iron fist, using what little air he could get to laugh at his own hilarity. A few others joined in the laughter, an air of relaxed joviality and anticipation seeping through the mists as they approached the arched oaked doors of the Abbey.

Niall shook his head, unable to fight a smirk at his friend's antics as he sized up the strength of the Abbey's defenses. It amazed him that a church of any religion would leave a building full of cloistered women with no defenses but stone walls exposed to the whims of the world.

To men such as himself.

An unmistakable sound hissed through the evening and reached his sensitive ears, and Niall held up a hand signaling for quiet.

Everyone froze.

Niall could hear through the walls what others could not. Angry voices. Anxious movement. Whispers. The sound of a whip connecting with flesh.

No cries of pain met the punishment, though, which to Niall meant one thing.

"Ready your weapons," he gave a hushed order. "I think there are *men* in the abbey. We may have to fight after all."

His favorite sounds in the world vibrated through mist toward him, abrading his most heightened Berserker sense. The rasp of metal against scabbard. The creak of a strong, sure grip on an axe handle, and the quickening of breath in anticipation of death or glory.

Niall gave a moment's pause in pity for the nuns and the slaughter about to be visited upon them. He was especially sorry for whoever was being whipped, for he would have to meet the wrath of Niall's Berserker whilst bound and injured and would have to watch his death coming at him with no way to shrink from it, or to fight it.

Not that either of those actions would save him.

The mist chose that moment to consolidate into rain, falling rather than gathering, streaking their hair to their scalps and muddying the dying autumn earth.

"These doors are heavy." Bulvark reached a hand to the tall arched gates, held with iron hinges and thick ingots.

Ingmar made a sound of juvenile anticipation comparable to that of a giggle, and rubbed his hands together. "Then it is good we brought our own battering ram." He slapped Niall on his shoulder and made a grand gesture toward the oak doors that doubtless were buttressed by a bar of thick wood on the inside. "After you my good man," he said, solicitously bowing in a mock gesture of the gallant English knights they'd fought in the fields.

"Thank you, Sir Ingmar," Niall replied, throwing his cloak of firs behind his wide shoulders as though casting aside a pretty lord's cape. "You are a most chivalrous gentleman."

At that, his troupe guffawed, but formed a crescent around him in preparation for bloodshed as Niall backed away from the door to get a running start.

He connected dead center, and the gates exploded open as though hit with thousands of stones worth of pressure rather than the shoulder of a lone warrior. His men rushed past him, spilling into the courtyard, half of them splitting along the right wall, half of them to the left, leaving Niall standing in the center of the gate, framed by the Highland storm.

Breasts.

The most incredible breasts he'd ever seen. Nipples the color of pink rose petals puckered against the rain streaming from flesh as white as skimmed cream.

It took Niall the space of two blinks and the sing of the whip to break the strange spell the sight had cast upon him. The whip connected with tender flesh.

Her flesh.

She still didn't scream, though a great shudder wracked

through her lithe form before she drooped against the ropes at her delicate wrists.

A hot anger built inside him, along with an alarming instinct he couldn't identify.

He'd been wrong. It wasn't a man who took the abuse of a whipping with admirable stoicism, it was a *woman*. A small woman, standing between two stakes, stripped to the waist and bound to each post with her arms open.

She looked so fragile slumped over like she was, her bonds becoming her only support as her dirty feet sagged in the mud of the courtyard. Hair the color of a brassier fire fell over her face and hung in long, wet streams, hiding her visage.

As far as Niall could tell, she'd lost consciousness.

And still the Valkyrie-sized nun drew her considerable arm back; her dark eyes alight with a feverish zeal as she let the whip fly toward the smaller nun once more.

Niall didn't know what drew him to intervene. Couldn't tell why he barreled through the small crowd of panicking women with his Berserker speed to catch the whip on his arm before it could mar one more inch of that pale, delicate skin.

The leather of the whip bit as it wrapped itself around his forearm, and Niall let it feed the rage building within him. With a jerk, he ripped the whip from the elder nun's hand and enjoyed her gasp of shock and pain as his presence registered through what seemed to be a fog of hatred in her eyes.

"What is the meaning of this?" she screeched, her chin straining against her wimple as she dared to reach past him for her instrument of punishment.

Niall sneered with disgust as he easily subdued her with one hand. "Are you too intent on hurting this tiny, weak woman to notice that you are being raided?" He shook her roughly for effect.

The woman, dressed in a longer, thicker habit than the rest of the nuns, blinked as though seeing him for the first time.

"Raided?" she whispered. "I—"

Niall turned and shoved her toward Bulvark, who caught her and compelled her toward the forty or so women gathered in the courtyard of the modest abbey.

"How dare you desecrate this holy ground with your Pagan blasphemies?" The woman shouted, throwing a strong yet gnarled finger toward the pale prisoner, who still remained alarmingly still. "She's a *witch*. The devil's handmaiden! And she must be castigated!"

Niall snorted, drawing himself up to his full height as he advanced on the nun, towering head and shoulders above her, though she was imposing even when compared to a Viking woman. "You would do well to fear me, old woman."

"I do not fear death!" she spat, squirming against Bulvark's unyielding grasp. "I fear nothing but damnation, the damnation this whore of Satan will bring down upon us. She's probably the reason you're here!"

"*Gold* is the reason I'm here. Gold and relics, and shelter from the storm."

"You'll find no sanctuary in these walls," she hissed. "God will punish you for any sins you commit against us or our *virtue*!"

A chorus of frightened gasps and soft exclamations of fear emitted from the nuns huddled together. The armed and leering Vikings surrounding them kept their frightened group from inching toward the archway of the overhang encircling the square courtyard. Torches lined the walls beneath the awnings, which threw wan light through the storm and turned droplets of rain into little reflections of fire.

"Trust me, lady," Ingmar chuckled as he sauntered up to them. "Your virtue is in no danger from us... or from anybody for that matter."

Bulvark actually laughed in agreement at that as the Nun's face puckered like the leather of an old shoe.

Niall drew a sharp dagger from a scabbard against his back, leaving his sword untouched. A few women screamed, chafing his sensitive ears with their histrionics. "Quiet!" he ordered sharply, and they complied, shrinking from him as though of one mind.

They'd probably never seen a man of his size before. Never laid eyes upon Vikings clad in leather, fur, and adorned with tattoos. His hoard was nothing like those prettily dressed holy men who liked to wear robes the color of blood. Those who never touched gore with their fingers, but were stained by plenty of it. "Stay still, stay silent, and cooperate and I vow, no harm will come to you."

He turned toward the bound woman, his ears pricking to her trembling breaths.

It wasn't just those impressive breasts that drew him forward. Nor was it the strange pressure against his heart. An alarming softening he'd only ever heard about.

Pity? Weakness?

Over some girl? A witch, at that.

He was Niall Thorson, the preeminent Berserker warrior at the temple of Freya, the pride of the elders and the first son of the oldest Berserker clan known to man.

He and his men laughed over the screams of the dying, broke bread over the bones of their enemies. It was said his line was descended from the god, Thor, himself. He was utterly pitiless. Fearless. Lethally dangerous. *And yet...* couldn't fathom why his hand was unsteady as he reached for *her*.

Her jaw felt as delicate as burned sugar in his rough hand. Easily shattered, utterly sweet. His breath stalled in his chest as he gently lifted her face toward him. Niall didn't know what he'd expected to see on her rain-streaked face. Fear, pain, shock, desperation, any of these would have been reasonable. He half expected her to be laconic from the trauma of a whipping.

But what flared at him from her eyes the color of smelted amber slowed time and tightened his skin as all the world receded from his heightened notice. *Fire.* The figurative kind, at first. Defiance and strength, licked by a sensual flicker that stunned him in light of their present circumstance.

Instant sensation took Niall in its thrall. The rivulets of rain running down his forearm to drip from his elbow became a physical caress. The rasp of his clothing against his burning skin an unexpected irritation he needed to be rid of. The muscles along his spine clenched and rolled with the need to be rhythmically thrusting.

Mine.

He'd thought such an instinct would belong to his Berserker, but the thought echoed from his head, not from within the cage of his ribs where the beast resided, dormant for the present moment.

Along with the unexpected sensual heat coiling through him, softer warmth began to glow through his veins as well, alarming him more than the uncontrolled lust. It was foreign, gentle, and damned unsettling.

"What are your crimes, priestess?" he murmured through lips aching for a taste of her.

"Not so many as yours, Berserker," she answered in a voice comprised entirely of smoke and sex.

Niall had to close his eyes for a moment to hide from her beauty like a coward he'd never been. Even in her wretched state, the startling perfection of her features burned themselves into his vision as though he'd been staring at the sun. When he looked away, the shadow was still branded into his eyes, blinding him to all but her radiance.

Fuck. What was happening to him?

"Are you going to try and kill me?" she asked, motioning to the dagger in his other hand with her eyes.

Niall had to blink again to stop from watching the way water slid along her proud, high cheekbones to collect in the corners of her sensuous mouth. "I am not your enemy," he insisted, and proved it by lifting his dagger and slicing through the ropes at her wrists.

With a weak sound, she collapsed, and Niall caught her before she fell to the mud, pulling her against him. The strength he'd seen in her eyes must not have existed in her legs.

Stepping into her, Niall pressed his body fully against hers, hiding her breasts from the unrepentantly hungry eyes of his men, hating the thickness of his leather armor as it hid their softness from his touch.

She hissed when his hands pressed against her back, and he drew them away instantly, not realizing the extent of her wounds until it was too late.

Blood.

Niall stared at it as though he'd never seen it before, watching the rainwater turn the crimson into a lighter pink in his palm. A familiar stirring radiated through him. Rage. Mayhem.

Panic?

Nie. He couldn't have saved this wounded nun only to be forced to violently take her life. She was different. He wanted her. Not only that, he wanted to *know* her. To see her. To save her. Not just from the pain of her wounds, but from himself.

"Run," he growled the last word his sharpening teeth would be able to utter before the beast completely overtook him in a voice darkened with animal rage. He could feel it mount. Feel his veins pulse with fury, bloodlust, and strength.

Niall pulled away from the woman as the vibrancy of the evening turned to predatory shadows of silver and grey. As usual all color disappeared, leaving only the shapes of his victims.

All color, but for the very real flames igniting *her* eyes.

"Everyone get back. Bar the door." Ingmar's voice was deadly serious, which underscored the danger of the situation. "Better start praying, ladies," he warned. "Make peace with your God, because you are about to meet him."

CHAPTER 2

To Kenna de Moray, watching a Berserker with the golden visage of a Norse God turn into a demon with eyes the color of charred coals had to be one of the most defining moments of her short life.

She'd known what he was, even when his clear, ice-blue gaze had heated from one of arrogant dispassion, to branding possession. It was as though she could feel the beast that lay dormant inside of him. Could sense the frenzy that was capable of bursting forth from the cold and capable leader.

She just hadn't known she would see that beast so soon.

Berserkers killed. It was all they did. They had no mercy. No control. Once the bloodlust took them, they indiscriminately slaughtered whatever life they could reach.

A flash of magick burned before her, bringing images of the near future. The stones of the courtyard painted with rivers of blood. The folds of habits, once lily-white, stained crimson. Rain washing gore and carnage into the gardens. The victorious roar of a Berserker beast, and then the tortured roar of a man...

Kenna and the Berserker would be the only two left standing. *What would happen then?*

There was no time to think. No time to philosophically

consider the good of the many versus the good of the few. She needed to live in order to keep the Doomsday Grimoire safe. In order to stay hidden, she couldn't use her magick. Not on purpose. But, could she allow this Berserker to be unleashed upon this cloistered order of nuns? Women who thought the worst of her, who stood by while she was beaten and berated?

Pain and weakness wrought by the lashes of hatred and the cold of the rain dissipated behind a surge of fear, and then of her fire. *Nay*. She couldn't let this man, who was turning into a creature more fearsome and beautiful than she'd ever seen, lay waste to the convent that had become her home.

These women weren't evil. They were afraid. Ignorant. They didn't deserve to be slaughtered like beasts.

The Berserker still held her, his grip becoming stronger, his teeth sharper, his eyes impossibly darker. Of all the abbey's in the world, why did this warrior have to pick *hers*?

When a terrified scream from a young novice drew his attention, Kenna knew she had to act now and live with the consequences.

Feeding on the anger of Mother Superior, the terror of her sisters, and the heat burning from the warrior before her, she drew the flames from the torches beneath the awning and created a wall of fire.

Battle-hewn Viking warriors jumped away from the blaze, lest it claim their flesh, and then their lives. Pagans had an innate fear of fire these days, as so many were sentenced to suffer a Christian death within walls just like these.

But this inferno couldn't be extinguished by the rain, could not be breached by the brave. And it cut Kenna and this frenzied creature of death from the rest of the world, from men now desperate to reach their leader, and from women desperate to escape him.

Kenna and the beast were truly alone.

And now that he was trapped with her between a wall of stone and a wall of flames, his soulless eyes promised retribution.

"You don't know what you've done," she told the terrifyingly handsome monster staring down at her with those fathomless eyes.

Nor did he seem to care.

Still caught in his clutches, she gasped when he swept her up and over one massive shoulder, his arms avoiding the raw lashes on her back. He carried her away from the comforting heat of the fire wall. Away from the frantic cacophony of whimpering women, and bellowing Vikings.

Where did he plan on taking her?

Ducking beneath the awning, he stopped and took in two quick breaths before selecting the door that led to the kitchens and then the chambers above. He none-too-gently climbed the back stone stairs of the abbey and stalked down two dank and narrow halls—hardly wide enough for his shoulders—before he kicked open a chamber door three down on the left.

Her chamber door.

His nose, it seemed, had led him here.

Choosing to ignore those implications, Kenna couldn't suppress a wince as the Viking lowered her to her feet, still taking care with her wounded back.

Beneath her weight, her legs buckled as though her muscles were made of bread dough, and the beast caught her by the shoulders, propping her up.

They shared a curious moment of investigation.

Kenna had to tilt her neck back at an alarming angle to meet eyes as perceptive as time and yet opaque as a moonless night. They could have belonged to the devil. Hadn't the Bible called Lucifer the *Star of the Morning*? Wouldn't a creator's favorite son be blessed with features such as these?

Golden-hued perfection. Skin like amber glass cut and shaped by raw bones and thick sinew. This warrior was a stoic mystery. Only a few weathered lines branching from his eyes hinted at age, or maybe just a restless spirit. His mouth, set with ruthless ferocity, called to her with an erotic challenge.

For a man emulating violence, he also seemed relaxed.

She wished she could step out of his grasp. It seethed with power, and power was something she needed at the moment. It called to her as though begging to be a part of her.

And, though it should have been impossible, her body answered that call.

Kenna considered her options, which weren't many. She'd saved the nuns of Westmire Abbey from a violent death at the hands of this Berserker, and in doing so, she may have brought about the end of days.

Goddess help her, but she was impetuous. Always had been. Acted with little regard and spoke with even less thought. She was supposed to be protecting the Doomsday Grimoire in this most unlikely of places. The only way she could stay hidden from the evil witches searching for it was to refrain from using her fire magick.

Now she'd not only used it, but drained the rest of the powers she'd been working so hard to suppress. Not only was her magick weak, but her body was also. Not just weak, but wounded, and she hadn't the gift for healing like her cousin Morgana did.

Kenna's element was fire. And, though it was one of the more powerful and dangerous elements, it wasn't among the earth's most abundant resources like air or water. It needed fuel. Ignition. Something upon which to burn. Those druids who were evil or lazy used powerful and plentiful resources upon which to feed their fire. Fear, anger, and hatred.

But those who were actual practitioners of elemental magick, who understood from where true power could be found, drew theirs from the well of the less profuse, but ultimately infinite. The potency of passion overcame fear and anger. The intensity of love always conquered hatred. It was from sensations such as these that Kenna knew she could revitalize her strength in order to face the dangers that lie ahead.

She thought of the nuns in the courtyard, most of whom

were generous, pious women. Of her cousins Malcom and Morgana with whom she shared the bond of blood, duty, and magick. Of the book hidden in the walls of her room that contained the secrets of the Goddess and the workings of the cosmos. Of all the souls who were and are and would ever be, who needed this earth upon which to live out their incarnations.

She thought of extraordinary men, like the one supporting her weight and staring at her as though she held his universe in her hands.

She did, after a fashion, and it was heavy.

He was supposed to be attempting to tear her limbs from her body in true Berserker form. The fact that he didn't only meant one thing.

Their eyes met and held. Hers heating with fire. His cold with a fathomless abyss, but unmistakable intent.

The Berserker wanted her, and that was just as well, because he was a powerful being with magick of his own. And his magick was *just* what she was after, and there was only one way to get it.

"Take off your clothes, warrior," she whispered. "I need you inside me."

CHAPTER 3

Heat raced through Kenna's veins, settling as a familiar and insistent throb between her legs. If her own reaction to the very idea of lying with this man was so powerful, she could only imagine how the act would feel.

The Berserker made a low sound, half warning, and half disbelief. Then another sound permeated the air, this one a rip, and the rest of her soiled dress slid to the floor.

"Nay," she whispered softly, trying to think beyond the haze of pain and lust and heat now permeating the chill left by the rainstorm. "'Tis *you* who should disrobe." She gestured to his layers of woven linen and leather armor belted and strapped with sharp-looking studs.

He didn't speak. Not once. And Kenna got the impression that it was impossible for him to do so in this form. But the look he gave her as he tore through the buckles of his armor—not stopping to undo them—could have steamed the rainwater from her skin.

She'd done this before, shared her passions with a man, taken his sex, his essence, to feed her power, but never with a man *this* potent. Never with one this lethal.

The skin of her back felt shredded and swollen and it

protested movement, but as the beast in front of her peeled his armor from his body, the pain faded beneath a surge of heat.

His light hair, darkened with rain, streamed glittering rivulets of water into the deep tracks of muscle he uncovered. He hissed great lung-fulls of air through his bared teeth, his abysmal gaze devouring the sight of her bared, chilly flesh. His long, water-spiked lashes lowered, those midnight eyes snagging on her nipples, puckered tight with the cold.

His muscles were not only large, but long, stretching over his bones as though holding together a frame as big and potent as his took a great deal of strength.

Unable to help herself, Kenna reached for him, enjoying the way his pectoral jumped and flinched beneath her hand as though even the lightest touch caused him pleasure. His skin was warm, burning, despite the chilly water, and the heat drew her forward. His armor hit the floor with a loud noise as she pressed her body against his hardness. The tension radiating from his body was hungry, predatory.

He bent to drag his mouth against the curve of her neck, drinking in the salt and rainwater he found there. The noise he made could have come from the throat of a wolf. A growl of need. A gentle threat.

Hurry, it warned, *I'll not be leashed for long.*

Right, Kenna thought. *To business.*

But *this* wasn't business, this wasn't just duty and magick and the cost of regaining her druid power. In the past, she'd been able to separate the fire of her passions from those few men she'd shared it with. Her emotions remained locked behind cold stone, and only her flesh and theirs were used as a conduit of pleasure, heat, and magick.

That would be nigh impossible tonight. Not only was her flesh raw and bruised, but her soul seemed to be, as well. And the fact that this big and lethal warrior—a deities' instrument of death—was now lavishing her skin with his tongue instead of spilling her blood was beginning to mean more with each passing moment they spent alone. She felt... exceptional, cherished somehow, by this man whose name and intent remained unknown. Indeed, his sense of honor was very much in question.

And she was about to take him into her body.

Kenna drew in a deep breath as excitement and lust flared beneath her misgivings. She'd just need to make sure to keep him *out* of her heart.

The delectable movement of his lips against her throat became more insistent, demanding, his teeth finding places to nip and gnaw that left her breathless. His hands bypassed her back to find her ass, pulling her in tighter against him to thrust the incomprehensibly sized erection burning from behind his trews against her belly.

The sound he made this time was no longer a gentle threat, but a savage one. And then his trews were gone, and Kenna knew they weren't going to make it to her small bed.

Suddenly she had difficulty breathing, the air in her cramped, spare room turned so hot, it scorched her lungs. To say he was magnificent would be as ridiculous as calling the Highland seascape beautiful. It applied, of course, but any of the descriptions she tried to conjure sounded trite and inadequate.

The effect was eerily similar. That rare moment a vision overwhelmed the eyes with its incredible, almost *impossible* perfection. When beauty stole the breath and quieted the mind, making one wish they could experience the sight with all the senses they possessed.

Laying both her hands on his powerful shoulders, she pressed him down. The thought of this hard, lethal beast on his knees before her caused a rush of desire to expel from between her thighs. She was slick and ready for him.

And well he knew it.

Allowing the gentle pressure of her hands to guide him down, he trailed his hot mouth over her rain-soaked skin, pausing to fill his hands with her breasts, to press a hot lick and a gentle tug against her nipple before leaving them with obvious reluctance. Before he could nuzzle at her sex, as it looked as though he wanted to do, Kenna sank down with him, splitting her legs over his hips and pushing him to the floor.

The heat radiating from him was alternately incredible and unbearable. His hips scalded her thighs. His chest burned her hands. His cock branded her belly as she slid it between their bodies.

Kenna almost felt sorry for what she was about to do to him. She felt guilty for taking power from a man so indescribably powerful.

But what choice had he left her?

Above that, how could she pass a man like this, with a body like his, without sampling the pleasure he could give her, and the bliss she could give him back?

They needed each other. The refugee and the marauder. The future held something for them, something they had to attain together. Kenna knew this with the certainty that she knew all things. And the exhilaration of the knowledge drove her to the brink of sanity.

"Lie still, Berserker," she rasped, lust lowering her voice by entire octaves. "Do not thrust." She had to control this, to make sure she knew exactly how much power she siphoned from him. Not too little, and not too much. The former would be useless, the latter, dangerous.

To them both.

His cold eyes speared her, reminding her he was not one to take orders, and yet he complied.

"You, who are so used to taking from others will know what it is to be taken," she drawled, caressing the heat of his flesh with the slickness of hers. "And you will be a willing victim of the flames. I will use what I take from you to save you and your men."

His lips parted as he began to pant, his big hands curled against her thighs in silent but insistent demand. She didn't think he heard her, or maybe he didn't mark her words, so intent was he on her breasts. Long, rough fingers ventured higher, seeking intimate flesh, but Kenna didn't wait long enough to let him find her sex.

Her back ached and stung as she rose above him. So to block out the pain, she focused on the feel of his hot, blunt sex stretching her slick passage as she impaled herself inch by agonizing inch on his cock.

His bold fingers didn't stop their questing just because she'd willed them to. Instead, they found the thin skin at the juncture of her thighs, so delicate and sensitive, and then reached even higher, to part the satin folds of her penetrated body.

She jerked with the shock of pleasure that thrilled through her at his touch. The muscles of her sex tightened with the movement, pulling a strangled sound from the Berserker's throat.

If she'd thought she'd been aroused before, she'd been lying to herself.

As the pad of his thumb brushed the sensitive, swelling nub of sensation, her sex drenched his with an embarrassment of slick moisture as she encompassed the pulsating column of his manhood with delicious difficulty.

Her body stretched to accommodate him, the pain a sharp burn that dulled to a pleasurable ache.

Goddess, but she'd never been so aroused. Her body never so eager to take a man. All of him.

His eyes were no longer cold, but burned with black fire as he bared his teeth in a hiss of pleasure. Though his gaze was lost, his clever fingers knew exactly what they were doing, drawing the moisture of her body toward the tight nub of sensation above where their bodies joined.

It took two lifts of her thighs and a few flicks of his thumb before Kenna was seized by a climax so quelling and unexpected all she could do was jerk and shudder on top of his cock. Her every movement was involuntary, her every breath a sob, as frantic pleasure coiled and broke upon her in relentless waves.

Somewhere, a dim part of her noted with some tingles and itches, a stitch and a burn, her back knitted itself together. The rent flesh and welts cauterized and mended until it was as though they had never been.

It had begun. She drew on him like a vampire, feeding on his passion, his need, and his brutality. His magick. It wasn't like her Druid magick. It was different, more of an ability, really, but it fed her like a gluttonous royal, filling the cracks and fissures in her body and soul.

The orgasm didn't ebb until she was red-faced and dazed with shock and repletion.

Beneath her, black-eyed and perfect, a sheen of moisture gave the Berserker an almost metallic patina in the fading light. The evening drew shadows along the paths carved by thick veins beneath his skin, gilding his frame with strength and vitality. As though he could feel her healing, he lifted himself until he could test the new, smooth skin of her back.

With a victorious snarl, he pulled her more tightly down over him, angling up in a demanding thrust.

How foolish she'd been to think he'd let her have control.

Before she could form a coherent thought, she was beneath him. He drew her knees up and thrust forward in strong, angled strokes.

Kenna panicked for a moment, feeling the force of his power surge within her. She was losing control of this quickly, but somehow, the delicious feel of his masculine weight pressing her hot flesh into the cold, clean floor seduced her as nothing else had.

He didn't hold back, didn't take care, but pounded all his desire, need, and passion into her body with fast, driving command.

Kenna didn't want him to stop. Couldn't allow him to continue. It was too much, too soon. He would give her more of his power than he could stand. She would take from him what he was not willing to part with.

"I can't," she whimpered, then cried out, pushing up against him with her hips and her arms. Her intimate flesh gripped at his cock in spasms that she fought, but they came upon her with hot, crushing inevitability.

He gave no quarter, his rhythm increasing. His brows drew together as though he was in pain, his eyes disappearing behind his lids. His muscles trembled, and still he took her.

And she took him.

She had to stop this, before she took *everything* from him.

Digging her foot into the floor, she bucked up with her hips and twisted, using the strength she'd siphoned. Rolling, she gained the top once again, barely breaking their rhythm as the sensations igniting in her core and flaring in her limbs burst into an inferno.

She groaned as her very soul caught fire and the searing bliss singed its way along her nerves like she'd never before experienced, or even imagined.

He shuddered beneath her, his hips arching, his hands grasping and finding nothing. His roar that of a beast facing immolation and giving into it. One last time, he shoved deep and held there.

She could feel the heat of his seed deep against her womb. The burn of his power deep within her soul.

And right as they culminated into a rush so intense it could have lit the night ablaze, a fire burst to life in the fireplace. The first to have warmed her since she'd arrived at the abbey.

NIALL SHUDDERED with a pleasure so deep, it seemed to brand itself into his bones, leaving the runic markings of magick and fate in their wake. But that pleasure replaced power and vigor that he could feel ebbing away the longer he stayed locked within the velvet sweetness of the witche's body.

Lifting arms that felt as though they were bound to the floor by invisible cords, he reached to push at the succubus riding him, but couldn't summon the strength. His mind screamed that he was in danger, but his body demanded he stay right where he was. That the sheath of her body now was his home.

Mine.

The witch's skin glowed in the firelight like the gossamer wings of a dragonfly. Creamy and iridescent with tiny veins visible at the places where her skin was most delicate and thin. Her wrists, the undersides of those lush breasts, the insides of her thighs, her neck.

A neck that should be encircled by his hands while he demanded that she return his—his—whatever it was she'd stolen from him that had weakened him so. Honey had replaced the blood in his veins. His bones had turned iron, anchoring his heavy body to the ground. His thoughts were sluggish and disturbingly...untroubled.

Her pulsating sex was a sweet prison, pulling the life from him, caging his Berserker beast, and turning him into a willing participant in his own death.

And what a glorious way to die, he thought watching the firelight set her hair aflame with embers of russet and copper as she gazed down at him through eyes drugged with pleasure and power.

His power. Power she'd stolen from him.

A sharp noise against the door and a familiar voice permeated the silken haze of Niall's thoughts. "Niall! Niall Halvard Thorsen, are you behind this door?" Ingmar's panicked question drove the witch off of his body with a gasp of pure feminine shock and mortification.

Niall wanted to call out to his general, but he couldn't seem to find his voice in order to do so.

The witch threw her tiny form against the door as another great succession of knocks caused the hinges and lock to tremble.

"Niall, you berserk bastard, answer me, or I'm coming in

there, and you'll have to live with the guilt if you eat me alive," Ingmar called. "Is that what you want? To have to explain to my mother how you killed me? Who's going to talk you off the ledge for killing that poor nun if I die?"

As soon as Niall could move *someone* was going to die. If only to prove to himself that he could still spill blood.

"Please," the witch called to Ingmar against the door, pressing her back to it in a way that made her breasts jiggle enticingly with each knock. "Please, leave us. He'll be down directly, I promise."

A speechless pause ticked off several seconds, which was a first since Niall could remember in Ingmar's intrepid company. The door rattled with another explosive knock. "Niall, if you want me to leave threateningly growl once, if you need me to break this door down and skewer a witch, threateningly growl twice."

The woman's amber eyes widened and she bit her lip.

Ingmar was used to Niall's Berserker, and had come up with a few strange tricks with which to stay alive around him, and even communicate upon occasion.

A genius, his wily general.

Niall opened his mouth to give a command, but only a pleasured groan escaped.

"Very well," came the disgruntled reply. "But let it be known that I'm going downstairs to stir malcontent among the men." Niall could hear every word as Ingmar retreated down the hall, even through a closed door and walls of stone. "Fucking orders *us* to touch nary a nun, and then has his way with the first pair of soft tits he sees. That'll hold as much weight with the lads as a fart in a whirlwind."

Who in the name of the All Father would interpret a weak groan as a threatening growl? A fucking imbecile, his general.

Chest depressing on what appeared to be a relieved sigh, the witch padded toward him with a regal grace very few naked women could attain. Kneeling at his shoulder, she pressed a hand to his forehead and then his cheeks. They were warm against his skin.

Mine, his beast purred.

If he didn't kill her first.

"I'm sorry," she crooned to him in a musical, lilting voice that reminded him of sex and mead. "I've always known I could take too much. I could have killed you, actually, but it's never happened before. Not with anyone."

Unable to tell if he was angrier about their dangerous sex, or that she'd had such amazing dangerous sex with others, Niall glared his fury at her.

"I know, I know," she soothed. "But just lie still for a few minutes and focus on breathing. Your strength will begin to return to you, and after some water and a hearty meal, you'll be back to your barbaric, pillaging self soon enough."

She had the breasts of a much larger woman, and they swayed and bobbed on her petite frame in such a way that made it impossible to keep any focus on his anger. With his sex still slick and aching with the aftermath of their unparalleled joining, and strange sense of well-being vibrating beneath the weakness in his limbs, Niall tried to breathe. She certainly didn't make it easy for him, with her bosoms brushing against his arm as she toured his jaw with those soft, warm hands.

Niall had the absurd thought that, in his experience, women tended to have chilly limbs. Her warmth was a pleasant change. A welcome one.

"I know you didn't realize what you were doing for me, but regardless, I want to thank you for..." She paused, blinked soft copper lashes against cheekbones kissed by a few freckles, and sucked her soft lower lip into her mouth before continuing. "I really don't have much of a gift for healing," she continued conversationally. "That is my cousin Morgana's realm of magick, but you are a very powerful man. I've never felt so..." A slight peach tinged her pale skin in a shade so pretty, Niall had to look away. "So *alive*. So full of vigor and potency. It's rather intoxicating."

Not as intoxicating as her fucking nipples rasping intimately against his shoulder as she reached to move a lock of his still-damp hair off his forehead. Though his body felt incapable of movement, his cock twitched and grew, ready to be inside her again.

Shit.

She noticed his growing arousal, her blush deepening, and knelt back, the sight not doing much to diminish his lust. "You should be able to speak now... Niall. That is your name, is it not?"

He liked his name on her lips. He wanted to make her moan it. He wanted her to use it while begging him in erotic supplication.

And he would, before they were through with each other.

The thought seemed to fill his muscles with a renewed energy, and he was able to lift his hands and push himself into a sitting position with her help.

"They whipped you, because you are a witch?" he asked carefully, testing the rasp of his voice.

"Aye," she confirmed, sadness touching her eyes.

"How?" he queried, trying to make sense of madness. "With power such as yours, you could subjugate them. You could make them respect you. Fear you. *Obey* you. You could visit harsh and torturous vengeance on them, bend them to your will."

She smiled as though he'd said something amusing, which irked him more than a little. "I could do that, I suppose," she acknowledged. "But I choose to forgive them, instead."

He turned and spit into the hearth, the sizzle hissing his disregard. "Forgiveness is a Christian concept. Are not our Gods more ancient and ruthless?"

"Yours certainly are," she murmured diplomatically. "But my Gods prefer different ways. Ways in which you leave people their own will, and bend the elements to yours, instead. You see, respect is not fear. Respect grows from love and trust. As does power."

Niall snorted, shaking the cobwebs from his head. "Woman's logic," he scoffed.

In a huff, the witch stood and pulled a shift from a small trunk at the foot of a bed that wouldn't have held the weight of his armor, let alone him.

"That logic comes from a man. A *powerful* man. One whom I both *love* and *respect*."

Once Niall found the name of this man, he would slaughter him. But first, he'd have to regain the use of his legs. Once a shift hid the lovely nun's perplexing breasts, Niall was able to think more clearly, or was it the effects of her siphoning magick wearing off?

"What did you do to me, woman?" he demanded, holding a hand to his head.

She glided to the fire in that graceful, regal way of hers, which made her tiny self seem much taller, though her copper brows drew together with sincere regret.

"The explanation is a little complicated, but for the sake of brevity, I'll tell you I'm a fire Druid, and fire needs fuel. Fuel which you *amply* provided." Her eyes drifted across the expanse of his body in a slow, appreciative caress before she reached to her small fireplace mantle for an earthenware bowl. Murmuring words he didn't understand, she tossed a handful of what appeared to be dried herbs onto the fire, causing it to flare treacherously.

"Kenna," a dominant voice crackled through the flames. The fire seemed to distort it, but couldn't hide the thick brogue of the Highland people. "Do ye realize what ye've done? Do ye have any idea the danger ye're in?"

"I have every idea, Malcolm," the witch, Kenna, said patiently. "'Tis why I can risk contacting you now."

"The Grimoire, is it safe?" the disembodied voice demanded.

"Of course," the witch assured him. "It is hidden away."

Niall couldn't believe what he was hearing. He wasn't a man prone to fits of panic, and he was also used to idea of magicks, but this was bordering on the fantastical. Before he could demand an explanation, the powerful shape of a man's torso and head appeared in the flames, congealing into a shadow, and then an actual specter of flesh and blood. Where Niall was broad and bulging, this man was lean and raw-boned. Yet his druid robes hung from powerful shoulders, and a short russet beard accentuated an angular jaw clenched as though he'd worn his teeth down to nubs.

A crown encircled his brow, one shaped like the broken antlers of the sacred elk.

Every man from Nordland to Rome knew who *this* man was.

Malcom de Moray, King of the Picts and Warden of the Highland peoples.

"What about ye?" Malcom's green eyes, shrewd to the point of pitiless, traveled Kenna's body with what might have been concern on features less cruel. "Are ye hurt?"

Niall had to suppress a growl. Was this the witch's man? Was he going to have to hunt him down and kill him in order to claim his mate? Breath escaped him as the full extent of his situation nearly knocked him back flat. He'd gone into Berserkergang around this woman, lay with her, and not tried to kill her. Not even once. That could only mean one thing.

Mine.

"I was hurt," she evaded. "But... someone helped me to heal."

Niall actually bristled. He did a bit more than just fucking *heal* her.

"How did ye get the power to do so in a nunnery—Ye know what, I doona want *those* details," the Druid King snorted in disgust. "But I demand an explanation for why ye just used enough magick to tickle the spine of every Druid from here to the shores of Inverness. And the reason had better be a good one, Kenna de Moray, for ye may have doomed us all."

Niall had a mind to rip the crown from the Pictish King's head and make him eat it.

"It wasn't my fault," Kenna remained calm in the face of the shrewd man's royal ire. "But now that it's done, I'll be needing you and Morgana to come to my aid."

"If the fault isna yers, who's is it?" the angry king demanded.

Biting her lip, Kenna stepped aside, allowing Malcolm a full view of Niall's hunched and naked body. "It's his," she said, as matter-of-factly as though she was telling her King about the weather. "And he and his men are going to help us fix it."

CHAPTER 4

Kenna had seen many powerful men interact in her life, lairds and warriors, chieftains and kings, sages and druids, even a shape-shifter once. But the look of utter contempt, challenge, and disgust that passed between the naked Berskerker on the floor and her beloved cousin and Liege lord beat them all.

"Kenna," The wrath in Malcolm's voice would have shriveled the manhood of the bravest of champions. Good thing she was a woman, and therefore immune. "Do. Not. Tell me. That ye mated. A *fucking Berserker*." Malcolm only spoke with such annunciation when truly infuriated.

She waved an impatient hand to cover a whispered spell that would trap the voice of the Berserker on her floor until she could get rid of Malcolm. "No, no, no," she soothed. "Not mated to just...borrowed from. He's quite...potent."

"Och, I canna know that!" Malcolm made the same sound of disgust he did as a boy. The only manner left about him that would ever remind anyone of those lovely, innocent days of their childhood. The days before Macbeth. Before the Wyrd Sisters. Back when her Uncle Duncan de Moray was still King and his sister, Kenna's mother, was alive. When mornings belonged to the mists, afternoons to Druid instruction, and evenings to laughter, play, feasting, and family.

"What have I done that the Gods curse me with lumbering, ungainly, ham-fisted Berserkers everywhere I turn? Tupping all the women in my family. It's not right." Malcolm lamented pinching the bridge of his nose as though nursing a headache.

Kenna put her fists on her hips. "Well, I don't think that's called for. I mean, I know he cocked up our plans, but in his defense, he couldn't have known he was raiding the abbey where the Doomsday Grimoire was hidden. It's not really his—wait," the full meaning of Malcolm's words widened her eyes. "What do you mean, everywhere you turn? Have you been raided as well?"

Malcolm heaved a heavy sigh. "After a fashion."

Kenna gasped. "What happened? Are you alright? Is Morgana—"

"She *mated* him, the bleeding oaf, and now ye canna lay yer eyes upon my sister without a dark shadow the size of a Roman wall looming behind her. Bloody irritating."

"Upon my word," Kenna sighed. "A Berserker." She turned to look at Niall, who was currently glaring daggers and attempting to regain his feet with what looked like murderous intent. He probably didn't take too well to the silencing spell. *Oops.*

"That can't be a coincidence, now can it?" she asked, which was more rhetorical than anything.

His look told her that when he regained his balance, he would *coincidentally* punish her in ways she'd never considered. It wasn't that she was a mind reader; only his intent was *that* unmistakable.

Turning back to Malcolm, she focused on the business at hand. "I've been hiding at—"

"I know ye're at Westmire Abbey," Malcolm said. "I felt it when ye used yer magick. Which means if I know, the Wyrd sisters know, and they're coming for ye and the book."

"What do I do?" Kenna tried to hide the terror in her voice from not just her cousin, but the Berserker as well. "I can't fight them on my own, and there are innocent women here. And Vikings," she added. Not so innocent, but she didn't necessarily want them dead. They'd been pretty accommodating and rather gentle, as raiding Vikings went.

"Have the Berserker and his men secure the Abbey, and ye stay with the Grimoire no matter what." The calculation left Malcolm's eyes for only a moment, and he gave her a look touched with affection. "I know I'm supposed to tell ye to guard the Grimoire with yer life," he rumbled. "But... I doona want ye hurt, Kenna, do what ye can to stay safe. We'll be there shortly after sundown tomorrow."

"Sundown?" Kenna asked. "But Moray Castle is nearly two days ride. How can you possibly get here so fast?"

Malcolm made another face, this one almost comically baleful. "Doona ask and I willna tell."

That brought a smile to Kenna's face, despite the circumstances. If she had to make a gamble, she'd bet it had something to do with Morgana's Berserker. She was excited to see her cousins, and hoped to live long enough to ask her closest friend about her new husband. Or mate, as it were.

"Hurry," Kenna pressed. "I'll get everyone here as ready as possible for what is to come." Though it wouldn't be easy, protecting a pagan relic in a Christian abbey.

"We will," Malcolm promised, his specter fading. "And whatever ye do, do *not* kiss that Berserker!"

"I won't," she vowed, then turned from the fire, which was now devoid of Druids, and ran headlong into a wall of muscle and rage. Oh dear, this Berserker had recovered quite a bit faster than she'd expected.

She waved her hand, releasing the silence spell, and prepared to defend her actions.

His features distorted into so many different emotions, Kenna couldn't distinguish them all. Some resembled outrage, others awe, but one she'd never seen before, at least not directed toward her.

Possession.

It was the last thing she saw before he crushed his lips to hers.

NIALL HAD MEANT to punish her, to threaten her with unthinkable consequences if she ever used her magick against him again. He wanted to curse and berate, to rage and bellow, to shake her... to spank her.

Perhaps he'd still do that, eventually.

He'd *wanted* to escape this tiny, spare chamber, with the Christian god watching their every sin from the cross above the bed, before he did something stupid.

Like binding his soul to hers for the rest of their natural lives with a kiss.

But she'd whirled from the fire with contrition in her eyes lit by sparks of amber mischief, and he'd been lost.

Mine, his beast had growled, and Niall had to completely agree.

Here was a woman who could not only take him, but tame him. One who could bring him to his knees with her magick. Who was he kidding? She could accomplish the same with only a few sultry words from her generous mouth. Her body tempted him like no other had. Her voice transfixed him in a way he'd never imagined. Their sex had pleasured him beyond comprehension.

And when he listened to her talking to Malcom de Moray with affection and respect, Niall knew he had to do *something*. Possessive instinct surged even before the Pictish King's warning against kissing him burned in his ears. Upon hearing that, Niall's body, soul, and beast came to a decision they could never retract.

He was not one to take orders, and neither would his mate.

Niall kissed her with the unrestrained hunger of an untried boy. He'd used his lips for many wicked, lustful things, but never this. The pure, bacchanalian delight he found in the sweetness of her mouth both aroused and humbled him.

He'd never known.

Gods be damned how could he not have known that pressing his mouth to that of his mate's would feel as though his heart might spill out of his chest and expire from the sheer pleasure of it? How could the illumination of just a simple act seem to resonate through him and radiate outward until it surely reached the sight of the Gods?

Every moment he'd lived, every drop of blood he'd shed, had lead him to *this*, to this woman, and how she was *his*.

When he dipped his tongue inside her warm mouth to taste her, exaltation didn't begin to describe the sensation. She was honeysuckle and cinnamon. She tasted of summer and smelled of sunshine, even through the rainwater.

He imagined it would be especially delightful when she decided to kiss him back.

Ah well, one thing at a time.

With a sound of protestation, she ripped her lips from his and pulled away, her eyes round with shock and accusation. "Why would you do that?" she gasped, holding trembling fingers to her bruised lips.

Niall shrugged shoulders now mobile with returning strength. "I wanted to."

"But—but doesn't that mean..."

"We're mated," he finished for her, smiling as her eyes went impossibly more round.

"Did you not just hear what Malcolm said? I promised not to kiss you!"

"In all honesty, I think you've kept that promise." Niall advanced on her with what he hoped was more charm than threat. "But, I'm hoping for more response next time."

Her lovely features filtered through a slew of emotions right before him. Shock melted into confusion, which quickly transformed into anger.

"I don't think your king's intentions are honorable," Niall continued. "He loves you. He likely wants you for himself." Jealousy was a new emotion, one he was sure to get used to with a mate as lovely as this one.

His woman regarded him like he'd just fed her Lutefisk for the first time. "Don't be disgusting. He's my cousin."

"I've heard about you English and your cousins."

"I'm a Pict, and a Druid one at that!" she spat, outrage flaring in her eyes and heating the air in the room to a temperature that steamed the last of the moisture out of his hair. "We're *not* English, and we know better than to marry cousins."

"As you say."

"And furthermore, Malcolm doesn't have the capacity for love. He's too busy, to studious, too... damaged. He barely tolerates Morgana and me, and we're the last family he has left in the world."

"And now he has two Berserkers to add to the count, the lucky Druid." Niall wondered to whom the King's sister was mated. Berserkers didn't usually stray far from the Nordic countries, and nearly all of them eventually found their way to the temple of Freya. Some took mercenary work abroad, and then there was the odd bastard or two.

"Nay, he does *not* have two Berserkers because *we* are not mated," she insisted, crossing two huffy arms beneath those fantastic breasts, lifting them to strain against the thin material of her shift.

"I am," Niall corrected, not missing the way her eyes followed the more intimate muscles of his body as he bent to reach for his trews and put them on. "And you *will* be." Just as soon as he talked her into it.

"Don't be so sure about that."

"What cause have I to doubt?"

She regarded him as though he were touched in the head. "The fact that I'm actively refusing you should lend you some pause."

Niall wasn't one to let something like that get in the way of eternal happiness. If she underestimated his tenacity, that was her fault. "You refuse me now, but I have time to seduce you. And from what I can tell, you're an easy catch, especially for a nun. I just had to lie there and you gave me your body. I don't imagine it'll be too much harder to win your heart."

He ducked as a book sailed past his head and the flames flared so high they shot up the thin chimney and heated the bricks of the walls. "You—you arrogant, thieving, base, wicked villain...you... you..." She seemed to run out of names, and this being a nunnery, projectiles were in blessedly short supply.

Niall didn't mind the name-calling, as all the words she hurled at him did generally apply.

"Did you not hear the conversation Malcolm and I just had?"

His little mate asked questions when she was angry. Niall shelved this information for future reference.

"There *is* no time! And even if there was, I would *never*—"

"Never is one of those words you *always* end up regretting," Niall interrupted her.

"*Ne-ver.* Accept *you*. As my mate," she finished with a very similar annunciation pattern as her cousin.

Niall just smirked at her. If there was one thing he'd learned about women in his half-century of life, it was that they never meant it when they said *never*.

"Tell me about this Grimoire," he prodded, hoping to distract her from her ire. "And these Wyrd sisters. Why are you in danger?"

"Why am I in danger? Because of *you*, that's why," she snipped.

"We've established that. But if my men and I are to protect

you, which we will, we'll need to know from whom and what for."

She glared at him for a moment, but then seemed to cede the point. "I barely know where to begin," she sighed. "On top of everything, the whipping, that kiss, this Viking raid... oh and let us not forget the pending apocalypse, I'm rather overwhelmed."

"Start with everything and go from there," Niall urged gently. They'd address the kiss again, of that she could be certain. Hopefully many times, and whilst naked, those breasts pressed against his—oh, she was speaking, he should pay attention.

"If you know of Malcolm, then you must know that his father, King Duncan, was killed by Macbeth, who usurped the throne and banished Malcolm to Goddess-knows-where, and gave Morgana, his sister, to the English King Harold for his own self-serving purposes." she began.

"I've heard as much." Niall eyed the bed upon which she sank to perch, and decided to remain standing.

"Well, Macbeth's actions were prompted by three de Moray witches who are known as The Wyrd Sisters. They're elemental Druids, like Morgana, Malcolm and I, except they use dark, evil magick and they were supposed to have died two hundred years past."

"Why are they still alive?" Niall asked. "Do Druids have longer life spans than usual?" If Berserkers did, it made sense that other powerful pagans would, as well.

Kenna shook her head. "I know not by what dark power they prolong their life, but the fact that they're here puts the survival of all the world in danger."

"How so?" he queried.

Scooting to the edge of her small bunk, she used lithe and nimble fingers to wriggle free a brick from her crumbling wall, then another, and another until a pile of a dozen stones sullied her bed.

Niall noticed that she didn't seem to care, as though she never expected to sleep there again.

Sobering thought, that.

She reverently extracted a tome that appeared ancient, even by his standards. The leather was too light to be animal, too thin to be sea creature, and tinted in only a way that a man who'd seen as much death as *he* would recognize.

Tanned *human* skin.

Blue wodish runes swirled in sacred spirals around the corners of the book and stretched toward the center in tribal arcs. There, in a script long forgotten, was a name he couldn't read written in a language far too ancient to still be uttered by a living soul.

Perhaps the first language of the first man. Or maybe the language of the Gods.

A kiss of power and lust touched the base of his spine, thrilling through his darker urges with the innate greed of man. This book wasn't exactly good, but neither could he call the feeling evil. Just potent on a scale he'd never before contemplated.

She handled it with reverence and not a little bit of misgiving, and opened its pages with the appropriate care. "This is the Doomsday Grimoire," she explained. "It is the book from which all other holy books were produced."

Niall's eyebrows shot toward his hairline. "Even—"

"*All* of them," she nodded solemnly.

"Contained within these pages is every prophecy, truth, mythology, and spell known to mankind." She caressed a page with suspiciously russet calligraphy that could have been ink, but was mostly likely dried blood.

Niall swallowed, truly feeling for the first time the direness of their situation.

"You see, the Goddess lends her power to three Druids of de Moray every generation. It has been thus since the evolution of man."

"Evolution?"

Kenna waved her hand, as though to signal that was for

another conversation and continued. "We are wielders of the four elements and keepers of the seasons. For example, Malcolm is Earth and Spring, I am Summer and Fire, and Morgana is Autumn and Water. You may note the absence of Air and Winter, and that is because the Goddess decided that four elemental Druids on the earth at once would be too much power for us mortals to wield, even though we're wielding them on *her* behalf."

"You said the Wyrd sisters were de Morays," he prompted with a growing sense of dread.

She nodded, as though pleased he understood which direction she lead him. "The most terrifying, powerful, and inevitable prediction is the Doomsday Prophecy, itself." She laid her hand on a page, reading a passage from a long paragraph scrawled in tiny symbols, her husky voice layered with the veracity of divination.

"Verily, when four elements are born to one house and are behind one gate, the seven seals will break. The first, Conquest, on his white horse with a crown. The second, War, on his red horse with his sword. Pestilence is third, on his black horse with his scales of balance. And finally, Death on his pale horse and he shall bring with him the might of the Underworld." She paused, taking in a shuddering breath and rubbing her arms. When the four Druids wield together from the Grimoire, they will hear thunder, the heavens will weep, the earth will tremble, the air will burn, and the rest of the seals will be broken, one by one."

Niall's own hairs lifted with trepidation. "Don't stop there." He chuckled, if only to let the air out of his burning lungs. "It was just getting good."

"The fifth seal has to do with raising an army of the dead," she continued. "An army of the slain innocent, the burned witches, and the wrongly executed to reap their vengeance upon the world. The sixth is elemental devastation as wrought by the four horsemen. You know, civil unrest, earthquakes, plague, war, dark suns, the moon dripping with blood— that whole bit. And then..." She looked up, her eyes swimming with moisture that comes from the shiver of truth.

"And then?" Niall asked breathlessly.

"The *reckoning*."

The ominous word speared his blood with ice.

"What reckoning?"

She shook her head. "It does not say, but I imagine with all that precedes it, it cannot be pleasant." Her eyes found his and they shared a desperate look. "Like I said before, the Wyrd sisters are of the de Moray line. They're of our house, so to speak. And with them is the witch Badb, and her element is Air and her season winter. You see, they've been after the Grimoire for two hundred years. It is their plan to set the apocalypse into motion, and now that there is an Earth Druid, Malcolm, that makes us *four*.

"When we realized King Duncan was dead and Morgana captured, Malcolm sent me away on his fastest horse. We knew the Wyrd sisters were after him *and* the book, and that we weren't powerful enough to fight them just yet. If they caught both Malcolm and the Grimoire in one place, all would be lost. So we decided I was to hide with the book somewhere the Wyrd sisters would never look, and as long as I didn't use fire magick, they couldn't find me." Her eyes became sad, tortured, and a desperate pain lodged in Niall's chest. "I'd heard that Macbeth had given Malcolm to the Wyrd sisters in exchange for the throne. I think they did terrible things to him. He didn't look the same..."

"And so when you used fire to save a bunch of thankless nuns from my Berserker..." Niall trailed off as a lead weight settled in his belly, realizing the true cost of his actions. He'd unwittingly set in motion the end of the world.

Well... Fuck.

His people had been raiders for generations. They celebrated the strong and preyed upon the weak. It was the way of nature. The way of the world. The strong survived, thrived, *deserved* to be here. The weak were culled and pillaged, preyed upon. But as he looked at his stalwart little mate, he realized that power came in many forms, and that he had a lot to think about.

The first consideration being that Kenna de Moray was *his* mate. More to the point, he was hers.

And if he had to stop the fucking Apocalypse to get her to accept him, then so be it.

CHAPTER 5

Kenna thought the dozen or so Viking warriors took the apocalyptic news rather well, all things considering. She supposed they were rather used to the idea of Gods, magick, war, and almost-certain death. They rallied around Niall, their undisputed leader, with a ferocity that both warmed and terrified her.

It was the nuns, and her fellow novices, that seemed to take the most issue with it all. Kenna had watched as the Vikings roused the anxious and bleary-eyed nuns from their beds and herded them into the courtyard, unmolested, whereupon Kenna tried to deliver the information regarding the Wyrd sisters, the Grimoire, and her Druid cousins with as much gentility as possible.

"Do you mean to tell us, that you've been hiding this evil book within these holy walls *all this time?*" Mother Superior demanded, her jowls shaking with obvious temper. "We knew you had tendencies toward witchcraft—that you might have been beset by a demon or two—but I was willing to help you find your way back to the Lord."

"You don't understand," Kenna argued. "These women will bring the wrath of evil here. They are possessed of powers you cannot comprehend, and they won't hesitate to hurt or *kill* each and every one of you."

"On your soul be it," the elderly nun hissed. "This is hallowed ground. The devil has no hold here and we are not a violent people. Besides, we are commanded to turn the other cheek."

"Not violent people?" Niall snarled at the old nun, causing her to jump before her features darkened with outrage. "Are you also commanded to whip defenseless women? Is that how your God teaches his wives and servants, through pain and humiliation?"

"That *witch* cursed young Brigit here, and Mary-Katherine with bodily injury," the bitter nun spat. "She's the devil in her heart, and likely her bed."

"That's not true." Kenna fought to keep her voice even. "I didn't curse them, I *warned* them. I told Brigit that if she didn't tuck her hem higher, she'd fall down the stairs, and so she did. And if I hadn't said something to Mary-Katherine about how to save herself from choking, that pit would have killed her." She turned to Mother Superior, hoping to soften her, though it hadn't ever worked before. "Sometimes, I can foresee what is to come in the flames. I don't do it on purpose. I don't even know when it is going to happen, but can't you understand that I was trying to help?"

"It says in the book of—"

Kenna squeaked as Niall shoved her behind him and towered over the woman with intimidating promise etched into his brutal features. "I don't give a dusty *fuck* about any book but the one we're trying to protect, and if you so much as look her way with questionable intent, so help me, I'll—"

To Kenna's utter surprise, Ingmar, Niall's tall and rather squirrelly-looking general stepped in-between his glaring leader and the battle-axe in charge of Westmire. "Look, woman, this isn't a man you'd like to see when he gets angry. And, from what we saw of this here Druid lady last night, she isn't a woman to be trifled with. So, if you want my advice, let's stop talking and start preparing for the end of the world. Which, to me means a good roast, some wine, and... let's be honest, how many of you really want to die virgins?"

Sputtering with outrage, Mother Superior whirled on Ingmar. "How dare you!"

"Mother Superior," Sister Judith stepped from the gathering of nuns who whispered together in a flurry of white habits and black wool. Kenna had always liked Sister Judith, as she was young and energetic, with soft grey eyes and a pretty sort of tranquility that brought peace to all her dealings. If Kenna tried to emulate anyone in the abbey, it would be Judith.

"Perhaps we could consider that God sent these men and Kenna here, to protect us from these evil witches." Judith cast Kenna a gentle smile. "He does work in mysterious ways, after all. Don't you think if he created all things, he must have created this Berserker and granted this Druid her—abilities for his own purposes? Perhaps it might be reasonable to help them intervene on our behalf, don't you think so, sisters?"

The sisters of Westmire appeared indecisive, but most of them seemed grateful to have a soft voice in such a hard time.

"Thank you, Sister Judith," Kenna breathed. "I promise, I will do all I can to ensure no harm comes to the abbey and the women here." Her greatest hope was that she could keep that promise.

"Marry me," Ingmar demanded of Judith, dropping to his knees at her feet.

Instead of seeming incensed, Judith gifted Ingmar with an amused, almost delighted smile. "Dear Northman," she chided, patting him on the shoulder. "Our heart and souls are promised to another, but we can slaughter a pig and offer you some very good barleywine and the best Highland whiskey."

Kenna thought capitulation would look odd on Viking features, and she'd been right. Though Ingmar brightened considerably at the mention of drink.

Mother Superior's deeply-lined face resembled that of a withered aubergine. "How can it be," she sputtered, "that my abbey is overrun by pagans and demons, witches and devils?"

"It does appear that you're I'*nun*'dated," Ingmar bowed to the enraged nun. "But we promise not to make a '*habit*' of invading your home." With a self-congratulatory chortle, he nudged Judith in the shoulder a few times, and she offered him a gracious smile, though no one else seemed amused.

"Tough crowd," he observed. "Someone say something about whiskey?"

Motioning to a few of her sisters, Judith led them to the kitchens, leaving Kenna and Niall to battle with Mother Superior and her many chins of disapproval.

"Do what you will," Niall informed the woman, obviously out of what little patience he'd ever had. "My men and I are going to help your nuns storm-proof this abbey and build what few defenses we can. Just don't get in our way."

Kenna watched as he gave orders and began to organize not just his people, but hers, as well. A horrible thought plagued her as she tried to figure where she would be the most help. It was the very last line of the Doomsday Prophesy, one upon which she and Malcolm had debated most spiritedly. One which alternately gave her hope, and terrified her.

It is not known who shall be left standing at the end of that great day of wrath.

CHAPTER 6

Niall found Kenna at the casement in the abbey's library, curled in the window seat, using moonlight and a few candles to pour over the Grimoire. The day had been long and productive, and at this moment, the small abbey was as prepared as it could ever be.

Would it be enough, he wondered, to stand against such power as these Druids wielded? Kenna had told him that the in the evil retinue of three, a Water Druid, Macha, and another fire Druid, Nemain, accompanied Badb, and that they used incredibly heinous means to feed their power. Blood magick, human sacrifices, and all manner of dark, torturous deeds. They were masterful witches, with more than two hundred years of practice and preparation on their side.

As calm as Kenna looked, studiously absorbing as much knowledge as possible, Niall could sense that she was terrified. The silver moon and golden candlelight turned the copper of her hair into a molten frenzy of precious metals. Her amber eyes were too dark as they tracked his entry into the room, as though the embers behind them were dangerously close to being extinguished.

"You should get some sleep," he prompted. "I'll sit watch over you."

"Nay," she sighed, returning to her book. "There will be no sleeping tonight. Not until I know that Malcolm and Morgana have arrived."

Niall moved closer, craving her eyes upon his. Her hands on his skin. That gentle smile upon her face. "I'm sure they're safe." He attempted comforting words, which sat upon his tongue less gently than he'd like.

Kenna just shook her head, not looking up from those ancient words in front of her. "No one is safe. Not anymore." Closing the disturbing cover of the Grimoire, she slid it beneath the faded cushion of the seat, as though the habit of concealing it was an unbreakable one. The moon illuminated her frown with an eerie blue cast when she turned from him to gaze out the window. "They're out there," she predicted. "The Wyrd Sisters. I can feel them casting. I wish I knew what they were up to. I wish I knew how to stop them."

Niall joined her in her inspection of the night, finding only a patina of shadow. "I am sorry I led them to your door," he murmured, the responsibility of her anxiety weighing heavy on his shoulders. On his heart.

She cast a soft glance his way. "I don't blame you," she comforted, much better at it than he. "I think it was inevitable that they find me here. That we were kidding ourselves to think that we could outrun a Prophecy as powerful as this one."

Niall hated that she sounded as though she'd already lost, the defeat etched into the hunch of her shoulders and the dips between her brows. He reached for her jaw, which felt as brittle as glass as he cupped it in his hand. "Accept me, Kenna, as your mate," he commanded in a husky whisper. "And together we will vanquish your enemies, or be sent to the afterlife in the attempt."

A tear snaked from the corner of her eye and dripped onto his palm where it branded all the way to his heart. "Don't you understand, Berserker?" she murmured. "This may be the end. Of *everything*. This is no time to begin a life together. To make promises we may not have made otherwise. I don't know you. I don't even think I like you very much—"

Niall lay a finger against her lips, wishing he could do anything to ease the burdens weighing his little mate down. "The Romans have a charming saying by which I have always lived. *Carpe Diem*. Seize the day." He motioned out the window. "Or the night, as the case may be. We're never promised tomorrow, little Druid, only this moment."

She stared at him for a second, her lips trembling behind his fingers doing strange and soft things to his insides. "I hate the Romans," she surprised him by saying, pulling out of his gentle palm to stand.

Niall let out a bark of amusement. "We all do, but they are a quotable lot. My point is, you should accept me. If you do, you'll make me nigh on five times as powerful as I am now. I'll conjure you fire that you cannot conjure yourself to wield as you desire. I'll give my life to protect you and pledge my Berserker beast to your service."

Feeling rather proud and poetic, he was certain there was no lass alive who could refuse such a declaration. He was Niall Thorsen, after all, pride of his people and slayer of armies. And finally he'd found a battle worth winning, and a woman worth fighting for. He could barely believe his good fortune.

"How do you know I cannot conjure fire?" she asked dubiously.

"Because my power belongs in my senses, and I've observed that you never create fire, only wield what is already burning."

She stared at him in stunned silence for a moment before whispering, "I'm sorry, but the answer is Nay."

"Nay?" he echoed, as though the word held no meaning to him. "Why not?"

"How can I? Moreover, how can *you* be thinking of such things now? Do you not understand? The servants of evil are out there, bringing the wrath of hell along with them. Everything, the fate of the entire world is on the line, waiting to be snatched out of our grasp. I don't have time to be anyone's mate."

Niall shook his head, careful not to scoff or condescend. She was young, and afraid. "Kenna," he crooned her name, crowding her into the bookshelf with his body and trailing his finger along the intriguing neckline of the red frock she'd donned.

A ceremonial color, if he had to guess.

"You shouldn't be so afraid of losing something that you don't let yourself have it. Life is to live, and I think you've forgotten that by locking yourself in this cold abbey devoid of happiness and focusing your every day on duty and prayer. If you don't allow yourself pleasure, leisure, risk and reward, then why bother?"

"Because I must!" She pushed against his chest, her tears of pain becoming ones of anger and bitterness. "Because it *is* my *duty* to keep the Grimoire safe and duty is all I have left! I've lost everyone I've ever loved. My parents. My uncle and king. Morgana and Malcolm. And now I've found them only in time to call them to what possibly could be their demise." She turned from him, her small body trembling with sobs that must have been locked away for the space of untold moons.

"Don't you see?" she lamented. "I can't bind my heart and soul to yours only to lose you. I will not let you be my last failure on this earth. *That* I could not bear."

His fingers closed around her heaving shoulders, drawing her back to lean against his chest so he could encompass her with his arms. "Don't cry, my mate," he murmured against her fragrant curls, her every sob tearing away a piece of his soul. "That is what *I* cannot bear."

She turned in his arms and collapsed against him, her shudders and convulsions increasing. "I feel I'm not strong enough," she sobbed against his chest, her tears tickling against his skin. "I fear I will not be able to stand against them. That I will let them defeat me."

Niall threaded his hands into her hair cupping her scalp and pulling her back to look at him. "Take me then, little Druid," he commanded. "Take my strength and use it in your battle. I will gladly give it to you, my mate, and let you wield it against our enemies."

"But..." she sniffed. "We'll have to..."

A wicked smile stretched Niall's lips as anticipatory lust speared him. "I'll just have to tolerate it, I suppose, benevolent marauder that I am."

The sparks rekindled in her eyes, as well, and Niall had never seen anything so beautiful in his life. "If you're offering your power, you'll have to give it to me where before I took."

"I'll give it to you," he promised with a husky growl, and yanked her dress from her body.

CHAPTER 7

H is fair eyes were even more disconcerting than the black pits his Berserker's had been. They were keen yet merciless as they traversed the curves and valleys of her naked body.

The air turned hot and heavy, thick with tension and passion, blooming with the scent of a storm. Whether it brewed outside, or between them, Kenna was too lost in the moment to care. All she knew was when it broke, she wanted to be clinging to this man, to his strength. Not just that of his massive shoulders or immense thighs, but also the strength of his character, the self-assured courage that bled from his every pore.

Niall's tunic and trews were discarded in a few jerks, and before Kenna had the time to do an appreciative inspection of her own, she was swept into his arms and deposited onto the window seat.

He remained standing, his impressive erection reaching toward her from a swirl of golden hair and sinewy hips.

To Kenna's shock, her mouth and loins flooded with moisture, rending an answering noise from Niall's throat. It rippled over her skin like silk and velvet, a sensual abrasion of sound and desire.

"Take me, Kenna," he commanded softly. "Taste my need."

His dark words sent her heart pounding against her breast bone. Heat welled within her veins and left her feeling shaky, jittery, and quite... aroused. The muscles in her loins clenched as though anticipating his intrusion, but first...

She parted her lips, letting her hot breath caress the bulbous head of his cock before closing her warm mouth around it. He tasted wild, like clean sweat and carnal sin.

An unnatural sound ripped from his throat as he gently cupped the back of her head, his fingers gliding through her thick fall of hair and then gripping it. His breath became rapid and shallow as she slid her tongue across the small slit at his head, indeed finding the slick drop as evidence of his need.

His shaft didn't go far inside her mouth before it became too much, but he didn't push. He stood, his knees locked, head thrown back to the moon as though about to howl like a Dire wolf, letting her mouth do with him what she would.

Only desperate gasps escaped him or sometimes guttural words in his harsh language as she began a rhythmic, pulling exploration of his sex. He was hot inside her mouth, and she felt her sensitive lips stretch around thick veins that she found curiously exciting.

She was about to take so much from him, of course she could give him this. His pleasure made her feel powerful in a way that had nothing to do with magick. It was as though she held his very soul in her hands, her mouth. His gasps and groans sounded as close to pleas as Kenna imagined a man such as he would ever make.

And he made them for her.

A gentle pulse in her mouth and a harsh sound was her only warning before she found herself shoved up against the window, her thighs wrenched open, and his heavy weight bearing her down. The smooth heat of his sex pressed against the slick warmth of hers, but he didn't shove inside her like she expected him to.

Instead he kissed her. Hard. Devouring her mouth as he took

her breasts in his hands, and thumbed the nipples until they were as hard as pearls.

"Take me," she sobbed against his lips. "Now."

He shocked her again by pulling back, his hands remaining possessively on her breasts. "I will fuck you," he vowed crudely. "But first I must taste you."

"Why," she lamented. "I need..."

A wicked smile split his demonically handsome face. "I will always give you what you need," he purred, rubbing against her so intimately that all she could think about was getting him inside her to ease the insistent ache. "But I will also take what I want." He slid down her body, his tongue and teeth wreaking havoc on her trembling muscles. "I am a Viking, after all. It is what we do."

He wasn't gentle with her breasts, tormenting them with his lips and teeth until she gripped and clawed at his shoulders, leaving marks and saying things that had likely never been uttered within the walls of the abbey.

His face, rough from a day's growth of beard, abraded the delicate skin of her belly as his hand found the auburn curls between her parted thighs. He didn't slip his fingers inside, didn't tease her or pleasure her, just held his hand over her mound, and dipped his tongue into her navel.

"I like to feel how warm you are," he breathed. "How hot and wet I make you."

Kenna arched, rubbing herself shamelessly against his hand, riding a wave of pure, desperation.

And still he remained motionless.

"Please, touch me," she begged.

His laugh was low, yet full of victory. "I'll do one better," he murmured, pushing her legs as wide as her trembling muscles could allow them to part.

With no preparation he burrowed his mouth into her moist cleft, latching on to her clitoris and lapping it until it was swollen and full.

Ragged sounds of relief and frustration tore from her in tight sobs as his tongue circled and flicked, teased and tormented her to the edge of release only to pull away and start again. She begged him for mercy, pleaded for it with the innocence of a virgin and demanded it with the abandon of a whore.

But he decided when his sweet torture would culminate, and he drew two fingers down her pink folds and slid them inside her.

Kenna's entire body tightened, arching and bucking against his mouth, releasing a rush of wetness against his fingers. For a moment nothing but the draw of his mouth existed. Nothing but the thrust of his fingers and the pulses they created surged through her body like a firestorm. She sang her pleasure in breathless screams that only lovers could hear as her soul burned with liquid desire.

"Fuck," Niall swore against her intimate flesh, his eyes burning as he watched his glistening fingers withdraw from her. "I was going to do this for hours," he mourned. "But if I don't take you now, I'll be unmanned. You're too fucking sweet."

He was on her again, big and demanding, drawing her beneath him and clamping her legs around his waist. "Take me now, my mate, take my body and my power. Take my heart along with my cock. It is all yours."

He sank inside her and Kenna moaned with relief. Tears pricked her eyes as she felt their connection deeper than before. Faster. His power was already transferring, fueling the inferno he'd ignited within her.

He was deep and she was tight. And they were bound. Not just as mates, but as two people with a common goal. One that reached beyond pleasure, beyond tonight, and past tomorrow that may be or never be.

The heat became hunger, then demand, and then was a lust so powerful Kenna came apart beneath it. His thrusts were rough and pulled a pleasure and pain that had simmered beneath her skin to a scorching rush through every nerve.

She could feel him weaken, and still he thrust forward, his jaw setting with a determined emotion that both frightened and humbled her. "Take me," he gritted through clenched teeth. "Take it from me."

She took it while he came, roaring and convulsing on top of her like the great, ancient predator he was. His power spread from her loins to her blood, kicking her into a climax that spun her through the stars. The candles flared and melted and for a blissful moment she couldn't think. Couldn't fear. Couldn't even breathe as her entire body locked with a fusion of the carnal and the divine.

In the moment he collapsed to the floor, words of surrender and adulation on his lips, Kenna felt her heart melt and knew she was dangerously close to losing it.

She tested her own limbs and felt a sense of strength and power she'd never before imagined. It was something like masculinity and invincibility combined with the feminine force of her own magick thrumming through her veins with a rather intoxicating, almost inebriating potency.

Sliding off the window seat to kneel next to him, Kenna used her thin shawl to clean them. She hated seeing him like this, such a large and dominant creature powerless and immobile. But, the look in his eyes seemed so soft for such a hard face, full of satiation and reverence, and an emotion she couldn't identify. Something deep and abiding.

Words that terrified her rushed to her tongue and choked her throat, making speech impossible. She should say something, shouldn't she? About how grateful she was for his trust and power. About how he would feel better soon enough. Or maybe about how she was feeling hopeful for the first time in a long while, because he'd given her perspective and perhaps a future worth fighting for.

She opened her mouth, but the crash of the library door against the wall cut off her reckless words.

Mother Superior stormed in like an avenging angel, all wrath and righteous indignation, followed by a black entourage of habits that milled into the room and surrounded her. "You *dare* to bring a demon into this house of God," she screeched. "Then you fornicate with him in this holy place, even as the minions of the devil are at our gates."

Kenna snatched her shift, holding it in front of her. "Mother Superior, I can explain." She looked for a friendly face in the crowd and found none. No Judith, or anyone of her ilk. "He gave me his power so I could protect you. It's the only way."

"Bite your tongue, slut," the old nun cursed. "There will be no tribunal for you. No inquisitor. You will burn for this, as will this barbarian and his savage men."

"What have you done?" Kenna demanded.

"I have reclaimed this abbey for God." Fanatical fire lit in the woman's rheumy blue eyes, and it sparked Kenna's temper. "All I have left to do is cleanse it of your evil." Mother Superior stepped forward, as though to seize upon her.

"Careful, old woman," Kenna warned, stepping protectively over Niall, who struggled to regain the use of his muscles. With a twitch of her fingers, the candles flared causing the women to start and scatter about the room in alarm. "My powers are no longer bound, and I won't allow you to get in my way. So if you want me to save you from a magick far more ancient and malevolent than mine, I suggest we cooperate."

Instead of being intimidated, Mother Superior curled her age-lined lips in the smug ghost of a smile. "I don't need you to save us from the Wyrd sisters," she sneered. "I already have."

Niall choked a warning, just as pain exploded in the back of her head and down her spine, and the world pitched into darkness.

CHAPTER 8

T he smell of smoke, acrid to most, was like a perfume to
Kenna. She could pick the scents of pine and larch trees
from their smoke with the relish of a wine connoisseur. Her nose
tickled with it, her throat filled with the taste of ashes and soot
and she lurched into consciousness with a frantic jolt.

She was tied to one of the large stakes that had been where
the whip had torn into her flesh. Firewood and kindling piled
high to her knees. Her head pounded like the inside of a
bodhran at Beltane, but the sight of Mother Superior carrying
the torch toward the adjacent pyre upon which Niall stood was
enough to force the pain into the background.

Vikings sprawled across the courtyard, though whether dead
or unconscious, she couldn't tell.

Flames licked at Kenna's feet, but they didn't burn, only fed
her ire, and the Berserker's power surging through her veins. Fire
might not be a danger to her flesh, but it would kill Niall, especially in his weakened state.

"What have you *done?*" she called above the crackle of the
flames.

Mother Superior turned at the sound of her voice, buying

Kenna precious seconds. "I have done what I must to protect those innocents under my care."

"By killing everyone?" Kenna asked, incredulous.

"Those pagans are not dead, only under the influence of the belladonna we slipped into their wine." A shadow of smug victory hung above her smile. "We hadn't the time to build enough pyres, but we will deal with the rest of them in due course." She lifted the flames to the firewood beneath Niall's feet as he struggled against his ropes as ineffectually as a mortal man might.

This was her fault. She shouldn't have let him weaken himself to save her. If she used her powers to redirect the flames, it would drain her strength against the Wyrd Sisters.

"Don't," she ordered. "You need him, and you need me against the witches who are, even now, plotting violence and terror without these walls."

"I have no need of you, harlot," the old nun hissed. "I've made my own deal with the devil."

"What deal?" Kenna gasped, the smoke now becoming a real threat. She'd need to do something soon, take action.

"All will be revealed," she hedged.

Kenna was so absorbed in the trajectory of the old woman's torch toward Niall's pyre as she tossed it onto the wood, that she almost missed the two nuns release the bolt to the abbey's heavy gates.

Mother Superior turned toward her, eyes glittering in the light of Kenna's own fire. "I *know* I'll be absolved before I die, which is more than I can say for you."

Kenna's heart leapt from its perch in her chest and took a dive into her stomach as three figures were outlined in the abbey's gates.

A maiden. A mother. A crone.

"You know nothing," Kenna addressed the wayward nun in a voice made low and dark, though she never took her eyes from the Wyrd Sisters. "For if you did, you'd realize the mistake you just made."

The Wyrd Sisters advanced in tandem, black-robed and coweled, a dark, malevolent ooze tainting the very air around them. Badb, on the left, the crone, her gnarled hands stirring the wind. Macha, the mother, on the right, calling upon the sea and darkening the clouds, promising the wrath of a storm.

And, in the middle Nemain, the girl with dark fire in her eyes and flames in her hands. Kenna's nemesis. It was because of her existence that Kenna's life was obsolete to these dark witches. They only needed one fire witch, and therefore could destroy her.

In Ireland they were thought to be the Morrigan, in England, the Wayward Sisters. Here in the Highlands, the home of their birth, they were the Wyrd Sisters. De Moray Druids who'd lost their way and let their greed for power take hold, turning them into creatures of darkness and avarice.

Kenna felt the ropes give as her clothes went up in flames. She yanked her arms free, letting the conflagration consume her robes. Heat spread through her body, a pleasurable singe with a punishing scorch at the end as she beckoned the blaze to heed her call.

Fire. Her element. A masculine, destructive, consuming force. It filled her, danced for her, and ignited a passion and a need for justice.

"Your fires of judgment could never hurt me," she taunted the speechless nun who'd just set the blaze to her lover's pyre. "It gives me the fuel to fight."

CHAPTER 9

Niall watched his mate disappear into the flames with a horrified sense of awe. Smoke curled into his already weakened lungs, and slowed the ineffectual struggles against his bonds.

Who knew nuns were so good at tying knots?

Had he his usual strength, he'd be able to rip through rope as though it was parchment. But he was weak, he'd given all of his essence, his potency, to the woman he and his Berserker had chosen.

And he'd do it again, gladly. Though, his heart wept for his men, scattered around the court yards like corpses, yet still drawing precious breaths.

This was no sort of death for a warrior of Freya. Rendered helpless by the poison from a gaggle of frightened women and left out in the storm for these fucking harpies to use as fodder.

Flames began to lick closer to his flesh, and despite himself, Niall felt a frantic sort of rage well within him at his impotency. If only he had more time. If only he could see blood.

If only...

She was like a goddess, standing on her pyre, her clothes turned to ash and her hair flowing behind her, lifted by the fingers of the flames. Her precious skin was unmarred by burns, but glowed with power and strength.

"Give us the Grimoire, Kenna de Moray, and we may spare your life," the witch in the middle spoke in a child's voice dripping with an eerie innocence that she'd likely never possessed.

"Not a fucking chance," Niall growled, knowing the depth of his woman's devotion to her cause. To humanity.

Three heads swiveled toward him in sinister synchronization. "Another Berserker," the crone hissed.

Their momentary distraction gave Kenna the time she needed to gather the flames to her body, creating a sort of human torch. Niall's skin had broken into a sweat as the fire arced closer to him, but she seduced it toward her, as well, leaving none for the evil witches to gain control of.

It crawled to her glowing body like a child to a mother, and once Kenna had it in her possession, she released an arc of flames toward the Wyrd Sisters with lyrical words spoken in her ancient language.

The older women leapt out of the way as the girl child deflected the arrow of flames with an arcane hand gesture and a few whispered words of her own. The fire illuminated the terrified, owlish eyes of cloistered women all huddled beneath the archway, desperately praying to a God who would not intervene.

Thunder roiled over the tops of the craggy Highland hills, bringing flashes of lightning forking toward them, just barely out of reach. The air promised moisture, and Niall knew that flames would be more difficult to maintain once the air and water Druids could concentrate storms to drench his mate.

"The book, Kenna," the Crone demanded. "It is *here*, I can feel it."

"It doesn't belong in your hands," Kenna called from the flames. "You cannot use it as an instrument for the end of days."

Despite what was happening around him, Niall couldn't tear his eyes away from his mate. Her clothes had been incinerated, her bonds no more than ashes at her feet. She was a vision of bliss and beauty ensconced in a deadly heat. A warrior of the elements, a protector of truth and power. A paladin, in her own right.

And she was *his*.

How could one man be so fortunate as to find such a mate, and so tragically cursed to perhaps lose her so soon?

The flames around her body seemed to culminate toward her middle as she gathered them within the shapes of her hands, and again arced fire toward the Wyrd Sisters.

This time, when Nemain deflected, the ball of fire hit the stupefied Mother Superior and engulfed her instantly. The woman didn't have time to scream before she was nothing but a pile of soot.

"She's the first casualty," the girl taunted. "We can slaughter these hundred virgins before you take your next breath, and then we'll flay the skins of the Vikings from their screaming bodies. Is that what you wish, Kenna, to be the cause of all that?"

Niall could see the way the old nun's death affected Kenna in the rapid, horrified blinks of her eyes, but she said nothing.

"We'll leave your Berserker for last." The Crone licked her dry lips and lifted herself toward him as though she floated on a pocket of air. "And we'll leave you alive long enough to endure their suffering, to relive it in your dreams. When the horror passes, and your soul dies, we'll end your life, as well, with the knowledge that Malcolm belongs to us."

"I can't," Kenna gasped, her frantic eyes touching each prone Viking body, and scanning the line of frightened nuns before resting upon Niall's face. "I won't. I must protect the Grimoire." She said this like an apology. For that's exactly what it was.

"I know," Niall acknowledged, pride welling in his heart along with a slew of other transcendent emotions. "I gave you my power, woman, I want you to use it to defeat your enemies. No matter the cost."

THE COST. The cost would be the future he represented to Kenna. The life they might have had. For those with responsibility such as hers, the cost was always too high.

Kenna couldn't let the crone drift any closer to Niall, so she threw one more flaming arc between her and the man who was very slowly gathering his strength, cutting him off from the evil sisters.

"I swear to the Goddess that I will destroy the Grimoire before I let you take it," she declared.

"Don't be foolish," the water witch, Macha, scoffed, the long sleeves of her dark robes rustling with hidden movement. "The Doomsday Grimoire has survived barbarians, genocide, Romans, fires, floods, and countless catastrophes. It is written in the blood of the First Druids and bound in the skin of their enemies. It is the height of arrogance to think that a slip of a fire witch like you could wield the power hidden within, let alone destroy it."

Lightning struck the spire of the abbey, punctuating the truth of Macha's words. Rain pelted the ground, and hissed through Kenna's fire, weakening her barrier between Niall and the witches.

Nemain was the first to step through her wall, as she was immune to the flames as Kenna. Then Macha, followed by the levitating Badb. They surrounded Niall in a triangle each of them running hands over his magnificent body.

"You feel for this one, I think," Badb sneered, her dry, white tongue snaking out to lick at his cheek.

Niall growled at her, and the witch growled back, uncovering rotten, sharp teeth.

"He tastes like fire and sex. Your doing, I believe," the crone continued.

Kenna wanted to lash out at her. The masculine power within her carried with it a bit of the man from which it was drained. A desperate fury called for her to murder the witch and peel the flesh from her bones to wear as a trophy. But she dare not strike, lest she miss, or the witches use her weapon against Niall.

Where are you Malcolm and Morgana? Please hurry! She silently prayed.

"The pain we could cause your Berserker," Badb crooned. "He would beg for death."

"Do your worst," Niall sneered, then laughed, his muscles seeming to come alive with his struggles, and the ropes creaking beneath his impressive weight. He was regaining his strength, just not fast enough. "I'm not afraid to die."

"My worst?" Badb cackled over the sound of the storm. "My worst, Barbarian is something you can not fathom. So much more terrifying than death, but just as final. You see, I know where your soul resides. I can reach for it with my dark magick through the empty spaces between the tiny fibers that comprise your thick, strong body. I can render you helpless. I can do things that you can't swing a sword at. I'll rattle the cage where your beast hides and rip your very essence through the cracks. It'll be bound to me, a slave to my bidding. And once I die, your soul will be trapped here, never to be reborn, never to see the Other World. Just a wraith for a lonely eternity until the end of days."

"You couldn't," Kenna gasped, her fire shield sputtering around her body weakened by her fear, and taking more energy to maintain. "The Goddess wouldn't allow it."

"I have done," Badb argued. "I have quite the collection of souls, already. But he would be my greatest acquisition. I no longer draw my power from the Goddess, but from something darker and more ancient than even *her*. Once they belong to me, their powers are mine, as well."

The possession she'd felt before exploded into a fury of frantic need, and Kenna made a decision that could forever alter her stars. "You cannot have his soul," she called, the flames whipping around her and reaching toward the triad of witches. "For it belongs to me, and I belong to him. *He* is my mate and I accept him as such."

Invisible cords, as soft and yet unyielding as silk reached through the ether and slid through the very fibers of her being.

Niall's handsome face registered so many things, she couldn't blink lest she miss something. Astonishment, pleasure, relief, victory, and finally, wrath. Storms and shadows gathered in his eyes and his lips pulled back from teeth as sharp as a predator's.

The Wyrd Sisters were about to meet his Berserker.

In one powerful flex, the ropes surrounding him snapped, and Macha flew through the air with a swipe of his hand, breaking on the wall and slumping to the mud. Niall leapt after her, clearly intent on murder.

Kenna attacked, as well, slinging her flames in great, lashing whips trying to keep both Nemain and Badb from Niall.

She failed; Nemain had fire of her own, and seemed to steal it from Kenna each time they fought, or lash back at her, forcing her to parry. They were at an impasse.

If only Morgana were here.

Levitating herself above the fray, Badb flew at Niall with a blood-curdling screech, her talon-like fingers clawed into the air and made a fist as though she grasped something ultimately difficult to hold. "His blood is strong, and his soul stronger, but I can still take it," she cackled gleefully, as Niall grunted his steps faltering. "He will serve me well. He will be locked in the cold darkness of the nether, always hungering, ever thirsting. And you'll be left with his perfectly preserved corpse as a reminder of what you've done to him."

"Stop!" Kenna cried out desperately, blasting Badb with a lash of flames that the old woman easily dodged.

Niall groaned and dropped to his knees, a strange illumination beginning to tear away from his back, rippling along his spine and arching as though struggling to stay inside of him.

"No!" Kenna cried. "Stop!"

The beast roared, not the roar of dominance or victory, but

that of a wounded bear, desperate and furious as more of his soul ripped out of his flesh with a sound so horrible Kenna wanted to cover her ears like a child.

That roar pierced her own soul, cutting through her as nothing else had. Never had a fear of loss been so great. Never had her heart beat so hard, not because of herself but *for* another.

She'd given that heart to him, and would lose it completely if she lost him.

"Come to me, Berserker," Badb taunted. "I will take you apart, and rebuild you. I will make you forget who you are. Who you love. Forget everything and everyone but *me* and my will. You will help me to bring about the Apocalypse and I will take my place among the demons to rule the afterlife."

The tragedy of that threat broke Kenna's will, at last. "I'll tell you where it is!" she cried. Hurling one last fire bolt at Nemain, knowing it would do no damage. "The Grimoire, you can have it. Just— let him go."

Badb's eyes glowed with silver light, so evil and malignant that Kenna wanted to claw them out. "Where?" she demanded.

Kenna's shoulder slumped, her lungs deflated, and her voice wavered as she forced out the words that may just damn the world. "The library," she croaked, pointing to the appropriate window. "Beneath the window seat."

Instead of rushing for it, Badb dropped Niall, curled her fingers again, and lifted Nemain from her feet. With a throwing motion, she hurled the girl at the window of the library. "Get the Grimoire," she hissed. "Do not fail me this time."

Wet, slick, and grotesque popping sounds echoed from the far wall of the courtyard, and Kenna turned to see Macha setting bones and mending them, the rain lending her powers of healing.

Niall faced the water witch still, shaking off the effect of Badb's terrifying grip, and rubbing his sternum as though to prove it was still there. Recovering, he rose from the mud like the warrior he was, comprised of parts earth, water, air and fire. Like all creatures.

Rivulets of rain ran into the cuts and groves of his muscles, disappearing into his trews. His back rippled with readiness and his hands curled at his sides.

Kenna could only see him from behind, but she knew how fierce his handsome face could be, and that Macha read murder in his eyes. His speed was blinding. Suddenly he had a sword, and then Macha had no head.

Her powers were quickly waning, and she lashed out again at Badb, who leapt toward Macha with a scream that shattered the clay pots in the courtyard. Kenna's arrows of flame pierced Badb's robes, but were quickly extinguished by the wind and rain.

"I will end you!" she screeched at Niall. "I will end everything!"

Kenna's legs gave as the earth beneath her shifted, plaster and stone dust fell from awnings and the short towers of Westmire Abbey. The rain abated, as though someone had swept the clouds aside, and the ground began to quake with a furious rumble.

"What fresh sorcery is this?" Niall demanded, whirling about with his sword raised.

Kenna stumbled toward him, though her heart lifted with relief. "Malcolm," she sobbed with relief. "Morgana."

Once again, three figures stood framed in the broken archway of the abbey. Only this time, the lone woman was Morgana de Moray, princess of the Highland Picts. She stood in the middle dwarfed by two very broad, very powerful men. One in the garb of a barbarian, holding an axe the size of a small man, and the other in rich, earth-toned robes, crowned with Pictish gold and holding a staff carved from the sacred ash tree.

Malcolm stepped forward, and forlorn howls and vicious snarls rang from outside the walls. He'd brought help, warriors of the animal world. His shrewd green eyes missed nothing, locking

KERRIGAN BYRNE

the scene away in his fantastic mind. Niall's bloody sword, Macha's headless corpse, Kenna's waning flames, and the scattered, stirring Viking bodies.

"This ends now," he decreed.

Lightning struck the ground, called down by the evil crone, and it sang along the nerves of everyone present. "That is where you're wrong, *King* Malcolm." Badb's lips curled into a disgusted sneer at the word. "This is just the beginning of the end. I will bring my army of souls and crush you and your people until there is nothing left but vague memories lost to the ages. I will bring with me the Horsemen of the Apocalypse, and they will trample your magick with their immortal might."

Malcolm's power rumbled through the earth again. The brutal angles of his regal face and the auburn hair that marked them all as de Morays promised the wrath of the Goddess and a deeper, more personal vengeance. "We are strong as three still," he observed. "And yer healer has been taken. Ye have no powers in which to do so."

"So you say," Badb levitated above them, out of their reach. "But we still have something you do not," she hissed.

Kenna dropped her head in defeat, as Niall reached her, his big form taking up vigil behind her as Malcolm whirled on her. "Kenna, where is the Grimoire?"

"It is here." Nemain stepped from the doorway beneath the awning, clutching the Grimoire to her middle.

Malcolm made a downward sweep with his hand, and the awning caved threatening to crush the leering witch, but Badb and Nemain anticipated his attack. The girl dove and Badb caught her with a whirlwind, lifting her above the walls of the abbey.

Without an air Druid, Malcolm, Morgana, and Kenna were bound to the earth.

"The Grimoire is ours and the day is won," Badb gloated. "We'll be coming for you next, Malcolm de Moray, and your

166

sister, as well. There are still four elements to wield, and I know how to break you. I've done it before."

Malcolm visibly paled, but he stepped forward, his lips forming ancient words of a binding spell. Kenna knew what he was doing, and began to recite the spell with him, hoping that it brought the witches to the ground. Morgana joined in as well, her dark Berserker looming over her like a black-eyed sentinel.

Badb was too shrewd, though, and with a gust of air, she and Nemain were gone, leaving them with the wet and dark aftermath of the battle they'd just lost.

CHAPTER 10

N iall stood by as the two lovely red-haired women rushed forward and embraced each other with sobs and words that only they could understand. The blue-cloaked Druid could only be Morgana de Moray, Kenna's beloved cousin. She was tall and voluptuous where Kenna was short and petite, but the family resemblance was unmistakable.

"Christ, Kenna, put some bloody clothes on," Malcolm growled, taking his cloak off and rushing to cover his cousin.

"Or don't!" sang a helpful voice from behind them. Niall whirled to see Ingmar struggling to his feet, his eyes round and bright as they appreciated Kenna's pale and lovely backside. "The only good witch is a naked witch, I always say." He brushed himself off, slinging mud from his fingertips.

"You'll look away if you want to keep your eyes in your head," Niall growled. "That is my mate."

Ingmar's eyes widened, and then he very intently began to study his boots. "Bound to a Gael, eh? Does that mean we're staying here?"

"I am. But it is your choice, and the choice of the men whether or not they will join me. I have to help my mate regain something she's lost. It's important to all of us."

"Well now, that is quite a Co'*nun*'drum," Ingmar chortled. "Speaking of, where are those lovely alchemists, they've made a *habit* of poison, I think."

Niall grunted. "They live, but you'll not take revenge, the old woman who led them has been slain."

Ingmar chuffed. "Revenge wasn't what I had in mind, I was going to see what other fun substances they have in their stores. I've built up too much of a tolerance for such things to last too long. And I want to raid the wares before the other lads wake up." He ambled toward one of the only doors left unscathed, stepping over still-unconsious Vikings in his wake.

"How did they get their hands on the Grimoire?" Malcolm demanded, "It should have been guarded."

"I let them have it," Kenna answered honestly. "To save Niall's soul from becoming their eternal prisoner."

Their gazes collided, Niall's and his lovely mate's, and for the first time, it truly occurred to him just exactly what she'd sacrificed to save his soul.

A shudder took him as the aftershocks of what that witch had done to him still lingered in his body. Being ripped away from one's self, it was the most terrifying experience he could imagine. Worse than death, more difficult than pain or torture, more soul-wrenching than regret or guilt. To feel the very essence of his being as a possible prisoner. It was unfathomable torment.

And she'd saved him from that horrible eternity.

"Why?g" Niall asked her through a throat tightened with emotion. "Why would you risk all that for one man?"

"My question, exactly," Malcolm gritted through obvious fury. "Of all the selfish, short-sighted, reckless—"

Niall stepped forward with a growl, wondering if his mate would forgive him for rearranging the arrogance that seemed to permanently reside on the Druid King's face.

Kenna stepped between them, clutching Malcolm's robes around her now shivering body. "Malcolm, I know this decision affects all of us. But hear me. I've always been able to glimpse the future in the flames, and when Mother Superior attempted to set his funeral pyre to burn, I saw *us*. I saw this man, this Berserker, and our children and grandchildren living—thriving—in our world. That is when I knew, I had to do what I must to save him. To love him. Because it is our fate."

A humbled awe overtook Niall as his little mate held out her hand to him, and he took it, engulfing her slim, warm fingers in his own. This hand, this elegant hand of hers was capable of such power, such awe-inspiring magick, and yet, also generously gave the sweetest caresses and most carnal of pleasures.

How could a man not love such a woman for the rest of his life?

"The Goddess grants us free will. I doona believe in fate," Malcolm muttered pinching the bridge of his nose in irritation. "And I doona understand how it is that the women in this triad of magick can possibly put their bloody mates above the fate of the entire God-forsaken world. Have ye no sense of responsibility? No *fucking* idea of the scope of the loss we just suffered?"

The dark-haired Berserker who'd been looming behind Morgana stepped forward, resting two enormous hands on the shoulders of his own mate. Niall recognized him instantly as Baelsar Bloodborn; Elder, half-breed, and the fastest mercenary Berserker to be born to the temple in a score of centuries.

They'd all thought him defeated at the Battle of Stamford Bridge, and since he was a bastard with no house, they'd not sent anyone after him, not even for his body. The sentiment shamed Niall, who'd been born to a wealthy house with a bloodline as old as the Gods, themselves.

"We can take the battle to them," Bael suggested, his dark, Persian eyes spearing Niall with equal parts wariness and conciliation. They were mated to cousins, which made them family now, didn't it? United in the same cause, for the love of these flame-haired Druid royals and their cantankerous King. "They are now two while you are still a sacred three, and Morgana tells me that your power is increased when you all cast together."

Niall nodded in agreement, wrapping his fingers around the shoulders of his own mate and pulling her back to rest against him. "You now have my sword, Druid King, and Bael's axe. For the sake of my mate, I will fight to regain what was lost on my behalf."

It spoke to Malcolm de Moray's courage and strength that he not only met the eyes of the two gigantic Berserkers in front of him, but he studied them with judiciousness not often seen in the eyes of a mortal. Niall even became a bit restless and uncomfortable, as though the King was stripping away his protection like the bark of a tree, to see the quality of the material beneath.

"Malcolm," Kenna sighed, reaching for her cousin's hand. "I'm sorry it happened this way, but just think, everything that has been done so far on our part has been for the sake of love. And, despite our many gifts and responsibilities, isn't that the most sacred and powerful magick of all? Is that not what the Goddess stands for?"

Morgana stepped forward. "Kenna is right, brother. We are stronger than our enemies, not because we are three, not because we are mated, and not because we are Druids. But because we are family, and we love each other."

The frigid anger in Malcolm's eyes softened, and Niall saw something within the Pictish King that made him flinch. This man did love his family. But there was a hatred deep in his soul, as well. One that covered a raw pain and a deep humiliation, that fractured his psyche in a way that only cold logic could keep the pieces together and in working order.

But for how long?

"I respect yer visions, Kenna," Malcolm finally addressed his cousin with a long-suffering breath. "And why ye did what ye did." He turned to his sister. "And I think yer husband is right." He cast his piercing green eyes to the headless corpse of Macha, still slumped in the mud against the wall, and a dark sort of satis-faction spread across his regal features.

"'Tis time for us to go to war."

Morgana and Kenna turned to each other, ferocity and forti-tude shining in their faces as well as they nodded to each other.

Niall hadn't understood until this moment the true strength of a woman's spirit. Courage was more difficult for such a deli-cate creature. War and bloodshed conflicted with their better natures. And yet, when called upon to defend the innocent, the weak, or in this case the whole fucking world, they became as stalwart as any general.

Kenna turned to him, wrapping her arms around his waist and pressing her body against his as two warm amber eyes gazed up at him, stealing whatever was left of his heart. "I'm asking a lot of you to abandon your homeland for mine, and your battles for our war."

Touched by her concern, Niall pulled her head against his chest, so she could feel his heart beating for her.

"Berserkers search the decades hoping to find a mate to fight for." He locked gazes with Bael, who nodded his understanding of what he was about to say. "We are fortunate among our kind because we have found mates to fight next to and a battle worth our legacy. I pledge my life for yours, Kenna de Moray, my magick, my strength, my heart, and my blood. They are all at your mercy and at your whim. My men will follow you, fight and die for you."

He felt a warm tear touch his chest from where it fell from her eye and he cupped her head with tenderness he didn't know he possessed. "Your fire will be the light, the beacon against this evil that threatens our world, and I will be your sword in the darkness."

He looked into Malcolm's eyes and silently reaffirmed his vow.

The Pictish King peered at him as though he were a queer

and fascinating thing, that their tenderness and intensity was something completely foreign and unfathomable to him.

"Just wait until you fall in love, brother," Morgana teased. "It will amaze you the sacrifices you're willing to make."

"Never going to happen," Malcolm scoffed, lifting his staff and pointing to the stables. "We're taking horses back to Dun Moray," he decreed.

Kenna pulled back, her eyes shining up at Niall with a laughter born of intimate secrets. "Remember what you said about *never*?" she asked.

There were, of course, Vikings to wake, nuns to settle, carnage to repair, and a war to plan. Sister Judith would be installed as the Mother Superior, a fair and generous woman. Ingmar and Bulvark would have to rally more men to fight the damned souls of the Wyrd Sister's army.

But before all that, Niall shared warm, knowing laughter, and a hot kiss with his mate.

HIGHLAND WARRIOR

The Wyrd Sisters:

*"By the pricking of my thumbs,
something wicked this way comes."*

~ William Shakespeare, Macbeth

CHAPTER 1

Badb:
"Sacred hate and ancient ire,
By the wind, water, and fire.
Reach through the souls now owned by me
And pluck the one who shall be freed.

A maiden fair, a beauty bold,
To ensnare a heart so cold.
She'll force a King to his knees,
And bring him to be ruled by me."

Wyrd Sisters:
"As we will, so mote it be!"

The Highland cave became as still as a tomb, and even the Wyrd sisters held their collective breath until one small bare foot stepped out of the nether, followed by a shapely calf, long, sensuous thighs, and a body that would have melted the hearts of the stoutest warriors.

Pale, luminous skin glowed in the light of the nether, illuminating eyes the color of amethysts and hair as dark as midnight.

"Mistress," the shade spoke, running elegant fingers along her bare flesh as though she couldn't believe what she felt. "What is your will?"

"Malcolm de Moray," Badb spat the name. "Bring him back to me, I haven't finished with him yet."

"Once we have the Druid King along with the Grimoire, the others will follow," Nemain drawled. "And since we are without Macha now, we'll need a third body to absorb the Magick we will claim from them."

That caught the shade's attention. "Me?" she asked hoarsely.

"Unless you'd like to spend another century in the nether."

"Nay," the ebony-haired maiden stepped forward. "Nay, I'll do whatever you ask. Just don't send me back there."

"Seduce him," Nemain ordered, stepping to the woman and running fingers through her thick hair. "Cripple him with lust and weaken him with pleasure."

Badb cackled at the idea. "Get him to trust you. Then his heart will be open and vulnerable for us to take. Then you'll say these words when he is at the peak of his pleasure, and all the power that is his, will be yours." She handed the shade a parchment with an ancient curse written upon it.

"*That* is when we'll strike." Nemain pulled a tattered, charcoal robe from her own shoulders and draped it across the shade. "A damsel in distress, I think, is just the tactic to disarm the King."

Badb spit into the cauldron she'd been stirring, and it hissed. "He'll be sorry he ever crossed us," she snarled.

Nemain smiled, her amber gaze gliding down the new woman's curves. "And sorrier still, that he ever laid eyes on you."

MALCOLM DE MORAY'S growl of frustration echoed off the stone wall of his laboratory. The looking glass he hurled shattered against it a scant second later.

By what ancient Magick had the Wyrd Sisters hidden the Grimoire from him? From *him*! The most powerful Earth Druid to be seen in a handful of centuries. The last potent male of his kind. The King of the fucking Picts. And he couldn't get a simple scrying spell to work.

His enemies were close, he knew it. The trees shuddered at their evil, and the fields swayed with whispers of sightings, but nothing tangible.

He'd be damned if he sat with his cock in hand and waited for them to strike. Nay, he'd find the vicious bitches and send them to hell where they belonged.

"Have you eaten today, Brother?" Morgana, his younger sister, flowed into his laboratory carrying a tray of food. Though breakfast or dinner, he couldn't be certain.

"I know not," he answered shortly, eyeing the doorway for the inevitable following of his sister's Berserker mate. "What day is it?"

"Would it matter if I told you?" Morgana's blue dress shimmered like crystalline water as she made her way past candles, lanterns, shelves, scrolls, and herbs to set his repast on the table in front of him.

"Nay," he admitted, the word almost drowned out by the loud, hungry sound his stomach made at the scent of salted pork, rosemary roasted potatoes, and beets.

Morgana reached up and took his stubbled jaw in her hands, and instantly he felt a relief that only a water Druid could give another human with her touch. His aches and pains dissipated, his tense muscles relaxed, and the pricking of the headache that had begun to pound behind his eyes disappeared.

"Dear Malcolm," she murmured softly. "When is the last time you slept?"

He blinked down into a face the feminine copy of his own. Unruly russet hair, pale skin, prominent jaw. Though hers was delicate, and his defined. Other than the obvious difference in their sexes, the only other thing that set them apart was the color of their eyes. Morgana's were as blue as the ocean in summer, while his were a mossy green.

Elemental colors.

"Who can sleep with all these bloody Vikings invading *my* castle?" he groused.

Unruffled, Morgana patted his cheek. "They're not invaders, dear, they're allies. *Guests.* Two of whom are mated to your sister and cousin. So they're family, as well."

Malcolm grunted. "That damned army of Niall's is picking our larder clean and planting bastards in all the kitchen maids."

"They've also pledged their swords and lives to help us defeat the Wyrd Sisters," she reminded brightly. "Now eat your supper, and I'll give you the gift that will make your search easier."

That arrested his attention. "What gift?"

The same mischief had lit her eyes for just over two decades now. Malcolm loved it, and he hated it. "Eat first," she ordered.

Malcolm took a step toward her, towering head and shoulders above her. "I am not a child, I am your king," he said darkly. "I command ye to give me what ye have." No one had ever dared disobey him when he was in such a mood.

Morgana burst out laughing and lifted onto her toes to give him a quick peck on the cheek. "When has that ever worked on me?" she giggled. "Eat up."

Nostrils flaring, Malcolm stabbed at a chunk of pork and brought it to his mouth, chewing furiously while holding out his hand to his sister.

"Your vegetables as well," Morgana reminded him.

"Give it to me, or I'll do ye violence," he threatened. They both knew he wouldn't. First, because he loved his sister and would never lay a hand on a woman, and second, because Baelsar Bloodborn, Morgana's Berserker mate, would tear his limbs from his body and throw them in the tall grasses. Magick be damned.

With a gusty sigh, Morgana reached into her pocket and held up a piece of twine on the end of which the most perfect quartz crystal he'd ever seen reflected the light of the candles.

"Where did ye get that?" he breathed, snatching it away from her grasp.

"From a toad Bael and I met by the river." Morgana shrugged. "And you're welcome."

"What were ye doing by the river?" Malcolm asked idly, running his fingers over the smooth, clear surface of the spear-shaped crystal. It fit in the palm of hand, and would be the most effective scrying tool of all time.

When he glanced up, Morgana's eyes were sparkling with that mischief again, and also with a lasciviousness that caused his belly to lurch with disgust.

"That's revolting," he spat.

"I said nothing," Morgana sang innocently, all but dancing toward the door.

"Ye didna have to," he complained.

"Now if you don't finish your supper by the time I return in an hour, I'll have Bael tie you up and shove it down your throat." With that cheerful threat, she closed the door to his workshop behind her.

"I'd like to see him try," he muttered to no one in particular.

Dinner forgotten, Malcolm retrieved the most recent map of his kingdom and uncurled it across his table. He murmured a Gaelic scrying spell as he sprinkled powdered mugwort, nutmeg, cinnamon, and yarrow onto the map. Licking his fingers, he let the crystal dangle over it and circle in the direction of the earth's rotation.

After a few minutes, the crystal stilled and skewered the map with its sharp point.

The Caledonian Forest. *Of course.* Within its ancient black depths any myriad of evils could hide. It was said that Fairy Magick still protected some of the forest, and that could be blocking each of the de Moray's attempts to find the Grimoire.

"Ha," he crowed in triumph. "I'm coming for ye." Grabbing his cloak and riding boots, Malcolm strode from his laboratory with vengeance lengthening his every step.

In his haste, he nearly knocked over his cousin, Kenna, when he rounded a corner on his way to the stables.

She jumped back into her mate, Niall's, broad chest and the man steadied her with gigantic, yet gentle hands whist glaring daggers at Malcolm.

"Malcolm," she exclaimed, her amber eyes glowing with genuine pleasure. "I haven't seen you in ages, you've been so isolated in your cave. Where are you off to?"

"The Caledonian Woods," he answered shortly, making to step around them.

"Going hunting are you?" she asked brightly, putting a fond hand on his arm.

"Aye."

"For game or for herbs?"

For evil. "I must be on my way."

"Of course." she kissed him on the cheek, which produced a soft sound of protest from her looming mate. "Ride past the west gate on your way out. My love and his men are erecting spear-tipped fence posts that would stop a war horse. It's really very clever."

Clever? Malcolm met Niall's light-eyed glare across Kenna's head and spoke to him in Gaelic. "My people were mapping the stars and discovering the mysteries of the universe while ye Nordic barbarians were still dragging your knuckles in your own people's blood and shit."

Niall's eyes narrowed even further with suspicion. "What did he just say to me?"

"They're just trying to help," Kenna answered back in the language of their fathers, putting a staying hand on her mate's chest.

"I should hex them all with a pox for making changes to *my* keep without *my* permission," Malcolm growled at Kenna, still in Gaelic.

"You've been locked in your laboratory for days," Kenna argued.

"Did he just threaten you?" Niall growled, taking a step forward with murder flashing in his eyes.

Malcolm made a fist, ready and willing to go to blows with the interloper.

"Oh... he said that you all are, indeed, quite clever," Kenna lied, sending Malcolm silent warnings of wrath. "*And*, he says *thank you* to you and your men for their hard work." She annunciated every word through gritted teeth.

The Nordic giant quirked a suspicious eyebrow. "That's not what it sounded like."

Kenna grabbed Niall's arm and guided him around Malcolm. "Oh, you know Gaelic, a rather harsh sounding language sometimes, isn't it? Let's go check on Ingmar and Bulvark, shall we?"

Malcolm watched as Kenna led her mate past him and disappeared around the corner in a hurry. He'd need to figure out what to do about these Berserker men. They weren't even properly married to his kin, and yet they'd begun living together as though they had been in an alarmingly short time.

Turning, he stalked down the corridor, his footfalls echoing off the stones. First, though, he needed to stop the impending Apocalypse. Everything else could wait.

Going after the remaining Wyrd Sisters on his own was reckless, he knew. But he had a secret vengeance to reap.

And if Malcolm was in a forest, he had more than enough weapons at his disposal.

CHAPTER 2

M y *name is Vían.* It was all she remembered. Anything else had disappeared into the nether ages ago. Her memories, her identity, and her humanity. She knew she used to be something. Someone. That she had loved, and had been betrayed. But even those details had begun to dissipate within the cold, dank void that had been her home for centuries.

When the madness set in, when she felt as though she'd fall through her prison that was as insubstantial as air, and yet as strong as iron, she'd press her cheek to the cold floor and chant the one thing she knew for certain over and over again.

My name is Vían.

Her name remained the only thing the Wyrd sisters hadn't taken from her. The only thing she hadn't pledged to them. Her last possession.

It seemed to be the purpose of the nether, to strip one's mind of all individuality. The longer one remained incarcerated there, the more of themselves they lost.

Though a thick mist shrouded the afternoon, and thicker trees blocked the sunlight, Vían blinked against the brilliance of the day. It had been precisely fifty years since she'd been called out of the nether. Fifty years since she'd seen any light whatso-ever, and before that it had been a few decades if she remem-bered correctly. In the hundred or so years she'd been incarcerated, she could count on one hand the number of times the Wyrd Sisters brought her forth to do their bidding. And once their objective had been acquired, it was back into the void with her. Alone and forgotten.

The dense forest shimmered with moisture. The leaves of trees, of which she'd forgotten the names, changed with the season, flaring into brilliant colors before they shriveled and fell to the earth. Her eyes ached with the sight, but she didn't dare close them, for fear the beauty would disappear. She'd need this memory to hold on to, in case the Wyrd sisters didn't hold up their end of the bargain and sent her back once her job was finished. The beauty of this forest would keep her for decades, until it, too, faded.

The damp flora beneath her feet felt like a carpet of clouds. She didn't even care about the biting chill, and couldn't help but run the moss between her toes with a child's relish.

Even the wet, cold air that reached through her threadbare cloak until she trembled with body-tensing shivers felt better than the perpetual dry cold of her prison. It was *something*. A sensation and, though unpleasant, it was life-affirming.

Watching her hot breath puff into the autumn air, Vían drifted forward, ignoring the strange rustlings and noises of the forest. She only had one purpose, and the Wyrd Sisters' evil Magick would protect her from all else.

She must seduce Malcolm de Moray, and say the spell Badb had given her upon his release into her body. With it, she would take his Druid Magick.

He approaches... the wind hissed with the voice of Badb, as she had dominion over the air. *Be ready... be ruthless.*

"Yes, mistress," Vían whispered just as trotting hoof beats drew near. Spotting a soft bit of ground beneath the corpse of a fallen tree, Vían threw herself down and made certain her threadbare shift only skimmed her slender thighs and bared one shoulder and half of her breast.

A damsel in distress. Noblemen couldn't help themselves.

As a dark shadow formed within the swirling mist and began to solidify, she moaned as piteously as she could.

"Help. Please sir. Help me?"

She didn't have to fake her open-mouthed gasp as the Shire steed obediently stopped, horse and rider peering down at her with nearly identical looks of astonished curiosity.

Malcolm de Moray, Druid King of the Picts, was nothing like she'd imagined. Indeed, Vían had expected an older king, grey-bearded, poxed, and portly from too much ignoble excess.

The man swinging down from his horse couldn't have yet seen five and thirty. He was tall and wide enough to merit such a giant steed, she could tell that even beneath his forest-green cloak and kilt.

"Christ," he swore, hurrying to her.

Vían couldn't make the assessments she needed, nor could she remember the plots and lies she'd worked on. His eyes were so mossy green and lovely in a face so raw with masculinity that the contrast rendered her speechless.

Locks of unruly russet hair fell over his braw forehead as he bent down to kneel beside her prone body.

"What happened to ye?" he demanded, ripping off his cloak and covering her with it.

So much for distracting him with her bare skin. She'd have to improvise.

The reasons she couldn't answer him were two-fold.

First, because the cloak was fur-lined and sumptuous, retaining the warmth of his body and sliding across her cold, bare skin like a lover's caress.

Second, because his shirt was unfastened to his torso, and she could see the swells of his chest and the dark shapes of his nipples hardened against the cold beneath the thin linen.

He was lean in the way that wolves were lean. Long limbs thickened with power and sinewed with grace, but also clinging to his braw frame in a spare, hungry way that made her wonder if he ate enough to support a man of his size.

Vían didn't quite know what to do in the presence of such a male, let alone what to say, so she merely stared at him in an open-mouthed stupor.

"Are ye hurt?" He made as though to put his hands on her, but then thought the better of it, studying her with shrewd, yet gentle eyes. "I doona see any blood. We're ye attacked, lass?"

"I—I don't know," she answered shakily. "I don't remember anything. I just... appeared here." Lies were more believable when peppered with the truth.

"Can ye move yer limbs? Yer fingers and toes?" he queried, still squinting at her alertly from beneath a cruel brow.

"Aye," she lifted her arm out of his cloak as though to show him, letting it fall down past her shoulder and breast.

There, he looked, she noted with pleasure. His gaze snagged on her creamy breast and pebbled nipple, before he tore it away and reached to cover her again.

"Were ye robbed?" he pressed, "Were ye—" He broke off, color crawling up his neck as his jaw clenched.

"My head." She pressed a hand to her forehead. "'Tis pounding, but I feel no pain elsewhere, and I have nothing of value to steal."

"Perhaps someone came up behind ye," he murmured. "May I?"

At her nod, he reached out and threaded big, careful fingers in her thick hair, probing her scalp with the expertise of an experienced physician.

"Are you a healer?" she asked, turning her head so her lips brushed against the skin of his arm.

"I have some experience with it," he hedged, pulling his arm away from her with a start. "I doona feel a lump, though that doesna mean one willna develop. Do ye think ye can stand? I'll want ye away from here in case they come back. There is much danger in these woods."

"I'll try," she said weakly, allowing him to help her upright. Immediately, Vían let his cloak fall to the earth, leaving her only with her almost transparent shift, as she swooned against him.

He caught her easily, and tensed as she pressed her body against his.

"Do ye live here in the forest with yer...father? Husband?" he asked uncomfortably.

"I live alone," she said against his chest. "I have naught but a cottage by the loch. Can I prevail upon you to take me there, sir? I don't think I can walk all that way back just yet."

Lifting her easily, he secured her on the back of his horse before bending to reclaim his cloak. Swinging up behind her, he wrapped them both in the fur, and pulled her back into the circle of his strong arms. "Lean against me, lass. Ye're like ice. I'll share my warmth with ye."

Vían leaned back, letting her head rest in between the grooves of his chest. Pangs of guilt and conscience stabbed at her belly, but she brushed them away. Though he was handsome and gallant, Malcolm de Moray was still a man. Still weak and prone to temptation. He'd take what she offered, or maybe he wouldn't even wait for her to offer.

And then she'd take from him.

She hoped he didn't hurry to the loch, though. His body fit so well against hers, and she soaked in the heat radiating from him. She couldn't remember anything feeling so incredible.

And she hadn't been warm in over a hundred years.

MALCOLM DID his best to keep his stallion's gait even. If the lass were concussed, jostling her overmuch could do irreparable damage. The mist seemed to thicken as they plodded toward Loch Doineann, which was more of a pond, in truth, surrounded by lush forest. He tried to keep his awareness on their surround-ings in case brigands were about. If he didn't, he'd focus on how her soft body fit against his, or how supple and tantalizing her breasts had looked. But the forest whispered warnings through the mist that unsettled him.

Beware. It said. *Enemies are near.*

If his enemies were near, then the Grimoire was too. The scrying stone had told him thus. So what was he doing escorting a peasant home when he should be searching for it?

"I've not seen you here in the forest before, how do you know where the loch is?" she asked, pulling his cloak tighter around herself and pressing her shoulders against his chest with a tremor of chill.

"I know every inch of these lands," he answered simply. *They're my responsibility.*

For some reason, he didn't want her to know who he was. Didn't want her to treat him with the deference she'd show the King of their Pictish people. For all she knew, he was a woods-man, doing a pretty lass a kindness. There was no Grimoire, Wyrd Sisters, Berserkers, or impending war. For just a moment, there in the mist, they were a man and a woman, making their way through the fragrant, loamy autumn forest.

"Do yer people hie from these woods?" he asked. "Do they live close by?"

"My people are all dead," she murmured, without much inflection. "I've been alone for many years."

It unsettled him how curious she made him. He wanted to press her, but knew the telling of her story would be painful. How did she come to be alone in these woods with nothing but a threadbare shift? Did her people die in the Lowland wars? Or by the hands of the English? Perhaps illness took them. Or plague. What family did she belong to?

Who had put the wounds and wariness behind her lovely, amethyst eyes?

"There." She pointed. "Just past that copse of trees."

Malcolm spotted the structure—if one could call it that—and frowned. Due to her dress, he hadn't expected much, but the rotting, dilapidated dwelling leaning against a few ancient trees was uninhabitable.

The roof, for lack of a better word, had rotted through and fallen in on one side. The door was a bunch of green branches lashed together and propped against the entry.

Malcolm tensed as they approached, stopping on the narrow sandy beach of the loch and gaping in silent protest for several minutes. When the lass began to squirm, he dismounted from behind her. "Stay here," he ordered. "I'll make certain no one is inside."

She nodded, her eyes growing rounder in her face, as though she hadn't considered intruders.

The interior was cozier than he expected, but only just. She'd been using the collapsed part of the roof as a chimney, with an old empty cauldron and cook fire laid, but unlit. A pallet of worn furs and a tattered blanket was the only protection from the chill of the dirt floor. A pestle, knife, tankard, wooden bowl, and a long-handled spoon were neatly lined up against the wall opposite the—well he couldn't rightly call it a bed, could he?

Forest fauna and the loch could sustain one person, he supposed, but surviving out here on one's own would be mighty difficult. Malcolm felt a pang slice through him at the thought of that lovely woman shivering alone on the dirt floor at night.

"I mean to mend the roof before winter sets in," she said from behind him.

He turned to her, unable to straighten to his full height in the cramped space. "Ye... *live* here?"

From the flash in her eyes, he could tell he'd said the wrong thing. "Aye, I live here, and it's a palace compared to where I was before."

At her words, his heart broke, but he tried to keep the pity from his eyes, lest she interpret it as condescension. "I didna mean to offend ye. It's only that this place seems..." cold, dark, broken, not fit for a forest creature's den, let alone a delicate woman. "Lonely," he finished. She didn't belong in this place, either. No one did. He prided himself on the prosperity of his people, upon the procedures he had in place to economically buoy those who were vulnerable.

"It does get rather lonely here." Her voice lowered to a husky rasp of honeyed suggestion. "Most especially at night...in the dark."

She moved closer to him, his cloak sliding down her shoulders to her elbows. Her lavender eyes glittered like gems in the fading light against the dreary surroundings. Ebony hair gleamed like silk and velvet.

Malcolm's body's reaction was instantaneous. Suffused by lust and awareness, he hardened beneath his kilt. A spell seemed to make the evening darker, and her skin brighter. It was as though his body was no longer his own. He couldn't even swallow, let alone step away from her as a nobleman in his position *should*.

It was invitation he read in her eyes, there was no mistaking it. But something else lurked in their depths, a hesitancy, a vulnerability maybe, that kept him in check.

And pain. There was plenty of that.

Giving himself a stern cursing, he remembered that she'd been hit over the head not an hour ago. "I want you lie down," he ordered gently.

She blinked as though he'd stunned her. "You want me to— lie with you?"

"Nay," he said vehemently, and at her puckered frown he amended. "Not, *nay*, just not... now. I mean, perhaps not at all. That is... I doona expect anything...but..." Christ, what was he, a pubescent youth? He clenched his teeth and tried again. "I want to examine yer head again, to make certain ye're not concussed."

She blinked a couple more times before replying. "I see."

Lowering to her furs, she cast his cloak to the side and

stretched out on her back, hair fanning out beneath her shoulders.

Malcolm could see her nipples beneath the thin garment she wore. It molded to her long torso, and flared with her hips, dipping in between legs that seemed to go on forever. To say her shape was fine would be like saying the night was dark or the December wind was bitter.

"You're staring." She smiled up at him.

"Sorry." Kneeling beside her, he reached for her scalp again. "May I examine ye?"

"I'm at your mercy."

Heat flared beneath the chill of the evening at her words, and Malcolm again reached into her soft tresses in search of a bump. Still finding none, he gently put his finger beneath each of her remarkable eyes and leaned in to check her pupils for signs of inconsistency. "Is yer vision blurry at all?" he queried.

"Nay."

"Are ye nauseated or faint?"

"Nay."

Her breath mingled with his, and a strange kinetic kind of energy seemed to leap between their skin. "Ye should stay warm," he said, lamenting the husky note in his voice as he reached for his cloak to cover her again.

Malcolm found it strange that she seemed perplexed as he tucked his cloak around her. She had to be chilly; it was colder than a sow's teat in autumn.

"What about yer headache?"

"It's better now." She shook her head back and forth as though to prove it.

Malcolm paused, his hand resting on her shoulder. There was naught left to do, and yet he didn't want to leave her here.

A soft hand snaked from beneath the cloak and covered his. "Is there... aught I can do to repay you for your kindness?" She moved his hand from her shoulder to her breast, emphasizing her meaning.

Malcolm had to force his next words around a throat gone dry. "Nay," he said. "I'd never take an offer like that as payment."

"Then what would it take, to get you to share my bed?"

CHAPTER 3

Ían thought Malcolm would hastily accept her invitation. Instead, he backed away and gained his feet, knocking his head on the ceiling in his haste. "I should... go." Moving the door, he ducked out and replaced it with a final-sounding *thunk*.

No man she'd been forced to seduce for the Wyrd Sisters in her century or more of confinement had ever turned her down. It seemed that the more odious her charge, the more willing they were to take her. There was not one thing odious about Malcolm de Moray. The man was built as strong as the castle he lorded over, and had features just as finely crafted.

Sitting up, Vían brought her knees to her chest and hugged them, staring at the hovel's entry. Maybe he'd seen past her beauty, to the demonic creature she'd become, and it drove him away. Maybe he suspected her intentions, or perhaps he would rather lie with a man than a woman. After all, a king his age and not married? A rare thing, indeed.

Or maybe he was married. Come to think of it, the Wyrd Sisters had never mentioned it.

Vían considered every last one of these options before landing on her real fear. What if he found her repugnant? Maybe the spark between them was one-sided and he was in a rush to quit her company. Instead of a damsel who enticed him, she might be a pauper who repulsed him.

The question was, what difference did that make to her? Why was she so forlorn over his rejection?

She hadn't been sent to *fall* for Malcolm de Moray. Her job was to get him to fall for her charms just long enough to fuck her. He'd hate her much worse than that when he found out who she was, who she worked for, and why she'd betrayed him.

And betray him, she would.

Vían's intention to stay out of the void that imprisoned her soul for more than a century had gone past desperation, past madness, into a determined ruthlessness that drove her like nothing before. If Malcolm de Moray had to be a casualty of regaining her freedom, then so be it. She couldn't go back into that place, the dark hole where despair swallowed her in endless torment, and she couldn't even look forward to death as a release.

There was no release. No escape. Only this.

Running her cheek along her drawn up knees, she reveled in the warmth of his fine cloak. He'd left it for her. Why? Because he pitied her? Because he was a decent man?

Most likely because he had a hundred more like it in his castle chambers and left this one to ease his conscience.

Well, it would give her the perfect opportunity to see him again. She could request an audience at Dun Moray under the guise of returning it to him. He'd be more relaxed in his own home, less guarded, and easier to seduce. There would be beds, candlelight, and maybe she could get Nemain to craft her a spell that would—

The collection of sticks that passed for a door moved again, stunning her thoughts to silence. Malcolm bent to enter, carrying a bundle of kindling and a few larger logs. "Yer wood pile is nigh empty," he chastised gently. "We'll need to remedy that."

Vían could only stare, as he bent to lay a fire in the meager circle of stones that passed for a fire pit.

"We?" she finally ventured.

He stood again and left just as abruptly as before, returning with his saddle bags. Retrieving implements from within them, he bent to start a fire on some tinder striking the flint together blowing on the spot where sparks began to catch.

Vían knew she should be re-strategizing her approach, and she would, just as soon as she could tear her eyes from the way his back and shoulders stretched at the seams of his fine shirt, or how his kilt rested on his bent backside.

His legs were so long. Lithe and powerful. Her fingers itched to get at what was under that kilt.

For the sake of freedom, of course, she reminded herself.

Vían got the impression that Malcolm wasn't a man of many words. He worked quietly, absorbed in the task of building a fire, and didn't look up until the blaze was stable and throwing off a furnace of heat. That accomplished, he reached again for the saddle bags and extracted a cloth wrapped around some cheese, some bread, and a few slices of cured meat. Next came a skein of something, hopefully spirits or ale.

It had been so long.

"If yer not nauseated, ye should eat and drink something," he murmured. Taking her knife, he crouched down and cut her generous portions of the food, handing it to her without truly looking at her. "I retrieved water from the spring trickling into the loch, there. While ye eat, I'll restock yer wood pile." He frowned, motioning for her to take the food he offered. "I'll not leave ye here with no axe to pick through frosty kindling. I'd have to question my manhood if I did."

Vían thought of the member that had twitched and throbbed against her rump while they'd shared the saddle. No one in the history of the world would ever be able to question *his* manhood. Lord, but it was generous.

Blinking down at the offered fare, shock and something else

entirely clouded her vision with moisture. Behind that was panic. Where was this coming from? Why did she suddenly have a lump in her throat so big she was unable to form words of thanks? And just how in the hell could she seduce a man if she was a sobbing mess?

If she failed, she'd go back to the void. She needed to pull herself together.

Now.

"Why?" she whispered before she could stop herself, hating that her voice was tight with tears.

"Why, what?"

She didn't look up from her lap, keeping her eyes firmly fixed on her knees. "If you do not want to lie with me, why are you being so kind?"

His big, warm hand reached out to cup her cheek, and he guided her face to turn toward him, his green eyes as sharp as cut emeralds and twice as brilliant in the firelight. "I'm kind because I am a Druid and yer king, and therefore kindness is not just my responsibility, but my way of life." He dropped his hand from her cheek then, but his next words reached so deep, they seared her very bones. "But make no mistake, lass, I want to take ye in ways that would wipe the word 'kind' from yer thoughts of me."

Her breath caught around a lump in her throat made of half emotion, and half elation. "Then, take me," she whispered.

"It wouldna be right," he forced through clenched teeth, his eyes those of a warrior valiantly fighting a losing battle.

"I need..." She didn't dare say it. Couldn't put into words what it was he made her want. She had to lie with him in order to take his powers, but this was the first time in a long time, maybe ever, that she truly wanted to.

Which made Malcolm de Moray more dangerous than she'd ever considered.

Through with words, she rose on her knees, and undid the ties of her garment, letting it fall to the earth beneath her. Malcolm regarded her from those jewel green eyes like one would an approaching viper. Which was closer to the truth than she'd like to admit.

His nostrils flared, and his fists clenched at his sides, but he remained where he was, obviously locked in a battle with his decency. His eyes devoured her like a starving man at a feast, but he didn't make one move toward her.

Decency be damned. Once he realized who she was and what she'd done to him, he'd wish he'd left her in the woods to rot.

Firmly pushing that thought to the side, she reached for him, sliding her hands up his shoulders and around his neck to lock behind him, pulling his head down to hers.

Her lips pressed against his, but Vían didn't have control of the situation for long.

Malcolm dragged her hard against his body in a deep, starving kiss. With a groan of surrender, he plunged his tongue into her welcoming mouth with a thrusting rhythm that set her loins on fire.

She'd have to try very hard to keep her wits about her. Already, her legs were beginning to fail, becoming weak enough that she leaned into him. Once he felt her submission, he lowered them to her furs and stretched his hard body above her supple one.

He whispered a few unfamiliar words against her mouth and the packed earth beneath her thin bedding suddenly became soft and fragrant with flora.

"Magick," she marveled aloud.

"Like yer skin," he murmured against her, before taking her mouth again. One moment his hot, silky tongue tangled with hers, the next he was nibbling and sucking at her lips, teasing her with alternating pleasures.

She shifted so her thighs could split beneath him, cradling that swollen, needy part of him against her sex. His clothes still separated them, but he ground against her instinctively, and Vían hissed at the intensity of the sensation.

Hungry for more of him, she lifted the hem of his shirt and wordlessly demanded that he help her peel it away.

The firelight threw shadows into the groves and valleys of his sinewed frame. He was light-skinned and fine, like the marble statues in the Roman ruins.

Vian stared as he lifted himself to sweep away his kilt and boots.

He stared at her, too. His eyes traveled her smooth skin and latched onto the apex of her parted thighs which she shamelessly bared to him.

"I've never seen a woman of yer like," he breathed. "Ye're so fucking beautiful."

He gave her the compliment with such ferocity, she had to hide behind her lashes for a moment and gather her strength.

He was beautiful, as well. Not in the lovely way a woman was, but in a raw-boned, utilitarian way. Each swell and dip and angle fashioned for power and purpose.

And all that power was about to be unleashed upon her.

Within her.

Vian's breath sped to a pant and she reached for him, suddenly feeling vulnerable stretched out and spread beneath him.

He came to her instantly, his hands roaming everywhere, his mouth capturing hers with a wild possession. Finding the softness of her bare ass, his fingers dug into the flesh there, pulling her firmly against his cock.

Vian would have liked to think she was not as affected with lust and wanting as he, but they both shuddered with the intensity of their connection, and it was her body that wept with slick desire.

Keep your heart encased in ice, she warned herself. *Let your body burn.*

His venturing fingers found her most private heat and, again, they both moaned their pleasure. He was gentle, crooning things into her ear as he kissed and licked the sensitive lobe. His words melted her core as his probing fingers drove her higher than she'd ever imagined.

"Come for me, lass," he commanded into her ear. When his teeth nipped down on her lobe, he pressed that pliant flesh with just enough pressure to launch her to the stars with an astonished cry.

When one lived the majority of their years in a hole looking up to where the mortals walked, flying seemed out the realm of possibility.

But fly she did.

And before she truly returned to earth, he was above her, then inside her, thrusting deep and long until their hips met. His fingers reached beneath her head and threaded into the hair at her scalp until her head rested in his palm, secured and immobile.

"Look at me while I love ye," he said, and began to move.

For all of his easy confidence, Malcolm de Moray made love like a doomed man, desperate for a safe harbor against the storms that loomed on the horizon. He fucked her like he knew tomorrow was not guaranteed and he needed the pleasure to fill whatever hollow pain lurked in his eyes.

She could only see the wounds now that they were this close, nose to nose, sharing each other's breath. And flesh.

It was like everything slipped away. The void. The witches. His Magick. Her lies. While his cock slid inside the tight, slippery skin of her sex, it was as though he had truly become a part of her, somehow. With each thrust, he branded her. Each moan and gasp was a wordless promise.

And the ecstasy was unparalleled.

Vían was too entranced to fight her second climax. It ripped through her with all the power and inevitability of a tempest. She saw it on the horizon, flashing with lightning and threatening with thunder, but she was just as helpless to stop it. And when the storm hit, it locked her in its verdant clutches with arching tremors and pleas for mercy.

He gave her none, but followed after her with thick, hot pulses of bliss against her womb and a roar of pleasure sent to the Gods.

❀

Vían stared at the fire for what seemed like an eternity after.

She'd failed her charge. She'd not said the curse.

Malcolm dropped to his side between her and the wall, and turned them both to face the flames. Tucking her bottom against his hips, he wrapped his strong arms around her and allowed them both to catch their breath.

His felt warm and strong, tickling her hair and brushing her skin with the sweetest of sensations. For the second time that night, her eyes filled with tears.

"Ye're going to think I'm daft," he said against her hair. "But I like it here, with ye."

"In my lonely hovel?" she said, fighting the frightening surge of emotion.

His soft chuckle brushed her face. "I truly didn't mean to offend ye," he rumbled, nuzzling through her hair and reaching her neck. "The earth in this forest is fragrant and soft. The night isna bitter, but chilly enough to enjoy the fire and yer warm body so close to mine." He pulled her deeper into the hollow he'd made with his frame. "It's different where I live, so much responsibility. So much always at stake. I am in charge of it all, and yet feel as though I control nothing. Here, the forest does my bidding and is simply happy at my presence."

"How can a forest be happy?" she wondered aloud.

Goosebumps flared on her skin as Malcolm's fingers idly ran over her shoulder and down her arm before dipping into her waist and flowing over the curve of her hip. Vían's tears overflowed her lids and slid across her cheeks and nose in a continuous hot path of pain.

"It's hard to explain," he continued, unable to see the effect his touch had on her. "But I am a protector of life, a vanguard of the earth and her forests. They welcome me, because I bring good Magick and nurture life. Here I am not but a Druid man and a creature of the earth."

Her breath caught on a sob, and her body jerked.

Instantly, Malcolm lifted to his elbow and leaned to look down at her.

Vían hid her face from him, but not in time.

"Why the tears? Are ye hurting?" he asked, his voice full of concern.

Damn him. Damn him for being a good man. "Nay," she croaked. "I just...just..." She tensed with a hiccup, and then sobbed again. "Please don't think I'm touched in the head, I can't tell you why I'm like this." In truth, she couldn't. It had been maybe a quarter century since she'd even had the energy to cry. Her despair had dipped below such shows of emotion.

Was he making her feel? Was he making her care?

Dear God, how much of this could she take?

"How long has it been since anyone's held ye?" he queried gently. "Since ye've been touched by another with affection?"

She sucked in a shaky breath. "It seems like... ages. Centuries, maybe."

He smiled against her neck, and pressed a kiss behind her ear. "Did ye know that our bodies require human touch?"

She shook her head as he ran his fingers over their previous path, and back up again, seeking the places that caused her to arch and moan. Distracting her from her tears.

"No matter how much ye feed a bairn, it willna thrive without the tender arms of a mother or nurse and will most likely die. Every caress, every embrace, every time our hands hold, like so." He traced her arm until he laced his fingers with hers. "It creates a substance within us that is vital to life."

"Magick?"

"Nay. It's just how we mortals are made. Call it what you will. Social beasts, souls in need of affectionate connection with another. Compassionate companionship." He released her hand to cup her face, kissing the tear from her cheek. "'Tis a gentle thing you're feeling," he murmured. "And I'm glad to be the one to touch ye. To ease yer loneliness. To liberate these tears of need." With utter tenderness, he pressed his lips against her temple, then her eyelid, then her cheek, and jaw.

Seized by raw emotion and instinct, Vían turned in his arms until she faced him and threw her leg over his hips. Forcing him to his back, she climbed atop him and filled herself with his hardening length.

Next time. Next time she'd say the spell, but this moment was for her. *For him.*

And what they could never have together.

"Give me yer name, woman," he gasped, his hands falling to her hips to help her set a rhythm as his eyes lazily enjoyed the sway of her generous breasts. "I want to know what to name to call when I'm inside ye."

"My name is Vían," she told him, then leaned in for a desperate kiss.

Now he knew the name of the woman he'd one day despise.

CHAPTER 4

I t never ceased to amaze Vían how quickly men could drop off to sleep after sex. She'd barely climbed off of his lean, talented hips before Malcolm had collapsed onto his back, pulled her to drape over his body, and given up consciousness in almost his very next breath.

She'd spent the last fifty years in a dark chasm, and thus didn't even like to blink, let alone fall asleep and miss one moment of her freedom. Besides, the flutters of his auburn lashes entertained her, as did the twitches of his limbs as he slept.

In fact, he reposed as though he and slumber were strangers. Perhaps he was as consumed with saving the earth as the Wyrd Sisters were with ending it. It would explain why he seemed so lean, hard, and stern.

It made the fact that he'd been nothing but gentle and patient with her that much more extraordinary. Here, on the floor of this hovel, he looked nothing like a king, but every inch the Earth Druid. The forest indeed seemed to welcome him.

Vían didn't know how long she watched him sleep. Long enough for the fire to die to glowing embers and the silver light of dawn to pierce the many cracks, holes, and weaknesses of the hovel.

She'd become accustomed to encompassing silence, so the sounds of the forest fascinated and lulled her. The rhythm of Malcolm's breath and the beat of his heart became the percussion to the forest's midnight melody, and the music transfixed her for splendid hours.

His body woke before he did, muscles lifting to press into her, and his manhood thickening beneath her thigh as it rested in between his legs. His breaths came deeper, and more quickly, and when she shifted atop him, he groaned and stretched.

Now was the time. The spell of the night was broken, and everyone had to face the hard truths in the light of day. If she were to work her curse on him, this would be the moment.

Vían bit her lip, hard, to cause herself physical discomfort that could match the sharp pang of guilt and sorrow.

"I'm sorry," she whispered. "There's no other way." Splitting her legs over him, she reached down to his hard, throbbing sex, meaning to guide it inside her and awaken him with the last bit of pleasure she could give, before she took everything from him.

The gentle nicker of a horse warned her a second before the entire hovel shook with the impact of the door being kicked in.

Malcolm shot up, his arms coming around her in a protective vice before he rolled her between the wall and the shield of his body.

"*Odin's bones*, Malcolm, your pale backside is the last thing I need to see this early in the morning." A dark masculine voice trembled with half amusement, half disgust.

Malcolm instantly relaxed, though his voice was laced with rage as he addressed the interloper. "Bael, if you doona get the fuck out of here, I'll forget ye're my brother-in-law and—"

"Malcolm you gave us a fright!" A flame-haired woman bent into the hovel, filling the poor structure to the brim. "What in the name of the Goddess are you doing all the way out—" She cut off when Vían poked her head above Malcolm's shoulder, her lovely blue eyes widening to the size of saucers. "Oh, my!" the lady exclaimed. "I thought... we assumed you were in danger... not...Oh my! Pardon us!"

Burning a bright pink, even in the dim light, the woman seized onto the dark-haired lummox next to her, and tugged at his arm toward the now ruined door.

The man relented, black eyes glittering with mirth. "My liege," he said in a strange, foreign accent before executing a mocking bow to Malcolm's back side, and ducking out of the hovel.

Their chuckles could be heard through the thin walls.

Malcolm's groan of frustration was more of a menacing growl. His morning erection still pulsed against her thigh, and he'd yet to let go of her. "Sometimes family isna the blessing others make it out to be," he grit out.

Vían began to panic. What would she do now? How could she face the Wyrd Sisters after her failure? They'd know she'd lain with him, and that she'd chosen not to carry out her charge. "I... suppose you must be going now." Fighting to keep her voice even, she mentally berated herself for the weakness he brought out in her. Was this the last morning she'd ever see?

"Aye," he sighed, pulling away and running his hands over his tired eyes. "Gather what things ye want to take with ye."

"What?"

Malcolm's jaw cracked on a yawn, and he reached for his discarded kilt and tunic. "I'll get ye home so we can finish what my sister and her husband so rudely interrupted." He kissed her forehead, and pulled his tunic over his unruly auburn curls.

Vían gaped at him in absolute shock, frozen in place.

He pulled his kilt over his tantalizing backside and then turned to her as though to ask her why she hadn't moved yet. Upon seeing her face, he crouched down to her and touched her cheek, obviously taking her astonishment for outrage.

"I doona mean to offer ye the dishonor of being my

mistress," he amended, green eyes sparkling with mischief. "I mean to make an honest woman out of ye."

He couldn't mean...

"What are you saying?" she breathed, her heart slamming against her ribcage.

"I'm saying I mean to make ye my wife." He grinned before leaning in for a kiss. "Now get dressed, dawn is upon us."

MALCOLM FELT LIGHTER than he had in months as he guided his steed over the moors toward Dun Moray. He ignored the silent, astonished glances of his sister and the smug, lifted eyebrow of his brother-in-law as they each followed behind him on their own horses.

He supposed he deserved both. Since Morgana had returned home from exile in England with a Berserker mate, he'd lectured both of them over the unwise speed of their union. He would reap what he'd sown, and try to keep a good humor about it. Morgana was full to bursting with questions, Malcolm could feel them swimming inside her, but she wouldn't ask him until Vían was no longer clinging to his back in dazed silence. If nothing else, his sister was a lady.

There were a myriad of noble reasons why he should marry Vían. He'd been found in her bed, such as it was, and therefore honor bound him to her. Though Picts didn't believe as the English did, that a woman exploring her sexuality was more sinful than a man doing the same, it still was a man's responsibility to take care of his offspring.

And what if their night together had resulted in a child?

The very idea terrified and humbled him. He was an Earth Druid after all, they were known to be more fertile than your average Celt.

And yet, that still didn't encompass the reason he was now

taking a bride home rather than searching for the Grimoire as he was bound to do.

The moment he'd seen Vían trembling and wounded on the ground, something inside him had shifted. For so long, he'd been consumed by his work, by the responsibility of being the king of a proud and clannish people, and by the charge he'd been tasked with by the Goddess.

A de Moray Druid.

With her soft amethyst eyes and skin that seemed as though it had never been kissed by the sun, Vían made him feel like a man. *Just* a man. A creature of blood and bones and hunger and lust. Nothing more.

In truth, he could have stayed with her in that hovel and lived out his days roaming the forest, fishing the lake, and planting wee babes in her belly every night by their fire. They'd tell stories, shape clay, weave baskets, and let the forest help them to forget that an Apocalypse loomed on the horizon.

"Is that Dun Moray?" Vían's question shattered his brooding fantasy as they broke over a rise and the Moray valley spread out beneath them. It shimmered like an emerald in the autumn sunlight, the village alive with activity.

"Aye," Malcolm answered, the mantle of obligation again beginning to weigh upon his shoulders.

"So, it's really true... You're King of the Picts." She said this as though the fact disappointed her, somehow, and that endeared her to him all the more.

Most women of his acquaintance chased him with the vigor of a pack of wolves. His crown being the prize rather than his heart. "Do ye think ye could take to being my Queen?"

"That remains to be seen," she whispered, and pressed her cheek to his back. "Why would you want me? I know naught of your world. I have no family. I'm nobody... nothing."

The forlorn words were made all the more bleak by her tone. She truly believed that about herself, which was a tragedy, and he planned to spend the rest of his life changing her mind.

"To me, ye're everything," he insisted, hoping she could hear the raw truth in his tone.

"How can that be? You don't know a thing about me. I don't know a thing about you. We've only just met."

A wise and careful woman, his lass. He liked that. "I know that ye're practical and resilient, which I appreciate. Ye know what ye want, and ye go after it." He was glad she couldn't see his lips twitch with the memory of how she'd persuaded him into her bed.

Not that it took much persuading.

"I know that ye're proud and lonely and that ye carry around a painful secret that ye doona want to share with anyone, least of all me."

Her gasp was audible. "How do you—what makes you think that?"

"I'm more perceptive than yer average man, lass," he tossed her a smile over his shoulder as they began to descend the hill into Moray Valley. "And we all have secrets."

"What are yours?" she asked after a pause.

Malcolm considered putting her off, perhaps until they knew each other better, but something about the open vulnerability in her question pushed him to answer her.

"When my father was killed, everyone thought I was in exile while Macbeth ruled, but in truth, I was in the hands of my enemies."

"The English?" she asked.

"Nay. Druids. Dark Druids. Women who have taken the powers of the Goddess and twisted them for their own evil purposes."

Vían was quiet behind him. Offering no words of sympathy, no empty platitudes, and somehow that prompted him to continue.

"I had no concept of time when I was in their clutches. They held me for months, but it felt like an eternity..." His hands tightened on his reins as the memories washed over him, spilling chill bumps over his flesh. "The worst of it is, I would have been able to break any chains wrought of iron or prison of stone, but... they didna imprison my body, they invaded my mind, held it captive with their black Magick."

Vían's arms tightened around his middle, offering him more comfort than any words.

"They tried to rip me from myself. To bring me to their side. And when they failed to do that, they used... terrible means to trick me into giving up my Druid powers to them."

"Obviously, they failed," she offered, her voice tighter than he'd yet heard it.

"Aye," he ground out. "But their attempts they... changed me... and not for the better." Bit by bit, Malcolm had felt his heart grow colder, his thoughts more bitter. He'd nearly lost himself in that place, in his own head, and the abyss he found within frightened him more than any physical pain he could imagine.

Even more than death.

"You ask me why I'm taking ye home," he murmured, placing a hand over the soft arms banded about his waist. "It's because when I'm with ye, I feel like myself for the first time in ages, and that is the most precious gift anyone could give."

Her breath had sped behind him, and she gave a few suspiciously rapid sniffs. It melted his heart that she was touched on his behalf. "Aren't you afraid they'll come for you again?"

"They will," he shrugged. "They already have. But we're all stronger with someone by our sides to remind us what we're fighting for. I see that now." He cast another look at Bael and Morgana, who were locked in a conversation of their own a ways off.

"You... know what they're after?" she asked.

Malcolm realized that this was a lot for a wee lass to take in, and that he'd likely just gave her cause to fear for her life. The best thing he knew to combat fear was information.

"There is a prophecy in the de Moray Grimoire that says that when four elemental de Moray Druids cast behind one gate, they are fated to bring about the Apocalypse," he explained. "We are only three. My sister, Morgana, my cousin, Kenna, and I. As long as one of us are behind castle grounds, we are able to ward them off, for now. 'Tis why Kenna didna join the search for me, I expect."

"How do you know the Wyrd Sisters cannot come for you?" she queried.

"Because my castle is warded."

"Warded how?"

"Do ye see the symbols carved in those stones?" He pointed to impossibly sized monoliths that they were beginning to pass. "They're placed all around the valley, and are strong enough that neither the Wyrd Sisters nor their minions can cross—."

With a cry, Vían's arms were jerked from around his waist as she was thrown from his horse and into the grass by the invisible barrier that protected his lands.

Malcolm slowly turned his horse, meeting Morgana's wide, blue eyes before he could bring himself to look at the woman who stared up at him from the ground.

A cold, bitter fury built in his gut as he realized, he'd never told her the names of his enemies, and yet she'd called them the Wyrd Sisters.

Because she was in league with them.

CHAPTER 5

Ían turned her shackled wrists this way and that, testing the security of the iron and her ability to slip out of it. Of course, it would figure that Malcolm's chains would hold fast, that his dungeon would be as absolute as the void had been. It was almost worse, because she could mark the passing of time through the narrow barred window at the top of the tall stone wall. The sunlight crept in a moving square across the floor, and every moment it passed was a moment she could mark her failures.

It had taken some considerable reworking of the wards to allow her into the castle, and still keep the Wyrd Sisters out. The power of the de Moray Druids was nothing like the dark workings she'd seen from her captors. Their spells were lyrical chants and prayers and even songs. Their runes pulsed with light instead of darkness, and their Magick was fortified with love rather than hatred.

But the wrath in Malcolm's eyes had been dangerous and terrifying. More frightening than any of the atrocities she'd witnessed as a captive of the Wyrd Sisters. In fact, it was the dark-haired, black-eyed Berserker, Bael, who'd shackled her and whisked her to the dungeon.

Because Malcolm couldn't bear to look at her, didn't trust himself to touch her without causing her harm. He'd said as much.

And who could blame him? He'd offered to make her his queen, and she'd betrayed him.

The irony weighed on her chest like a load of bricks.

As the shadows grew long, and the meager light from the outside began to dissipate, Vían fought an encompassing, paralyzing panic. Her chains became heavier, the stones colder and more unforgiving. The scuttles of vermin, unseen or just imagined, were more frightening than the complete isolation of the void.

You've failed us, Vían. Badb's voice hissed on the wind. *We're coming with the Grimoire, and if you don't take what we bade you when we break the wards, then you'll be returned to the void for eternity. But first we'll make you watch as we toy with your lover, and slaughter everyone he loves...*

"No," she whimpered, dropping to her knees. Even in this dungeon she wasn't safe from their evil. The darkness always found her. That was her curse. She'd traded her soul to it, and now had to live with an eternity of tormented regrets.

The sound of the heavy bolt and the scrape of the door against the stones brought Vían to her feet. Never let it be said that she faced her fate on her knees.

Never again. Not even before Malcolm de Moray.

His climb down the dungeon steps was long, as though he didn't want to reach the bottom any more than she wanted him to. Golden light from his torch spilled over the stones from the entry a moment before his wide frame filled the archway.

Vían's heart leapt into her throat and stayed there, rendering her mute, as she watched him mount the torch in its sconce.

Gone was the gentle, patient lover of the prior night. Gone was the noble, beloved ruler of the Pictish people. The man who stalked into her prison trembled with a fury that covered wounds. Wounds that she'd created. Scars she'd ripped open.

As he loomed over her, a creature of cold rage and hot blood, one word ripped from his lips that surprised them both.

"*Why?*"

The question encompassed so much, and yet Vían didn't know where to start. He had such control, and such power. She realized now that the Wyrd Sisters, as potent as their dark Magick was, underestimated this Druid.

"You have no right to ask me that," she answered, cursing the tremor in her voice. "My reasons are my own." And they were many.

"I have every right!" he exploded, the walls of the prison trembling with the force of his emotion. He captured both her shoulders in a brutal grip, and pulled her to him so his eyes burned down into hers. "But I wasna asking why ye're a minion of those evil hags." He gathered a cold, lethal calm back into his voice. "I was asking *why* I still desire ye as desperately as I do. Even after everything ye've done."

Vían didn't have time to process the question as he crushed his lips to hers in a punishing kiss. He didn't plunder or explore, didn't give her time to respond, but instead kissed her long enough to bruise her lips and then ripped his mouth from hers with a sound of aggravation.

"Damn ye," he forced through gritted teeth, and bent to kiss her again.

"No!" Vían cried out, her chains scraping the earth as she lifted her hands and pushed against his chest. "Damn *you*," she spat. "Damn you for making me care!"

They circled each other like suspicious wolves, but her shackles restricted too much movement. Emotions swooped and flew about them like bats in a cave, blindly searching for a safe place to rest and finding none.

"You know what it's like as their prisoner," she accused. "Can you blame me for doing anything they asked to escape their wrath?"

"Ye could have told me. I would have protected ye."

His words both touched and angered her at the same time. "How can you be so arrogant? They threaten me even now, within these walls. I am not their prisoner as you were Malcolm, I am their *possession*. They own me, body and soul."

Malcolm froze in place, his eyes daggers of emerald fire within the sharp planes of his masculine face, his chest lifting and falling as though he'd run a league at full speed. "The only way that could be is if ye..."

"*Yes*," she hissed, a bit of her soul flickering and dying like a candle in a storm at the disgust and disbelief in his eyes. "Yes, I made a deal with them. I sold my soul, more than a century ago, and I became one of their *minions*, as you call it."

He took a step toward her and opened his mouth, but Vían backed away, holding a hand up against him.

"Don't you dare ask me why," she warned. "It doesn't matter anymore. Just comfort yourself with the knowledge that whatever happens here tonight, whether you win or lose this battle, I'll be thrown back in the dark void that has been my personal hell for the rest of eternity." Her voice wavered on that last sentence, so she kicked her chin up a notch. "You'll be done with me forever."

"I'm not done with ye," he growled. "I'll *never* be done with ye." Tearing off his shirt, Malcolm tossed it to the stones. This time he stalked her like a predator, reaching out and dragging her against his hard, corded torso with punishing force. "Ye've bewitched me, somehow," he accused, giving her a shake for emphasis. "Ye canna belong to them, Vían, because ye are *mine*."

Oh, how she wished that could be true.

Even if her soul were to be set free, she'd instantly die. "Malcolm—"

His fingers pressed against her lips. "Doona speak," he commanded as his lips descended once more. He had to know. The tension in his muscles, the bruising desperation of his lips told her that he realized the futility of their connection, but refused to accept it.

It was the anger of a man who was a Druid in his spirit and a King in his land. He was used to controlling his environment. To bending others to his will.

But she was something he could neither control nor possess.

With a frustrated groan, he shoved her tattered shift above her waist, baring her sex. In an astonishingly graceful maneuver, he turned her to the bars and forced her to cling to them as his kilt hit the stones at their feet.

His body was a muscular mass of coiled strain behind her as he gripped her ass with bruising fingers and maneuvered his erection to her entrance.

She went wet for him, panting as alarm and shock heightened the blood and lust racing through her veins. His growl of possession drowned out her whimper of submission and he surged inside her with a powerful stroke.

Pleasure rocked her, flooding her limbs, and she threw back her head with a moan.

"I'm sorry," she gasped, as he thrust forward again, harder this time. Deeper.

"Shut up." He wrapped her hair in his fist and secured her neck in place as he shoved inside her with such force, her teeth clacked together.

"Forgive me," she panted.

"*Never.*" He thrust forward again and again, his hips bucking against her ass with jarring force. It took all her strength to brace herself against the bars, so the power of his body didn't crush her against them. Her arms trembled and burned with the effort, and sweat bloomed on her skin.

He thrust so deep he evoked sensations she'd never before experienced. Her body wanted to thrust back, to seek release and to meet his need. But his relentless rhythm was too brutal and too fast, so Vían helplessly took what he gave her. His growls became groans, and the friction intensified.

"Come for me, temptress," he commanded against her ear, tugging on her hair in a way that caused her inner muscles to clench with a spiraling pleasure. "Scream my name as ye knew it all along."

She obeyed. Pleasure seized her in its unrelenting hold and his name poured from her lips again and again. First as a plea, then as a prayer. And at last a worshipful gasp as wave after wave of bliss pulled her from the void and lights exploded even in the darkness behind her eyelids.

When the climax began to fade, the Wyrd Sister's cruel threat permeated her pleasure with a raw pain.

We'll toy with your lover, and slaughter everyone he loves...

Inside her heat, Malcolm grew impossibly thicker, hotter, and his breath sped with his approaching climax. Conjuring her courage, she squeezed her eyes shut once more and whispered the words Badb had made her memorize. Three times. She had to whisper them three times and it would be over.

Her life would be over. Freedom beckoned.

"Blackened blood and tainted soul, from this Druid Magick pull.
Into the nether set it free, then by darkness grant unto me—"

His strong hand clamped over her mouth as his movements became jerky and frenzied. The entire castle seemed to tremble with the strength of his roar, and for a long moment, Vían feared that the stones would bury them both.

Maybe that would be for the best.

Lightning singed the air and screamed through the night as it touched down close by.

Malcolm withdrew with a groan and lowered his head to her back, running his cheek along the rough fabric of her shift as their breaths exploded into the silent aftermath.

They'd just entered the eye of the tornado, and neither of them had an anchor.

"They're here," she whispered, dropping her forehead against the cold bars, her lungs seizing with despair. "They've come for us both."

CHAPTER 6

M alcolm gripped Vían's delicate shoulders and turned her to face him, his eyes searching hers for a truth he was almost afraid to find.

"Before I face them... answer me this. Why didna ye do the spell last night in the woods when we made love over and over again?" His guard had been down. He was embarrassed to admit to himself that she would have been successful.

Vían's eyes dropped to his chest and her chin wobbled in such a way that it tore at his heart. "Because I'm a fool," she gave a harsh, humorless laugh. "I'd planned to. But you touched me and every‑thing...changed." She blinked up at him as though trying to under‑stand it, herself. "And I've given up my soul for a *man*, a second time."

Malcolm seized upon that bit of information. "What do ye mean?"

She hesitated, but he shook her as though doing so would rattle the answers from her. "Tell me what happened," he demanded. "Help me make sense of this before I go to face my fate."

After a long moment, she nodded, so he released her and she turned from him, only able to speak her truth to the stones.

Malcolm used the moment to dress as she gathered her thoughts, watching the way the firelight threw gold and blue hues into her raven-black hair.

"More than a century ago, I fell in love with a War Chief named Kenneth McManus," she began.

Malcolm instantly hated the man, though he realized the bastard had been dead a few decades, the jealousy that swirled within him was unreasonably violent.

"The McManus and the Gregor were at war," she continued. "And at the time, the Wyrd Sisters were summoned by the Chieftain of the Gregor and paid for their dark Magick to help win the skirmish. The price, was the soul of an enemy."

She paused then for such a long time, Malcolm wondered if she was going to finish, but he remained quiet while she gathered her words.

"I thought Kenneth was so brave. That he was a man who could unite a warring people. I was proud that he chose to love me, when all the lasses chased him. But when he fell into the Wyrd Sister's clutches, he told them to contact me. Do you know why he did that?"

Of course Malcolm knew, but he wasn't about to say it.

Vían turned to him, her eyes filled with such bitterness and self-loathing it surprised even him. "He *knew* somehow, that I was weak and gullible enough to make such a stupid offer. That I would give my soul in his stead. That I loved him almost as much as he loved himself. And when it was done, he promised to find a way to liberate me..."

Unable to stand the sadness and pain radiating from her, Malcolm went to her, enfolding her in his arms and tucking her against his body. "He couldna find a way?" he asked.

She shook her head against him, a tear falling from her cheek to his bare chest. "He never even tried," she whispered. "He married another lass, and forgot about me."

Malcolm held her even tighter, cursing the man's name. "If it makes ye feel better, the Gregors decimated the McManus, and took their lands."

She gave a short laugh, and then a sniff. "It does help a bit," she said fondly pressing herself closer to him. "Since I've been in the void, Malcolm, I've suffered every form of madness imaginable. I've prayed to every God and Goddess known, and they've all abandoned me to the darkness, just like Kenneth did. And so, you see, I made a vow that if I ever had the chance to escape the void, I would take it, no matter who became a casualty of the circumstance."

In that moment, Malcolm not only understood her choices, he sympathized with them. His anger drained away, and he was left with a helpless sympathy that unsettled his very soul.

"But ye didna, lass," he murmured. "Here I still am, in command of my people and my powers."

She made a bitter sound, but didn't pull away. "Like I said, I'm a fool. I promised myself that I would never again sacrifice my interest for a man or his cause."

"I doona blame ye." Malcolm stroked her hair, thinking that he ought to take the shackles from around her wrists. She didn't deserve them. She'd been imprisoned enough.

Lifting her chin, she rose on her toes to press a kiss to his jaw, her lips seeking his own. Malcolm tilted his head down to cover her mouth with his. The kiss was soft and achingly sweet. Malcolm drew his lips over hers again and again, the tenderness passing between him blooming to life against his soul.

She pulled back, her lovely eyes shimmering with unshed tears. "I lied," she whispered. "I lied to myself."

"How do you mean?" Malcolm brushed her hair away from the pale perfection of her cheek. She was such a beauty.

"Your cause is to save humanity from the Apocalypse. That is a cause worth giving my soul for."

"Vían, *no*." Malcolm panicked, clutching her to him with all his strength. "Doona do anything foolish."

A tear slid down her cheek, but her features were serene.

"And you, Malcolm de Moray, are a man worth the sacrifice, because it's one you'd never ask me to make."

He gasped her name, but in the next instant he was only clutching her thin, empty garment as the manacles that had once shackled her wrists clattered to the stones.

The inhuman sound that ripped from him shook the entire castle and brought his family storming into the dungeon.

"Malcolm!" Kenna gasped, her amber eyes wide with astonishment. "What's happening?"

Malcolm turned to them slowly, shaking with the force of his rage and loss, trying to summon the cold wrath of which he knew himself capable.

"Arm yourselves," he ordered his Druid family, and their Berserker mates in a dark voice he'd never heard before. "We're going to war."

Even Bael and Niall stepped out of Malcolm's way as he stalked toward the stairs, aiming to make preparations for the battle to come. First, he was going to defeat the Wyrd Sisters and stave off the Apocalypse. Then, he was going to fetch his woman, even if he had to claw his way through the depths of hell to do so.

CHAPTER 7

S unset turned the Berserker knights and their Viking comrades into dark silhouettes against the flaming sky. Loch Fyne glimmered like a lake of fire as it buffeted against the western side of the castle. Thirteen men, including Bael and Niall, stood bravely in front of the fence of wooden stakes, angled to impale an advancing enemy. Across the expanse of the Moray Valley, a vast army crested the rough Highland peaks and began a syncopated march down toward Dun Moray and the village.

Ingmar—a general of Niall's who would have been a jester but for his voracious bloodlust—turned to address Malcolm and his small garrison of kilted countrymen as they approached the Vikings from behind. "You should stay behind your wards, King Malcolm, and let *us* battle your enemies," he said smugly. "You've marched to the front lines with no armor, flanked by women and mostly naked men, which, in my opinion, should be the other way around." He hit his leather jerkin with his shield. "Leave us the glory of plunging into battle and bloodying our armor."

"I believe we shall," Malcolm replied absently, as he scanned the approaching army for the Wyrd Sisters. They were yet too far away to make out distinct features, but Malcolm knew they were out there. The distinct stench of evil flowed on the Highland breezes, and demoralizing threats whispered on the chill winds.

"Who are they, Colm?" Morgana touched his elbow and squinted into the gathering shadows that seemed to follow the endless swarm of the advancing enemy. "They wear no colors."

"I think it's an army of the damned," Kenna drew up to his other side. "Badb said that she had countless souls at her disposal. I think she's unleashed them all upon us at once."

Souls like Vían. Some innocent. Some malevolent. All desperate to do whatever it took for the promise of redemption. Or maybe just for the release of death.

"Do you think she's out there?" Morgana whispered, the compassion in her eyes cutting Malcolm to the quick.

He knew to whom his sister was referring.

"Nay. The Wyrd Sisters know Vían wouldna march against me. 'Tis why they took her from me." Malcolm fought to keep his composure, and reminded himself that a village full of women and children relied on his protection.

The future of humanity, itself, relied on the strength of his principle and power.

How would they feel if they knew he was tempted to sacrifice it all for *her*?

"I expect the village bard will be writing lyrics to our valor and ingenuity," Ingmar was still taunting them.

"I told ye not to touch my castle grounds weeks ago. Not to cut down trees to make yer fences," Malcolm said slowly.

Niall turned, ignoring the warning look from Kenna. "What would your people have done without our fortifications?"

"What if the army breaks through the line?" Ingmar asked smugly. "Not that it's likely," he added. "But Dun Moray would have been defenseless if not for us."

Malcolm made a slight gesture to his men, and the forty archers spread out, making enough space between them to reach the edge of the loch.

With a whispered spell, Malcolm stretched his arms out, palms up, and lifted them from his sides. As he did, the earth trembled beneath them, and then separated, lifting him, Morgana, Kenna, and the entire line of archers above the slack-jawed Vikings, and their wooden fortifications, on an impenetrable rock wall thrice as high as Bael, the tallest Berserker.

Standing on the corner of the wall, he wrapped the structure of stone around the village, using the edge of his wards for a guide.

As preoccupied as he was with Vían, with revenge, and with the inevitable battle, Malcolm enjoyed a victorious moment over the Viking's rare, awe-struck silence. "You see." He lifted an eyebrow. "Your fortifications were not needed. And I would *never* leave my people unprotected."

"I'd like it to be noted that *I* never doubted you." Bael twirled his axe and winked at Morgana, his dark eyes glittering with anticipation of bloodshed.

The army of souls began to run forward as they reached the edge of the loch, their weapons raised. The Vikings drew their own weapons and clustered into a shield formation. Bael and Niall growled their pleasure as *Berserkergang* overtook their bodies, their eyes turning into black voids, promising a quick death to their enemies.

If they were lucky.

"I can feel the Grimoire," Malcolm told the Druids on either side of him.

"It's close," Kenna agreed. "They're close, but I can't see them."

"Do you think they can die?" Morgana worried. "This army of souls?"

Malcolm watched them advance, his hand clenched around the staff made from the sacred Ash, a relic of the de Moray Earth Druids that transcended written history. He drew strength from it, the strength of patience, and the strength of survival. "We're about to find out."

Kenna called for a torch that was handed to her by an awaiting warrior. With a flare of her powers, the flame rippled across the line of archers, igniting their arrows. "We are they who repelled the Romans," she said in their Gaelic tongue. "Protect the Viking army with your arrows, and slay our enemies." Upon her order, they let loose their first barrage, dropping the first line of the Army of Souls and igniting the flames of war.

"Malcolm, look!" Morgana pointed east, to the crest of the hill opposite the loch.

Four silhouettes appeared as statues atop their magnificent horses. The rise was far off, but the figures were unmistakable. They neither advanced nor retreated, but stood as sentinels, witnesses to the most important battle humanity had faced thus far.

The Four Horseman. Conquest, War, Pestilence, and Death.

They'd come to watch him battle for the salvation of the world.

Malcolm sent a silent prayer to the heavens. It was a heavy thing to think that the fate of the eternities rested on the outcome of the day.

Malcolm found himself wondering which side The Horsemen were on. Did they want to bring about the Apocalypse? Were they expecting him to fail?

If so, they would be sorely disappointed.

Now was not the time. Not like this, by dark measures and blood Magick. The prophecy said that four de Morays would wield behind one gate and the Seals would be broken. Malcolm had always interpreted that to mean that four de Moray's would be born to *one* generation. He could not let the Wyrd sisters force the End of Days for their personal gain. There was still so much life left to be lived. So much progress and enlightenment and invention to discover. How could it end now when, it seemed, that the world was still so young?

A prickling of the fine hairs of his body heralded the notice of the Four honing in on him, even as the Army of Souls broke upon the Viking frontlines, and the fighting began in earnest.

Though the souls were neither alive nor dead, but some macabre version of *in between*, they still bled when Bael's axe culled a dozen down in one mighty sweep. They still screamed, and writhed when Niall's sword cut them navel to throat before kicking them off into the red-stained field. Their flesh sizzled and stunk as flaming arrows and bolts of Kenna's magickal fire decimated and illuminated the carnage.

Malcolm mourned for his lush valley, and for the souls of those he claimed as he used his magick to pull the black, sharp boulders from the earth and roll them through the advancing horde. The crunch was sickening, but the tactic effective, cutting neat swaths of blood and bone.

And still foes spilled from the gathering shadows of the night as new waves of enemies broke upon his walls.

"I cannot see the Wyrd Sisters, Malcolm." Morgana grasped his elbow. "Something's not right. Where are they?"

Turning to search, Malcolm noticed the Four Horsemen had begun a slow and steady advance down into his valley until they stood at the edge of the battle.

Apart from it, and yet an inevitable part *of* it.

Conquest, with his white stallion and silver armor looked like an arc angel sent by a vengeful god. Whereas War, with his horse almost the same color as his blood-red breastplate resembled some kind of Hell spawn.

Next to them, Pestilence, his visage hidden in dark robes, perched atop his nightmare steed more regally than Malcolm would have imagined. And Death, his horse pale and dappled, his armor dark and antiquated, surveyed the carnage with a relentless power that could only belong to an immortal such as him.

"Ye will not have this day," Malcolm vowed at them, in a voice too low for anyone but him to hear.

Death's head turned slowly toward him, far enough away that Malcolm barely marked the movement.

The question is, will you?

The words were not spoken, and yet Malcolm heard them clear as day.

Death lifted a finger, and pointed to the edge of Malcolm's land, where Dun Moray's keep was buffeted by craggy Highland peaks. At first Malcolm saw nothing. Then a shimmer of disturbance in the air around his wards caught his eye the moment before lightning flashed, and two women straddling broomsticks flew through the air and pierced the protection of his magick.

"Nay," he growled. "How is this possible?"

"The Grimoire!" Morgana pointed. "They have it."

That *had* to be how they got through the wards. Cradled under Badb's left arm was the book filled with all the secrets of his Druid family since the beginning of time.

We're after you both now... Badb's eerie voice brushed past his ear on a chilling breeze. Even as he watched her hag's robes draping below her as she circled his keep on her broomstick, it was as though she whispered right next to him.

Fear sliced through him, followed quickly by a cold fury the likes of which he'd never before felt. Moray Village, full of innocent souls, separated the space between his walls and the castle. Could he get to them in time?

A sister for a sister... Badb's cruel winds hissed. With a deafening crash, she called down a silver fork of lightning. It struck his parapets and half the roof of Dun Moray gave a great shudder, and then collapsed.

With a harsh sound of strain and rage, Malcolm did all he could to keep the stones from crushing any of the inhabitants of the castle, but knew that from this distance, he had to have failed.

Come to us and we'll let the wee Moray babes and their mothers live...

Malcolm hesitated, though his heart bled. Of course it was a trap. One that if sprung, could seal the fate of the entire world. And yet, what of his people? How could they make him choose between those whom he loved most dear, and—everyone who was or would ever be?

*Bring Morgana, and we'll give you what you want, or should I say who *you want...*

Vían.

The thought of her locked away in their hellish void nearly drove him to his knees. The sounds of the battle receded into the background. Though Vían had been the one imprisoned all these decades, Malcolm felt as though it was *him* that had found deliverance in her presence. He'd felt more wealthy in that hovel in the forest than he ever had in the halls of his own castle. A chance to be who he truly was. No pretenses, no expectations, and no barriers. He wanted nothing more from this life then to be given the chance to show her the same kind of freedom.

A love that never bound, but liberated.

Cursing the prophecy, the Fates, the Wyrd Sisters and the *fucking* gods, he turned to his beloved sister, a void of his own opening inside his heart.

"Keep me strong," he ground out a command and a plea in one breath.

She met his gaze with her soft blue eyes, clarity and determination sparking in their depths. "Nay," she murmured.

Malcolm flinched, and then glared a warning at her. "What are ye saying?"

Grasping his elbow, Morgana turned them both toward his keep, where Badb and Nemain touched down on the flagstones of his home. Lightning sheeted across the Highland sky, warning that their time was running out.

"We take the fight to them, Malcolm," Morgana said, closing her eyes and pressing her forehead against his shoulder as though gathering strength.

Gritting his teeth, Malcolm nodded, lowering them to the

ground on his piece of earth. "It's time we end this," he agreed. "One way or another."

"I'm going with you," Kenna announced, taking a moment to break from the line of archers. "Lower me down."

"Nay," Malcolm held his hand out to her. "Ye stay where ye are and help the Berserkers fend off the attack. They need yer fire."

Kenna stood upon the wall, her amber skirts flapping against her legs in the increasingly violent winds. "I know you could have loved her." Her eyes glowed with the fire of prophecy. "I'm sorry that you could not keep Vían and also your word as a Druid. But your decisions today will echo for millennia, one way or the other."

Her words affected Malcolm more than he could ever have expected. So much so that all he could summon for her was a nod before he turned with his sister toward Dun Moray. It wasn't sadness that welled up inside him as he stalked the thoroughfare of Moray Village toward where Badb stood, clutching her broom in one hand and the book in the other.

Rage. A helpless, impotent fury Malcolm had never had to grapple with in his entire life. He was a de Moray. The King of the Highland people. His family had held off the Vikings, the Romans, and the English with their might and magick.

How was it that this one crone and her coven were more dangerous than all the sword-wielding warriors who'd been after this isle since the beginning? How could it be possible that no matter which side won the day, the ultimate loss would be his? He'd always done everything required of him. Respected the earth. Studied his craft. Learned herbs, potions, incantations, leadership, justice, and mercy. Some of those lessons had been hard-won. Others had come easily.

But after decades of sacrifice for his people and his Goddess, he was denied the only thing that truly mattered in this world. The one thing that would strengthen and solidify his power and allow him to become the man, the *King*, he was meant to be.

Love.

It was love that saved the souls of the mated Berserkers who now cherished and protected his kinswomen. Malcolm craved such love. The love of a woman willing to sacrifice her eternal soul for his sake. The rare emotion that filled in the cracks of one's being and fortified the weaknesses with a power greater than any other.

Hatred boiled in the absence of that love, filling him with a dark power that surged dangerously just beneath the surface.

"Keep Nemain busy," he instructed Morgana. "Her fire is useless against your water. Draw from the Loch and drown her if need be."

"What are you going to do?" Morgana asked.

"Whatever is necessary."

The sky darkened as they stopped at the bottom of the stone steps to Dun Moray. The spires of his home now seemed sinister against the backdrop of the roiling clouds, occasionally illuminated with flashes of lightning.

Energy crackled in the very air between them. The ground was alive with it, and it sparked from the Crone's silver eyes as he approached.

"I've never understood you, King Malcolm," Badb spoke down at him from the top of the stairs, where she and the vicious girl/child, Nemain, blocked the entrance to the keep. "For a man of such power, you certainly lack vision."

"I'm envisioning ye in yer grave," Malcolm growled.

Badb's cackle sounded like the crunch of gravel beneath a boot. "To say such things to your family," she tisked.

"You're no kin of ours," Morgana said, her fingers twitching as she drew power into her hands and connected with the waters of the loch.

"I am a de Moray." Badb lifted the Grimoire, the wind flipping the pages of the ancient tome until it fell open. "There are four de Moray's behind one gate. The *Prophecy of Four* has foretold that we will be the ones to open the Seven Seals and bring about the Apocalypse."

"Ye know I'd never do that," Malcolm vowed. "I'd die before I succumbed to yer evil."

Badb's eyes flared, and she stepped forward, brandishing the book at him as she descended the stairs with the languor of a victor. "Evil?" she purred. "You men are always so short-sighted. You think there is only good, and only evil. You plant your flag on one side or the other and you fight to the death in service to the light or to the dark."

"I will *always* choose the light." He said this without hesitation, and still the crone laughed at him.

"It is easy for evil to take purchase in the soul of a good man." Badb stopped three steps above him, bringing them all but face to face. "Bliss can be found in a sin, and bitterness often follows a good deed, is this not so?"

Victorious cries from the wall heralded a triumph over the Army of Souls. Smoke curled into the sky, mixing with the dark clouds and reflecting Kenna's flames as though they licked skyward from the bowels of the Underworld.

"Your minions are defeated," Malcolm informed his enemies.

Badb shrugged. "What need have I of them when I have the two of you? Once I help our master rise from the deep and seize what is left after the Apocalypse, the Army of the Damned will be my minions, and I will rule them with unimaginable power."

"Ye're delusional," Malcolm spat.

"I'm a visionary," she corrected. "And I'm willing to share that power with you, King Malcolm. I'll give you a piece of my paradise when this is all over. And also, grant you what you desire most in this world, if you and your sister do what I want."

With a wave of her gnarled finger and a whispered curse, a portal opened up on the steps right in front of them, a window to the Void. There, naked and curled in on herself, was Vían, shivering in a hole of desolation and anguish, whispering his name as though it were a prayer to the gods.

Morgana's gasp seemed far away as Malcolm lunged for the portal, calling out to the woman on the ground.

Vían's dark head lifted, sightless amethyst eyes searching blindly for his voice.

"Malcolm?" she choked as desperate tears streaked the grime on her face. Struggling to her feet, she put out her arms as if to reach for him, though it was obvious that she couldn't see in her pitch-black prison. "Malcolm, are you here? I can hear you."

Badb clenched her fist and the portal disappeared.

"She'll think you came for her," Nemain giggled. "How cruel."

Morgana lifted both of her hands, making an intricate sign with her fingers and commanded a pillar of water to rise from the loch and douse the small fire witch. "Silence, you vicious harpy, or I'll forget that I've taken a vow never to take a life."

"Let her go," Malcolm commanded, the ground beneath them trembling with the force of his rage.

"You know my price," Badb countered. "Cast with us, and open the First Seal. Help me unleash the Horsemen into this world and wipe out all the useless tribes of people who will only become like a scourge to this earth whom you love so much."

"We are not a scourge of this earth, we are her children, and I am her protector." They knew this, but Malcolm wanted them to remember that he had the power of the Goddess behind him.

Badb slammed the book shut, pulling it close into her robes. "Nemain has seen the future of this world. If we don't end it now, people will multiply until they spread over every continent and every land. They will build machines that belch poison into the sky and taint the rivers with their rubbish. They'll use everything the earth and the seas have to give and still demand more. You are not saving this world for anyone who matters. You can prevent all that. Join me now."

"Don't you dare!" Kenna threatened as she, Bael, and Niall drew up behind them leading none other than the Four Horsemen in their wake like giant, mounted sentinels.

They looked both mortal and inhuman, mounted on horses unlike any Malcolm had seen on this earth, their colors as vivid as the book prophesied, and their potency just as terrifying.

"I'll not believe your lies." Malcolm addressed the Crone. "Now hand over the book or I'll crush you to claim it."

"I'm not lying!" she screeched. "Ask her!"

Kenna jumped as Badb thrust a finger in her direction.

"Ask your seer if what I say is not the truth."

Malcolm turned to Kenna, whose eyes were filled with pain. "She's not lying... I've seen this in the flames, as well."

The image of Vían's despair flashed in his mind's eye. Could he carve out a life for them in this new world of darkness and subjugation Badb wanted to cultivate? Would it be any worse than the picture she'd just painted of earth's own future?

"You would be dooming poor Vían forever, and for what?" Badb pressed. "For a species bent on destroying themselves. They can't escape the inevitable, King Malcolm. Someday, somehow, the prophecy must be fulfilled. Why not now, when we can seize the outcome and turn it to our favor?"

Shame burned beneath the temptation, and Malcolm turned to glare up at the Horsemen, searching for answers in their inscrutable eyes. "You want this?" he asked them. "You want me to cast with them? To unleash you to wreak the bloody swath of your destiny on this earth?"

The pale horse stepped away from the line, and Death turned his dark head to survey the gathering Druids and Berserkers, poised on the brink of the End, ready to fight the final battle and finally put to rest the argument of destiny versus free will.

His voice evoked brimstone as he spoke. "If the Apocalypse begins this day, we will fulfill our final duties. And then, what is left for immortals such as us? What purpose will we have but to become agents of chaos and devastation? We will be what we are meant to be, and whatever is left after the End will be an unyielding temptation for the four of us... Think on that, Druid King, before you make your decision."

Death's answer chilled Malcolm to the very core of his essence. Badb's paradise could easily be turned into an unimaginable hell were these Horsemen to challenge her, or each other, for it.

Malcolm reeled as he cast his gaze about, to his family, to his enemies, to the smoke covering the sky, and to the faces of his people, who poked out from behind the village walls, awaiting his word to seal their fates.

A gentle hand touched his arm, and he looked down at Kenna as though she might be a stranger, willing his pounding heart to slow. "Dear Malcolm," she said quietly, her voice a warm flicker like a candle in the gathering darkness. "I have seen the shadows and suffering in the days to come, as the Wyrd Sisters predicted, but there is a reason I have not succumbed to despair, as you are about to do."

Despair didn't seem like a strong enough word for the bleak void inside of him.

"I've seen other things, as well," Kenna continued. "Sparks of transcendence from within the devastation. Marvels of ingenuity. I've heard poetry that would make your heart sing, and music that would cause the wounded to dance. There are those whose love will inspire entire generations toward change and hope. There is a limitless potential within us all, and how can we, in this very moment, take that potential away from those who would realize it?"

"Don't be a fool!" Badb scoffed, the wind blustering through the gathering with an angry hiss. "Humanity will always be ruled by fear like the sheep they are. They will be controlled with rhetoric and lies, and ultimately, their stupidity will be their downfall. Why prolong the inevitable?"

"The future is never certain," Kenna insisted. "But we owe the world a chance for redemption."

Malcolm stared down at his cousin with new eyes. She was

right, *damn her*. He was wrong to be tempted by a future at the cost of humanity. How could he have even contemplated it?

Because the part of his heart he usually saved to encompass the entire world had been stolen by a raven-haired beauty, and then broken by their star-crossed fate.

"We'll not cast." Malcolm addressed the Wyrd sisters with unyielding certainty.

"Don't be so certain." In a confusing flurry of robes, Badb hurled her broomstick on a powerful gust of wind. It impaled Kenna with such force, she was knocked from her feet and propelled backward before crashing to the stones.

Niall was at her side in a moment, his golden hair brushing her face as he gasped her name.

Bael ran for the Crone, but Nemain stopped him with an explosion of her fire, the strength of it knocking him to the ground, as well.

Reflexively, Malcolm lifted a flagstone from the earth and hurled it at Badb. She didn't counter in enough time to completely avoid it and her legs became crushed beneath its staggering weight, pinning her to the earth. The Grimoire went flying, sliding in a flesh-colored heap toward Nemain.

Badb tried to lift the stone with her powerful gusts of wind, but Malcolm used his magic to keep it in place, locking them in a battle of elements.

Nemain lashed out with her hands and a wall of fire crawled across the courtyard, effectively cutting Kenna, Niall and Bael away from the Four Horsemen and the four Druids.

Malcolm advanced on Badb, his hands out, intensifying the pressure of the stone crushing her legs.

Instead of shrinking in fear, Badb sneered triumphantly up at him, blood beginning to stain a few of her teeth that had been broken in the fall. "That makes three of us casting at once," she cackled. "Now Morgana must heal your cousin, or she'll die."

"Malcolm?" Morgana inched toward the fire. "I can't just do nothing. Let me heal her."

"You're running out of time, Druid King," Badb taunted. "How much are you willing to lose to save the world?"

The void in Malcolm's heart suddenly became a cavern, and all the loss, rage, and helpless fury rushed to fill it until his heart did slow, and his breathing stabilized as the answer to everything became startlingly clear. "Nothing," he answered coolly. "I'm done with sacrificing what is mine for the greater good."

CHAPTER 8

I t was a reckless risk, but he seized it. Whirling to face the Horsemen, Malcolm addressed Death once again. "This Druid has taken tens of thousands of souls from you, including her own, and locked them in the Void."

Death narrowed dark, soulless eyes at Badb. "So she has."

"I doona think that ye want us to break the Seals." It was a stab in the dark, but something in the eyes of the Horsemen, in the way their steeds pawed the ground in impatience verified what he'd begun to suspect.

"We will unleash the might of the Underworld on this plane, whether we will it or not. Make no mistake of that." Death gestured toward the book, lying innocuously on the stones. "The prophecy demands it."

"Until then, it is yer duty to escort the souls to the Other World."

His statement was met with expectant silence.

"I could offer her to ye." Malcolm gestured to the Crone. "Ye could take her and the souls in her possession to do with as ye will."

"You can't!" Badb hissed. "Not in time to save your fire witch."

"Heal her!" Niall demanded of Morgana. "Now!"

"Wait," Malcolm ordered. "Doona cast."

"Malcolm, Kenna is dying!" Her blood was now running into the grooves between the stones, creating gruesome rivers in his courtyard.

"I am your King," Malcolm commanded. "You will obey me for once."

The eyes of the man called Death were shrewd and unnerving as they narrowed on Malcolm.

"And what is your price for this trade?" Death inquired.

"One soul," Malcolm answered.

"The Fire Druid?"

"Nay." His throat tightened as he spoke her name. "Vían."

"Malcolm!" Morgana cried, tears running down her cheeks. "Malcolm don't do this!"

"I'll kill you *and* your woman if you let her die," Niall threatened through the flames. "Your magic is *nothing* against my wrath."

Badb screeched, her powers flaring as she tried desperately to escape his hold. "I am immortal! I serve a master greater and more powerful than any of you! I'll return and my vengeance will turn the green Highlands into nothing but blood and ashes!"

Malcolm ignored them all, gazes locked with the man who eventually held all the souls in the world in his grasp at one time or another.

"I don't make deals," Death said evenly.

"This isn't a deal," Malcolm replied. "It's a threat. One that I don't make lightly. Give her to me, or I cast with them and force yer hand."

The time it took for him to draw his next breath felt like an eternity. Through the wall of flame, he could see Kenna twitching, her eyes beginning to flutter closed. His heart bled just as much as her body did, but he knew what would happen to her soul if she were lost.

She'd be taken to the Other World to wait until she was reunited with her mate.

Vían would be locked in a prison that not even Death could breach to set her free.

He couldn't let that happen.

A silent look passed between the horsemen, and then Death nodded. "Your descendants will pay the price, Druid King," he predicted, nudging his horse forward and up the stairs of Dun Moray.

Even Malcolm stepped out of his way as the harbinger of the Apocalypse swooped down and scooped up a spitting, cursing Crone before disappearing in a swirl of dark mist.

Bael used the distraction to leap through the flames, singing his dark hair, and beheading Nemain with a speed almost undetectable by the human eye.

Somewhere in the distance, a raven cawed.

And then Vían stood in the center of the courtyard, naked and trembling, her face wet with the evidence of her grief, and her beautiful eyes wide with disbelieving astonishment.

Malcolm was only dimly aware of the fire disappearing. Of Morgana rushing for Kenna. Of the three remaining Horsemen turning and disappearing into the shadows.

He could see nothing but her eyes. Those lovely irises such an unnatural shade of blue, they seemed purple. The color of Scottish heather in bloom. The color of Pictish royalty.

The color painted on his heart.

"Malcolm?"

His name on her lips was the most beautiful melody he'd ever heard. It was better than rustling leaves, waving grasses, or shifting stones.

Her legs gave with a sob as she collapsed to her knees.

Malcolm flew down the steps, and seized her. Reminding himself to be gentle as he pulled her back to her feet and into his arms. The last time his hands had been on her, he'd been punishing, but never again.

"You came for me," she whispered against his neck. "Tell me I'm not dreaming."

Dreams never felt like this.

"I'd have crawled into hell to come for ye," he said against her hair. He left out the part where he'd nearly brought it to this world for her. She didn't need that weight on her shoulders.

"I like your Druid wars!" Ingmar interrupted, leading a band of battle-weary, but generally good-spirited Vikings into the courtyard. How they'd gotten over his walls, Malcolm could only guess.

The Viking general sent a leer in Vían's direction. "They always seem to end with explosions and naked women. What could be better?"

"Avert yer eyes, or I'll pluck them out," Malcolm growled harshly, ripping off his robes and spreading them around Vían's perfect skin.

With a few guffaws, the Vikings complied.

"Malcolm," Kenna croaked, pushing herself up on weak elbows.

Her blood still stained the stones, but through the blemished hole in her dress, new, healthy skin appeared. Morgana had been able to heal her, and Malcolm had never doubted that she would, even for a moment.

Shame settled in his gut, though not regret. "Kenna, I—"

"I forgive you," she interrupted.

"I don't!" Niall stood, his enormous shoulders taut and ready for a fight. "How dare you allow my mate to come to harm. I'm going to rip your limbs off with my bare—"

"Look at them, my love." Kenna admonished. Struggling to push herself up for a second before her mate leaned down and lifted her. "Would you not have done the same for me in such an instance?"

Niall's hard blue eyes softened down at his mate. "I'd slay every last soul alive if you asked me to."

Kenna rested her head on his shoulder. "Then how can you be angry?"

Niall's brows drew together, but he was silent.

Bael took Morgana into his arms, as well, sharing a silent and desperate embrace with his mate. Keeping a hand locked with his, she went to the Grimoire and retrieved it, unsurprised that it was completely intact.

"You heard what the Horseman said." She ran fingers across the pages. "It is your descendants who will be the prophesied Four. The de Morays who will... who will break the Seals."

Malcolm nodded. "I'll do everything I can to make certain that they are ready when the time comes, to defeat the Horsemen in need be."

"Is such a thing possible?" Vían murmured.

Malcolm blinked down at her, his heart too full for him to form any words for an answer.

She looked like the goddess, herself, swathed in his robes of green and gold, her ebony curls flowing over his colors.

He knew he looked like nothing more than an average man left in only his kilt and tunic. Stripped of all artifice, pomp, and duty, he could be only a man. A man who devoted his everything to her. A man who could give her what he'd given no other living soul. Could do what he'd done for none other.

Slowly, he bent his knees, lowering himself until they rested on the cold stones and he was kneeling at her feet.

A King, and yet her loyal subject.

"Though I rule this land, I know it will not be thus forever." He took her trembling hand, his blood quickening at the adoration shining down at him from her eyes. That indefinable spark passing between them as it had in the very beginning. "Our ways will die, but our line never will. Do ye ken how I know that?"

Wordlessly, she shook her head, as fresh tears spilled from her eyes.

"Because my worship of ye is the most sacred magic there is, and if they are raised as a product of that love, then they will have every chance to write their own destiny."

"As we have." Vían smiled.

"No, *mo ghaol*, my love." He rose and gathered her close. "Ye were always my destiny."

A HEARTFELT THANK YOU!

Thank you from the bottom of my heart for reading The de Moray Druids. If you enjoyed this book, please consider posting a review. Reviews don't just help the author, they help other readers discover our books and, no matter how long or short, I sincerely appreciate every review.

Would you like to know when my next book is available? Sign up for my newsletter:

♥ Thank you! ♥

WWW.KERRIGANBYRNE.COM

Also, please follow me on BookBub to be notified of deals and new releases.

Let's hang out! I have a Facebook group:

💜 Let's Hang Out! 💜

FACEBOOK.COM/GROUPS/KERRIGANS
YRNEZ

Thank you again for reading and for your support.

ALSO BY KERRIGAN BYRNE

THE MACLAUCHLAN BERSERKERS

Highland Secret

Highland Shadow

Highland Stranger

To Seduce a Highlander

THE MACKAY BANSHEES

Highland Darkness

Highland Devil

Highland Destiny

To Desire a Highlander

THE DE MORAY DRUIDS

Highland Warlord

Highland Witch

Highland Warrior

To Wed a Highlander

THE BUSINESS OF BLOOD SERIES

The Business of Blood

A Treacherous Trade

A Vocation of Violence (Coming 2020)

CONTEMPORARY SUSPENSE

A Righteous Kill

VICTORIAN REBELS

The Highwayman

The Hunter

The Highlander

The Duke

The Scot Beds His Wife

The Duke With the Dragon Tattoo

A Dark and Stormy Knight

ALSO BY KERRIGAN

The Highwayman

The Hunter

The Highlander

The Duke

The Scot Beds His Wife

The Duke With the Dragon Tattoo

How to Love a Duke in Ten Days

All Scot And Bothered (Coming in March of 2020)

ABOUT THE AUTHOR

 Kerrigan Byrne is the USA Today Bestselling and award winning author of THE DUKE WITH THE DRAGON TATTOO. She has authored a dozen novels in both the romance and mystery genre. Her newest mystery release THE BUSINESS OF BLOOD is available October 24th, 2019

She lives on the Olympic Peninsula in Washington with her dream boat husband. When she's not writing and researching, you'll find her on the water sailing and kayaking, or on land eating, drinking, shopping, and taking the dogs to play on the beach.

Kerrigan loves to hear from her readers! To contact her or learn more about her books, please visit her site: www.kerriganbyrne.com

CPSIA information can be obtained
at www.ICGtesting.com
Printed in the USA
LVHW031539210520
656176LV00014B/1360/J